D1244623

Death Overdue

Death Overdue

A HAUNTED LIBRARY MYSTERY

Allison Brook

NEW YORK

This is a work of fiction. All the names, characters, organizations, places, and events portrayed in this novel are either products of the author's imagination or used fictitiously. Any resemblance to real or actual events, locales, or persons, living or dead, is entirely coincidental.

Published in the United States by Crooked Lane Books, an imprint of The Quick Brown Fox & Company LLC.

Crooked Lane Books and its logo are trademarks of The Quick Brown Fox & Company LLC.

Library of Congress Catalog-in-Publication data available upon request.

ISBN (hardcover): 978-1-68331-386-1
ISBN (ePub): 978-1-68331-387-8
ISBN (ePDF): 978-1-68331-389-2

Cover illustration by Griesbach/Martucci
Book design by Jennifer Canzone

Printed in the United States.

www.crookedlanebooks.com

Crooked Lane Books
34 West 27th St., 10th Floor
New York, NY 10001

First Edition: October 2017

10 9 8 7 6 5 4 3 2 1

Chapter One

Time to move on. I crossed the Green and headed for the library. A gust of wind bowed the branches of the nearby trees, showering me with red and yellow leaves. I paused to inhale the tangy air. It was a glorious October morning, and I stood in the center of the most glorious setting—the historic town of Clover Ridge, Connecticut. This was my family's hometown, where I'd spent my summers as a kid. Elegant, well-preserved homes bordered one side of the Green, and an array of shops, Zagat-rated restaurants, and galleries bordered the other three sides. We were a stone's throw from the Long Island Sound and a few miles from the river, with a low mountain range to the west. Picturesque by anyone's standards—mine included—but my need to leave was growing stronger every day.

Since graduating from college seven years ago, I'd held five jobs in as many states. Practically a new job every year until I began my online library science degree. Even then, I'd worked in three different libraries before coming here. I sometimes wondered if I'd inherited my wanderlust from my father. He was always away traveling . . . when he wasn't in prison. Now he was off somewhere—I had no idea where—and my mom was remarried and living in California. I'd come to Clover Ridge for a visit, and my departure was long overdue.

I approached the Clover Ridge Library, which was once a private home and still exuded a warm and cozy ambience. I loved libraries and felt most secure and happy surrounded by books. Still, I wished I were off hiking in the nearby mountains instead of spending the day carrying out tasks any ten-year-old could handle. The wind cut through my cotton poncho, sending shivers down my back. Winter was coming. Time to move on to someplace warm. Someplace new. I yanked open the heavy wooden door and entered.

Where would Sally put me today? In reference with prune-faced Dorothy Hawkins, who would order me to weed the collection? In the children's room to read a story to the pre-Ks? Actually, I wouldn't mind that. Only please don't make me spend the day reshelving returns like I did last week. That wasn't why I'd gotten my library science degree.

"Hey, Carrie," Angela called out as I passed the circulation desk. "Great day, isn't it?"

I grinned back. Angela was in her late twenties, like me, and one of the few library employees who'd befriended me. "Sure is."

She winked. "I love the new color of your hair."

I ran my fingers through the spikes sticking up from my scalp. Ever since high school, I'd been a rebel in the looks department. It irked my proper-minded mother because it reminded her so much of my errant father.

"I got tired of red. Thought I'd go for purple this week."

Angela shot me a look that conveyed sympathy, conspiracy, and warning. "Sally wants to see you in her office ASAP."

"I'm on my way." Against my orders, my heart began to race. "I wonder what she wants."

"Beats me." Angela turned to a patron to check out her books.

California would be nice. Or Florida. I hurried past the reference desk, glad that Dorothy was mesmerized by something on her computer screen, and turned the corner to Sally's office. "Library Director" shouted the sign over the doorway in big bold caps.

I stood before the closed door, reminding myself that Sally had no real authority over me. I was working as a floating librarian—a temp—and I could quit any time I liked. If she gave me another lecture on proper attire, this time I knew my rights. The library hadn't had a dress code for its employees since 1963. Still, I tugged at the ends of my tunic, which refused to budge any lower than midthigh over my leggings.

Besides, I was leaving. I felt a twinge of guilt, knowing Uncle Bosco would be upset when I gave him the news. But I'd told him back in May that I was only visiting. I couldn't help it if he wanted me to stay so badly he'd made himself believe I'd be settling down in Clover Ridge.

I knocked. As I entered Sally's office, a draft of wind blew by, as though someone were entering the office beside me.

"Good morning, Carrie." Sally looked up from her desk. She frowned when her glance reached my hair. "I'm glad you finally got here."

"I arrived on time. It's now three past nine." I wished I hadn't risen to the bait. Sally loved to put people on the defensive.

"So it is. Please have a seat."

Uh-oh. What am I in for? I'd sat in this office only once before—the day Uncle Bosco had introduced me to Sally and all but ordered her to take me on as an assistant librarian. I perched on the edge of the chair and hoped my expression was pleasant. I waited as the silence continued.

Finally Sally spoke. "Your job application indicates that before coming here, most of your library experience was in adult programming."

"It's true." I knew I sounded as puzzled as I felt. In the five months I'd been working there, I'd spent no more than ten days in programs and events.

"You had a stint as programs coordinator in a small New Jersey library."

"Yes. Filling in while the coordinator was out on leave."

"The director has given you an excellent reference." Sally sounded unhappy about that fact. She sighed. "I don't know if you're aware of it, but Barbara Sills has had to resign her position as head of programs and events. Her husband took a job in California, and they're leaving at the end of the month."

"No, I didn't know."

"We need a new head of programs and events, and I"—she cleared her throat—"would like to offer you the position."

"Really?" I stared at Sally.

She looked sullen. I opened my mouth to say I didn't want any part of this when she spoke.

"I can't imagine you get much satisfaction floating from one section of the library to the other."

"I don't. To tell you the truth, I've been thinking of lea—"

A draft chilled my neck as a voice whispered softly in my ear, "Don't be a fool! Tell her you'll think it over and give her your answer tomorrow."

I looked around. Only Sally and I were in the room.

"Go on. Tell her!" the voice hissed. "Or she'll think you're a moron and withdraw the offer."

Startled, I cleared my throat and obeyed the mysterious voice. Was this my conscience telling me my vagabond days were over? "The offer sounds very tempting. And I have been thinking about my future." Mostly my future outside Clover Ridge.

"Of course you have!" Sally said in a hearty manner not at all like her. "You're almost thirty. You have to consider what you'll be doing for the rest of your life."

I cringed. Did she have to remind me my big birthday was just two months away?

"What does this new position entail?" I asked.

She proceeded to tell me about the various classes, programs, and events that filled almost every hour of the week the library was open to the public. The movies. The trips. How the bimonthly newsletter had to be planned and written three months in advance. By the time she started in on acquiring guest speakers, instructors, and performers, my head was spinning.

Could I handle it all?

Did I want to handle it all?

"That's quite a workload," I said. "How many assistant librarians help Barbara?"

Sally's head jerked back. Clearly, my question had offended. "Two part-timers: Trish Templeton is here every weekday afternoon, and Susan Roberts comes in four evenings a week."

"Oh."

"The position is demanding. It requires a good deal of time and effort, but the salary's quite good."

I bit back a gasp when I heard the amount. I could pay off my car. I could get my own place. I could—

"However, if you don't feel comfortable undertaking the position—"

"I can handle it," I said firmly, a reaction to her dismissive attitude rather than a sureness that I could manage all that would be required.

Sally eyed me speculatively. "I certainly hope so. There are librarians here with more experience and seniority. But considering certain factors and that programs and events is your specialty, the job is yours if you so decide."

"I appreciate the offer. Still, I must think it over very carefully. I'll let you know my decision first thing tomorrow morning."

"That's understandable," she said, surprising me. "Why don't you work with Barbara today? That way, you'll see how she runs the department. I'll expect you here tomorrow at nine sharp. I'd like to get this settled once and for all."

I was dismissed. I closed the door behind me, careful not to slam it as I wanted to. Sally had all but told me she disapproved of me for the job. Obviously, I was being offered the job because Uncle Bosco sat on the library board and had made a hefty donation for the future library extension. What's more, Sally'd had someone else in mind for the position.

"You did admirably well," a voice whispered in my ear.

I glanced down and was shocked to find a frail-looking elderly woman at my side. I was no giant, but she couldn't have been more than five feet two inches in her black "old lady" shoes. "Who are you? How do you know—?"

"Shhh." She pointed across the room, where prune-faced Dorothy sat glaring at me from her seat behind the reference desk.

"I bet she wants the position," I murmured.

"I think she'd kill for it."

"Oh."

"She always was a spiteful child," the woman said. "Once, when her younger sister received a stuffed elephant for her birthday, Dorothy threw it into the pond. Of course, she denied it, but we all knew she'd done it."

"How do you know?" I asked.

"I was there. Dorothy's my niece."

I shivered. "Who are you?"

The woman crooked her finger. "Follow me and I'll explain."

She led me into an empty office and asked me to close the door. When we were seated and facing one another across a desk, I said, "Okay. Talk."

She cleared her throat. She seemed almost transparent. "I'm Mrs. Havers. Evelyn Havers. I used to work here in the library."

"Used to?" I leaned across the desk. "You're looking . . . rather pale."

"I'm fading is what you mean, dear."

"Fading?" I was having difficulty following her end of the conversation. "Were you in the room with Sally and me? I couldn't see you when you spoke to me. You told me . . ." I jerked back and gawked at her.

Mrs. Havers exhaled loudly. "Do us both a favor and don't get hysterical when I tell you I'm a ghost."

"A ghost!" I echoed, feeling hot and then cold and too numb to move. "I always wondered if ghosts really exist. I've always wanted to meet one. One that was friendly, I mean." I was babbling, but I couldn't stop myself. "You seem friendly." I blinked. "And you're real."

"That I am," Mrs. Havers agreed. "Both friendly and real. I would explain more, but we don't have much time. I must soon return to where I go when I'm not in the library."

I shook my head. I closed my eyes. "This is a delusion. I'm hallucinating. Is this the result of drinking two glasses of wine last night?"

"Don't be silly! Try to pay attention, Carrie, in these few remaining minutes. Very few people can see me. I realized you have the gift, so I've been hiding from you until today. I saw you were bored with the mindless tasks they had you do. Why show myself if you were planning to leave? But now that you have the chance to stay on as head of P and E, it's time we got acquainted."

My mouth fell open as I watched her grow more transparent by the second. I leaped to my feet and yanked open the door, ready to bolt.

"Please don't be frightened," she pleaded. "I'll never hurt you."

I turned slowly. "Why are you here?"

"I'm not sure. I believe I'm supposed to help in some way, but I've no idea how."

"Who else can see you?" *Was I the only freak?*

"Only a little girl named Tacey. She's four. She sometimes brings me cookies, though I've told her enough times I can't eat them." Mrs. Havers smiled. "She's afraid I'll go hungry."

"Why did you follow me into Sally's office?" I asked.

"I knew she'd called you in for something important. And I was right. I hope you'll take the position."

"I'm not sure what I'll do. It sounds like a lot of work and responsibility. Besides, I was thinking it was time I left Clover Ridge."

"You can't run away from yourself or your history."

"You know nothing about me!"

Mrs. Havers didn't answer because she was no longer on this plane. What a bizarre day this was turning out to be. First an amazing job offer, then an encounter with a ghost. I opened the door and headed for Barbara Sills's office.

* * *

"So Sally's finally made up her mind," Barbara said when I told her why I'd come. She was a petite brunette in her midforties, with sparkling brown eyes and a touch of ADD, which I figured helped carry her through her many tasks. "I suggested she consider you as my replacement a month ago." Barbara winked. "It took a push from the board to get her in gear."

"Thanks for your vote of confidence," I said. "I'm still thinking it over."

"Don't take too long. She's interviewed a few applicants, but so far, no one's been a good fit. Dorothy's dying for the position and pressuring her best friend to wield her influence. But Sally's smart enough to know Dorothy would make a total mess of things. However, if you won't take it, she might have no choice but to give it to Dorothy."

Barbara put me to work laying out and typing up the January–February newsletter. We worked side by side in companionable silence. Suddenly it was lunchtime.

"Shall we?" She reached for her jacket.

"Of course," I said, as if we'd been eating lunch together these last few months.

We walked around the corner to the Cozy Corner Café, whose lunch menu featured giant-sized sandwiches on homemade bread and two hearty soups that changed daily. I ordered a turkey and bean sprout sandwich on their eight-grain bread and ate every crumb. I took mental notes as Barbara filled me in on the various programs she'd recently set up, but we were constantly interrupted by people stopping by to tell her how much they were going to miss her and her husband.

"I'm going to miss all this," she said as we were paying the bill. "Clover Ridge is such a friendly place. Doug and I moved here nine years ago, and it seems we've lived here all our lives. You must know the feeling. I understand your family's been here for generations."

"My grandfather and Uncle Bosco, who's actually my great-uncle, grew up on Singleton's Farm, three miles outside of town. I used to spend summers here when I was little, before they sold the farm." I laughed. "My job was to feed the chickens."

"And now you're back," Barbara said.

I shrugged. "I'm thinking of moving on—maybe to California like you. Or to Florida."

Barbara looked upset. "I thought you were seriously considering taking over P and E."

"I am thinking about it. I told Sally I'd let her know my decision tomorrow morning."

We walked back to the library in silence. It was obvious I'd disappointed Barbara, even though I'd told her my intentions from the get-go. I sighed. People heard what they wanted to hear.

The truth was, part of me—the part that longed to run my own program and events department in a small library—was ready to rush into Sally's office and shout, "I'll take it!" But the other part of me shied away from anything permanent, especially in a town where people knew the type of man my father was and that he'd been in prison.

We entered the library and passed a line of patrons waiting to check out books and films at the circulation desk.

Barbara took off her jacket. "Trish will have come in by now. She's a dynamite worker and can handle any job. She'll work overtime as long as you give her enough notice so she can get someone to babysit her two kids." She grimaced. "Don't expect the same level of work from Susan, though she does her best."

"Good to know."

Trish was typing away on one of the computers. She was short and round, with rosy cheeks and dark-brown hair that framed her face. She reminded me of one of those Russian nesting dolls.

"May I tell her?" Barbara asked.

"Of course."

After Barbara finished explaining that I'd been offered her job, Trish got up and hugged me.

"This is the best news I've heard today. I think I'd have to quit if Dorothy got the position."

I sat at the table to finish laying out the newsletter. When I was done, Barbara had me write blurbs for handouts for next month's programs and events.

"How do you decide on new programs?" I asked after I'd done a few.

"I keep my eyes and ears open for guest speakers. I have a long list of people who've contacted me wanting to do a program." She laughed. "Tomorrow we'll go through the list together. Too many of them are downright boring."

"We have a real exciting program coming up in two weeks." Trish's eyes lit up with excitement.

"You mean Al Buckley's talk," Barbara said. "I'm sorry I'll be missing it. You'll have to e-mail me all about it."

"Who's Al Buckley?" I asked.

"Al was a detective on the local police force. Fifteen years ago, he was in charge of a murder case that was never solved," Trish said.

A chill snaked up my back. "Around here? Who was murdered?"

"A lovely woman named Laura Foster," Barbara said. "She was married and had two boys in high school. Someone came into the house and struck her when no one else was home."

"How awful," I said. "And how awful that they never found out who killed her."

Barbara and Trish exchanged glances.

"What is it?" I asked.

"The word is that Al was drinking a lot in those days and wasn't on top of things like he should have been," Barbara said. "In fact, there was a hearing, and he ended up leaving the force."

"But he's cleaned up his act," Trish said, "and feels terrible about not finding Laura's killer."

Barbara nodded. "When he called a few months ago, he said he hadn't been able to get the case out of his head.

He started investigating on his own a year or so ago and has found what he believes is new evidence that will put the killer away."

I shook my head. "I don't get it. Why didn't he go to the police with what he's found?"

"He did, but Al doesn't know if they'll follow up on it, given his history with the department."

"They should listen to him!" Trish said. "Al's a great guy and a terrific detective. He and my dad have been friends for years. I know what a bad time he was going through when Laura was murdered. Now all he wants is to solve the case and write a book about it."

"It will make for an interesting program," Barbara said, "but now we have to get to work."

* * *

At ten minutes past five, I retraced my morning walk, my head abuzz with the many surprises of the day. Aunt Harriet and Uncle Bosco's home stood on the far side of the Green—a large, white, wooden-framed house of the same architectural style as the library and most of the other houses in the area. I'd arrived in May, despondent and lethargic, grateful for my aunt and uncle's loving hospitality. I immediately felt at home in their large, beautifully decorated guest room and never tired of gazing out the window at Aunt Harriet's gardens and the mountains in the distance.

They'd bought the house from another old Clover Ridge family seventeen years ago after selling the family farm. Uncle Bosco liked that it was located smack in the middle of town yet had a deep front lawn that afforded them a sense of privacy. Aunt Harriet appreciated the acre of backyard, which was large enough for a good-sized vegetable garden as well as the floral and shrub arrangements she loved to design.

My aunt and uncle were where they always were at this time of day—in the den, ensconced in matching lounge chairs, enjoying a glass of wine. I kissed them both and then went to get my glass of Chardonnay chilling in the refrigerator.

"Have a nice day at the library?" Uncle Bosco called after me.

"It was okay." I sat on the sofa and sipped my wine.

"Just okay?" Aunt Harriet asked.

I bit back my smile. "Why? Is there anything special about today?" Obviously, they knew about the job offer—just as they knew about everything that went on in Clover Ridge.

Uncle Bosco cleared his throat. "We're asking because we want our favorite grandniece to be happy."

I burst out laughing. "Uncle Bosco, did you twist Sally's arm until she agreed to give me the library position?"

"Of course not. I simply pointed out that you're the most qualified for the job."

"Though I've worked in programming for less than two years?"

"It's more hands-on experience than anyone else has." Uncle Bosco eyed me closely. "You don't sound as glad as I thought you'd be."

I frowned. "I didn't plan on staying here long-term. This job sounds so . . . permanent."

My great-aunt and uncle exchanged glances.

"But you've seemed happy lately," Aunt Harriet said. "Much happier than when you arrived."

"I am happier," I agreed. "Who wouldn't be, living with you guys? You spoil me. Never letting me do more than help with the dishes and the grocery shopping. Only, I don't think Clover Ridge is the right place for me."

"Nonsense!" Uncle Bosco boomed as he always did when brushing aside opposing opinions. "We Singletons have lived in Clover Ridge for generations. You have cousins here and in the neighboring towns."

"Their father wasn't a thief who lived apart from his family even when he wasn't in prison. Sooner or later, people are going to figure out I'm Jim Singleton's daughter."

"Let them," Uncle Bosco said. "You're your own person, Carrie. You're beautiful and smart, and it's time you thought about settling down."

Why is everyone telling me to settle down?

"Besides, I'd forgotten how cold it gets here in the winter," I said. "I'm thinking of heading south to Florida."

"The job's a wonderful opportunity," Aunt Harriet said. "You'd be doing work that you love."

"Why don't you give it a shot?" Uncle Bosco said. "Offers like this don't come along very often."

"True," I agreed.

"If you don't like it for some reason, you can always leave," Aunt Harriet said.

"Maybe I'll do that." A weight slid off my shoulders. It was a decision I could live with—taking a job I loved, yet knowing I could leave at any time.

You call this a decision? All you're doing is putting it off, my critical voice scolded.

Perhaps, but this way, I'm giving the job a chance, I answered back.

Aunt Harriet pushed herself to her feet. "I'll go and see to dinner. We're having meatloaf, veggies, and garlic mashed potatoes."

"Can I help?" I got up too.

"No, you can't." She pressed my shoulder down. "You put in a day's work at the library. Relax here with your Uncle Bosco."

I suddenly remembered my odd experience earlier in the day. "Did you know Evelyn Havers?"

"Of course. Everyone knew poor Evelyn," Aunt Harriet said. "Why are you asking about her?"

"Someone mentioned her name in passing—and that she died."

Uncle Bosco let out a sigh. "Evelyn worked in the library for as long as I can remember. The sweetest woman you could ever hope to meet. Always helping anyone who needed a hand. She fell in the parking lot. I'm ashamed something like this happened here in Clover Ridge, where we look after one another."

Aunt Harriet nodded. "It was a bitter cold February evening five years ago. No, six. Evelyn was one of the last people to leave the library. She must have slipped and fallen on a patch of black ice, hit her head, and lost consciousness. They found her the following morning a few feet from her car. Poor dear. The only consolation is that she didn't suffer. Someone set up a shrine where she fell; people left flowers in her memory for months afterward."

"How awful," I said. "Didn't anyone realize she never made it home?"

"Evelyn lived alone after her husband died." Aunt Harriet smiled. "Such a good-hearted soul. She's been gone all this time, but I still expect to see her whenever I'm in the library. It's as though her spirit lives on in the place she loved best."

Chapter Two

The next morning, I told Sally that I'd be happy to accept the position of head of programs and events.

"I thought you'd reach that decision." She wore a smug little smile as she handed me a pile of forms to fill out. "I need these back ASAP. Now remember, your appointment isn't official until the board meeting this Friday. Meanwhile, you'll continue to work with Barbara to learn as much as you can. Thursday is her last day on the job. Good luck."

"Thank you." I turned to leave, but apparently Sally wasn't finished.

Her gaze went from my dark-fuchsia lipstick to the silver dangling earrings that almost brushed my shoulders.

"Your position comes with responsibilities and obligations, and that includes your appearance. You're required to dress and groom yourself in a manner befitting a Clover Ridge Library administrator."

I opened my mouth to say I'd dress any way I liked when I felt a poke to my ribs.

"She's right, you know," Evelyn Havers whispered in my ear. "Tell her you'll be the poster girl of cooperation and proper attire."

Annoyed, I whispered back, "Stop telling me what to say."

"Excuse me?" Sally sounded offended.

The second nudge was more of a jab. "Stop acting like a rebellious teenager. You're a professional woman about to hit thirty," Evelyn said.

I rubbed my side and cleared my throat. "I'll be happy to appear more—er, in the manner befitting my new position."

Sally gave me a broad smile, the first she'd ever directed my way. "Your words are music to my ears."

Evelyn Havers left me to wend my way slowly to Barbara's office. Slowly because my brain whirred with ideas for future programs and events: trips to Manhattan, an adopt a dog or cat day, presenting musicals in the meeting room. It was time the Clover Ridge Library entered the twenty-first century.

"Go slowly," Barbara advised after I'd rattled off a few of my future project ideas. "We have plenty of ongoing programs that our patrons enjoy. Movies, craft programs, and exercise classes filled to capacity. I scratch whatever programs aren't well attended."

"I'll keep that in mind." I was disappointed but grateful for her guidance.

Barbara had me print out the handouts I'd written and then place them in the holders scattered about the library.

"Why bother?" I asked. "All this information is in the newsletter and available on the online calendar."

"Of course it is, but many of our patrons don't bother to read the newsletter carefully. Like every other merchant and vendor, we have to advertise and promote what we offer. In this case, library programs and events. We need to catch our patrons' attention. The number of attendees counts, my dear. Never forget it."

Now that I knew I was taking over as head of programs and events, I peppered Barbara with questions as I tried to learn everything there was to learn. Today was Tuesday. She'd be gone after Thursday. Two more days and I'd be on my own!

"Calm down," Barbara said when I tried to write down everything she was telling me about library grants. "We've literature up the wazoo on the subject. And Sally will help you. She knows you have lots to learn. Every library has its own way of doing things."

Evelyn Havers remained out of sight, which pleased me to no end. I didn't need a ghost acting as my private Jiminy Cricket, instructing me how to behave. Only Dorothy Hawkins remained a thorn in my side. She resented my having taken the position and glowered at me every time I passed the reference desk.

Get over it, I silently told her. *You don't have the required courses for the position.* But I knew I never would have been offered the job if it weren't for Uncle Bosco and felt a pang of guilt each time I walked by Dorothy.

We hosted a farewell dinner for Barbara Wednesday night. I was surprised to find myself close to tears when I hugged her good night.

"You'll do a great job, Carrie," she told me. "California's only an e-mail away. Write if ever you need my help."

"Thanks, Barbara. I'll take you up on it."

Thursday night, I dyed my hair a light golden brown, which I thought was its natural color. For the first time in months, I blow-dried it so it framed my face instead of forming it into spikes with lots of gel. Then I rummaged through my tunics and leggings until I found a skirt and top I'd saved from my administrative assistant days in Manhattan. *Good-bye, Goth Carrie*, I thought as I unearthed a pair of heels hidden away in the back of my closet. I wasn't going to miss my Goth persona too much. I'd only adopted it as a lark, and because everyone else in Clover Ridge wore such proper clothes. I made a mental note to revamp my wardrobe at the local shopping mall the first chance I got. Besides, I could always slip into my Doc Martens, leggings, and tunic on my days off.

The next morning, Angela called out to me as I passed the circulation desk. "Hey, Carrie, don't you look cool!"

All eyes turned to stare at me. My face heated up, and I hurried along as fast as my high heels would allow.

Her voice followed after me. "Meeting in the conference room at nine thirty. Don't be late, Miss New Head of Programs and Events."

My small audience broke into applause as I ran the rest of the way to my office.

By nine twenty-nine, the four library heads, three librarians, and four assistant librarians were seated around the mahogany oval table in the conference room. Sally made her appearance at precisely nine thirty. Her first order of business was to announce my appointment. The others clapped with enthusiasm. Only Dorothy sat, arms crossed over her chest, in silent disapproval. When it was my turn to present my report, I heeded Barbara's suggestions and mentioned upcoming events without offering any of my new ideas. Sally nodded her approval, and I released a sigh of relief.

I spent the weekend preparing for my new life. Saturday, I went on a shopping spree, buying pants and jackets, sweaters and blouses, and low-heeled shoes as if I had an unlimited supply of money. I even indulged in a pair of sexy brown leather high-heeled boots—so different from the Doc Martens I normally wore every day. I charged it all so I wouldn't have to start paying for my purchases until the following month.

Now that I had a good job, I suddenly longed for a place of my own. I scanned the classified ads on Sunday morning and circled several rentals I planned to check out. By day's end, I was despondent. The few in my price range proved to be truly awful—a dank apartment in someone's smelly basement or three tiny rooms over a dry cleaner's. All the nice apartments cost more than I could afford right now. This was going to take time.

Be positive. Something will turn up soon.

* * *

Monday morning, I dressed with care in my new brown trousers, ribbed beige turtleneck, and low-heeled shoes. I blow-dried my hair and dabbed on mascara and green eye shadow while my heart raced like a tom-tom. I refused Aunt Harriet's offer of breakfast—except for a cup of coffee—slipped into my leather jacket, and set out for my first solo day as head of programs and events.

The day went more smoothly than I could have hoped—probably because Barbara had talked me through every contingency imaginable. Having Trish at my side, at least from one o'clock on, was another big help both for moral support and because she knew what had to be done. Unfortunately, Susan Roberts was Trish's opposite in every important way. She was slow and dim-witted and didn't have even a smidgen of initiative in her body.

On Tuesday, I arrived at one o'clock because it was one of my late nights. According to my contract, I was to work two evenings each week and two Saturdays and two Sundays every month. Sally made up the schedule, which changed weekly. Trish and I went through a pile of possible new programs and made some headway on the next newsletter. At six, Susan arrived. Trish went home, and I walked over to the deli around the corner and ate my dinner—a bowl of chicken soup, a turkey sandwich, and a salad.

I knew something was wrong the minute I returned to the library. Susan stood hovering in the doorway, a look of panic on her face.

"Carrie, thank God you're here! I didn't want to bother you while you were having your dinner, but I've looked everywhere. The movie is gone!"

"The one we're showing tonight?" I looked at my watch. "That was supposed to start five minutes ago?"

"Ye-e-e-ss!" Susan wailed.

I reined in my annoyance and pasted a smile on my face. "I know Trish took the movie out of circulation. Are you sure it's not in the cabinet where we keep the films to be shown in the meeting room?"

"Of course I looked. It's not there. Twenty-two people are in the meeting room waiting to see the movie. They're growing impatient."

"I'll speak to them, then we'll look for it together. Maybe it got misplaced somehow."

"It's a popular movie," Susan said. "I bet someone took it home to see it."

I stared at her. "Now who would do a thing like that?"

"I don't know!" Susan blinked feverishly. I hoped she wasn't going to burst into tears.

I hurried to the meeting room. "Sorry, there's been a delay. I'll get to the bottom of it."

"Susan seems to think someone absconded with the movie," an elderly gentleman said. "Is that so?"

I cocked my head. "I intend to find out. Be back as soon as I can."

I hurried to my office, where Susan was rummaging through the shelves in the cabinet. When she heard me, she turned around. "It's not here."

"Call Trish. Ask her where and when she saw it last."

Susan picked up the phone, seemingly glad to have something to do. I wished I knew what to do next.

"Where is that movie?" I muttered to myself as I made a mad dash to the shelves of movies on the odd chance someone had put it there. Or, if I was lucky, there might be another copy. Then it hit me: Dorothy had taken it!

This wasn't her first bit of sabotage either. The day before, she'd called one of the monthly program presenters, identified herself as me, and told him the program had been canceled. Good thing Trish had called him shortly afterward because he was in the habit of mixing up his dates. And to think Dorothy was Evelyn's niece.

Where did she hide that movie? I couldn't very well insist on searching the reference desk. If it wasn't there, I'd look like an idiot.

"Where did Dorothy put it?" I muttered to myself.

"So you figured it out." Evelyn was walking beside me and keeping pace, quite a feat for an older woman. But then again, she was a ghost.

"It wasn't difficult."

"Don't blame me. Dorothy inherited her spiteful tendencies from the other side of the family. Her mother—my sister, Frieda—was the most amiable woman."

"Where is it?" I asked. Too loudly, judging by the scowl a patron sent my way.

"Nestled among the documentaries, I'm afraid."

A minute later, film in hand, I rushed down to the meeting room. "I have it!" I inserted the DVD in the player, dimmed the lights, and walked slowly back to my office.

"Evelyn, are you still with me?" I whispered.

"Right beside you. I faded to conserve energy."

"Tell me, what does your niece Dorothy hate?"

"Crowds, broccoli, people talking during a movie. Why do you ask?"

"Why do you think? What is she afraid of?"

"Flying, spiders—"

"Spiders!" I grinned. "Thanks, Evelyn. You're a dear."

A band of cold gripped my arm. "Promise me you won't hurt her."

"Of course not. I simply want her to stop harassing me."

* * *

After lunch the following day, I browsed through the party store until I found exactly what I wanted—a big black rubber spider. Back in my office, I scribbled a note: "Any more of your little tricks, and you'll find a real one in your desk. Or maybe your car. Or perhaps your bed."

Of course, I hadn't the foggiest idea how I'd get a spider into Dorothy's car or bed, but I thought it best to cover all three bases. I worked with one eye on the reference desk and bided my time. The moment Dorothy headed for the ladies' room, I dropped off the spider and note. When she returned ten minutes later, I grabbed my iPhone, but was too late to snap a photo. No matter. Dorothy's shriek and expression of horror were fixed in my memory for years to come.

Chapter Three

I awoke on Thursday morning with a sense of anticipation. Like most people, I loved the idea of a cold case being solved, and I couldn't wait to hear what former detective Buckley had discovered.

I stopped at the bakery on my way to work. It was the library's policy to serve coffee and cake at major programs. Trish had offered to pick up a few cakes at the supermarket, but I wanted bakery cookies for my first big event. After some deliberation, I settled on a pound of chocolate chip cookies, a pound of mini Linzer tarts, and two pounds of blueberry yogurt cookies.

I hummed as I worked through the afternoon. My first major program! And such a fascinating subject. I could hardly wait for seven thirty to come.

Al Buckley's upcoming talk had stirred up both interest and controversy. Laura Foster's older son, Ryan, had called Sally a few times to try to convince her to cancel the program. He doubted Buckley had unearthed any new evidence regarding his mother's murder and thought he was only after publicity for the book he was writing about the case. For once,

Sally was unsure of what to do. I advised her to go ahead with the program. She agreed, but I think it was only because she knew it would draw an audience large enough to fill all sixty seats in the library's meeting room. She asked both Trish and Susan to be on hand to deal with the mob we expected. My two assistants were only too eager to oblige.

At five, I asked our two custodians to start setting up chairs in the meeting room, which was long and narrow and devoid of windows and character. The proposed library renovations included plans for a stadium-seating auditorium. I couldn't wait for the work to begin in the coming year.

At seven, Trish filled the large coffeemaker while I arranged the cookies on trays. I placed a glass and bottle of water on the table our guest would be using. At seven fifteen, the man himself strode into the room carrying an iPad and a huge board, which he placed on the easel he'd requested we provide. Former detective Al Buckley stood about six feet tall and had brown eyes and salt-and-pepper hair. He appeared to be about sixty, imposing rather than handsome in his black turtleneck and gray sports jacket. He was well on his way to developing a paunch, which led me to believe he was a big fan of beer or desserts.

"Good evening, Detective Buckley. I'm Carrie Singleton, the head of programs and events. It's my pleasure to welcome you to the Clover Ridge Library."

He placed his iPad on the table and took my hand in both of his. "I'm glad to meet you, Carrie. Call me Al, why don't you?"

His grasp, like his voice, was firm yet gentle. He gazed into my eyes, making me the focus of his attention. He must have been one hell of a detective. I hardly knew this man, yet in his presence I felt protected from the evils of the world. I had to look away so he couldn't see the tears that had sprung to my eyes. The last time I'd felt this way, I was ten and in my father's arms—minutes before he took off on one of his long absences.

Al gestured to the doorway, where Sally was standing guard until seven thirty. "I see we have a good-sized audience tonight."

"People are eager to find out what new information you've uncovered about the case," I said.

"I'm glad Laura's nearest and dearest are here. I want to hear what they have to say."

Startled, I said, "You mean you'd like them to hear what you have to say."

"That too."

"Did you know they'd be coming?"

"Laura's son Jared filled me in this afternoon." I must have looked surprised, because he added, "We've kept in touch."

"His older brother wanted us to cancel the program." I felt drawn to this man and wanted to prepare him for possible hostile comments.

Al's smile held amusement and irony. "Still, Ryan couldn't resist showing up. Along with their lawyer, I see. The guy called last night to warn me I run the risk of being sued if, in the course of my presentation, I defame anyone's character by falsely accusing him or her of having murdered Laura."

"How odd. You'd think they'd want to know who killed her."

"You'd think."

"What did you tell the lawyer?" I asked.

"I hung up on him. Now, if you'll excuse me . . ."

Al turned on his iPad, and I headed for the refreshment table. Too late, I realized I should have asked how he liked his coffee. At least I could bring him some cookies to munch on before the crowd descended and devoured them all. I selected a Linzer tart, a chocolate chip, and a blueberry yogurt cookie and carried the plate to his table. Al nodded his appreciation without looking up from his iPad.

"Coffee?" I asked.

"Black. Thanks."

I brought him his coffee and then joined Sally. The sound of voices coming from the hall on the other side of the door was surprisingly loud. Sally put her hand to her temple as though she had a headache.

"Trish and Susan are out there on mob control. Keep the first row empty for the family. Bryce Foster and his two sons are here, along with their lawyer. Jared expects his uncle George will show up as well." Sally lowered her voice. "Though he probably won't sit with them. George Ruskin's convinced Bryce killed Laura or had her killed."

"The husband's always Suspect Number One."

Sally glared at me, her eyes bright with fury. "Watch what you say, Carrie. I've known Bryce Foster all my life. He'd never kill anyone, least of all the wife he adored."

"Sorry," I muttered.

She blinked as though she were emerging from a dark place. "Forgive me. This program is difficult for everyone who knows the Foster family. I'll be happy the moment it's over."

When the minute hand on the clock above us moved to six, Sally opened the door. Men and women spilled into the room, making a mad dash for the chairs in the front. It took all my strength and effort to keep the first row free.

"You're welcome to coffee and cookies, then please take your seats," I shouted to be heard above the din. "The program will begin in ten minutes."

Sally pointed to the four men walking toward me. The family entourage. Two were in their fifties. The two younger men—Laura's sons—were in their late twenties, early thirties. Both were good-looking, with dark hair and eyes and nice, even features. I assumed the taller, scowling brother was Ryan.

"We've saved these seats for you," I said.

"Thanks." Jared flashed me a smile, which I returned.

"Much appreciated," muttered one of the older men. His face was red, and the sweater he wore under his open jacket stretched across his bulging stomach. I figured he must be either Laura's husband or her brother because the handsome, gray-haired man beside him wore a three-piece suit, announcing to one and all that he was the family lawyer, attending the program in his professional capacity.

A fifth man trailed after the others. He was tall and well built, like Laura's sons, and looked dapper in a brown leather jacket and charcoal slacks that appeared to be expensive. He walked over to Jared and whispered in his ear. Jared said something to the red-faced man sitting next to him, whom I'd decided was his father, Bryce. Father and son exchanged animated whispers until Jared, Bryce, and the lawyer moved down a seat so George Ruskin could sit between his two nephews.

A woman in her fifties rushed over to the first row and, with various squeals and giggles, hugged each family member in turn. She was plump and attractive in a look-at-me sort of way. Her bleach-blonde hair framed her heart-shaped face most becomingly, and the purple scarf draped stylishly around her neck set off her green-and-purple outfit.

"Sorry to interrupt," I told the family group, "but please help yourselves to coffee and cookies before we begin the program."

I pointed to the line snaking past Al's table as people made their way to the refreshments in the far corner of the room. Still chatting with one another, the Fosters joined the queue.

I glanced at the clock. It was seven thirty-eight. The line was almost as long as it had been five minutes ago. People were in socializing mode, as if they were attending a party. No way was this program getting under way in two minutes. My stomach quivered. I'd miscalculated. I had to tell Al there would be a delay. He'd probably timed his talk down to the minute and wouldn't appreciate its being cut short.

But Al wasn't at his table. The quivers turned into spasms. Where on earth could he be?

Frantically, I looked around the crowded room and gave a sigh of relief when I saw him, coffee cup in hand, talking to Jared a few feet from the refreshments table.

I hurried over to them. "Al, I'm afraid we'll be starting a bit later than planned. I didn't expect this part to take so long."

He smiled. "Not to worry." He gestured with the hand holding his coffee. "Jared, meet Carrie Singleton. Carrie, Jared Foster."

Jared and I exchanged smiles again. This time we shook hands.

"Pleased to meet you, Carrie. And thanks for setting up this program. I can't wait to hear what new evidence Al's uncovered. I want my mother's murderer put away, no matter how long it takes."

"I can well imagine," I said. "But I must admit, tonight's program wasn't my doing. I only took over this position last week."

Trish appeared at my side. "Sally's pissed," she whispered in my ear. "She's begun another line to the refreshments so we can get started ASAP."

Sure enough, about fifteen people were following Sally across the back of the room. "Oh, no! Why didn't I think of that?"

"My bad. I should have remembered we always form two lines when there's a crowd like this." Trish turned to leave and almost collided with Ryan Foster stomping toward us, his gaze fixed on Al.

"So what's this new evidence you have, Buckley? Don't you think you should bring it to the police instead of writing a book about it?"

"I talked to them," Al said. "What they'll do with it is another matter."

Ryan's expression grew angrier with every word. "What's your big find? Something you overlooked fifteen years ago?"

The air crackled with hostility.

"I admit I made mistakes during the investigation," Al said. "I regret it every day."

"Mistakes! You screwed up royally."

Jared put a hand on his brother's arm. "Chill out, Ryan. You gave your word you wouldn't make a scene."

Ryan shrugged free. "He's just playing with us, aren't you, Buckley? You're bored, with nothing to do, so you pretend you've found our mother's murderer."

Any minute now, Ryan was going to take a swing at Al. I had to do something.

"That's enough!" I was amazed at how assertive and calm I sounded. "Our program's about to begin." I cleared my throat. "Our program's about to begin," I shouted so everyone could hear. "Please take your seats."

Thank goodness the audience took heed and began to settle down. Those still in line grabbed a cookie or two and returned to their seats. Jared shot me a look of gratitude. Al was halfway to his table. I hurried after him, mentally running through what I'd planned to say in my introduction.

I told the audience about Al's work in the police department, something most of them already knew, then took the last seat in the first row as he started his lecture. He described his role as the detective in charge of the investigation into the death of Laura Foster. He explained that Laura had been alone in the house that night because Bryce had gone to a meeting and the boys were out—Ryan visiting a friend and Jared at basketball practice.

He walked over to the easel, which held a large diagram of the floor plan of the Foster home. "There was no sign of a break-in, which means Laura probably knew her killer."

"We know all this. Where's your new evidence?" Ryan called out.

"All in good time." Al sipped his coffee, then ate the Linzer tart I'd brought him earlier.

Like everyone else in the room, I watched him chew as I waited to hear what he'd say next.

"Many of you here knew Laura as a friend or neighbor, a member of the civic association, or a library aide. Before I talk about the evidence I've uncovered, I'm asking those of you who knew Laura to share your memories about her." He paused. "Especially those memories that are yours alone."

Murmurs coursed through the audience as couples and friends turned to one another. Al finished off the chocolate chip cookie in two bites. Two cookies remained. Interesting. I'd placed three cookies on his plate. I supposed he'd brought another one over from the refreshment table.

As he lifted the blueberry yogurt cookie to his mouth, I noticed the remaining cookie was dark brown. Chocolate! No wonder. Al was probably a chocolate freak. Someone must have brought it, because I didn't remember buying any chocolate cookies.

Silence reigned. I nearly sighed with relief when Sally began to speak.

"Laura was a valued aide here at the library. She was warm and friendly to patrons and put everything she had into the job. Once, she spent an entire hour researching an obscure fact for someone. That was the Laura Foster I knew."

"Thank you, Sally." Al chomped on the last of his blueberry yogurt cookie. "Anyone else?" He grinned, looking mischievous. "Anyone remember Laura doing something out of character? Something completely un-Laura-like? Did she hate anything? Or anyone?"

Ryan leaped to his feet. "This is pathetic. A thief murdered my mother."

"Is that so?" Al asked calmly.

"Yeah!" Ryan answered. "Her antique peacock pin was stolen, along with her favorite gold bracelet. Or have you forgotten?"

"I haven't forgotten." Al downed the last of his coffee. "We always knew robbery was a possible motive, though no other jewelry was taken." He bit into the chocolate cookie. "Was Laura really as perfect as everyone claims?"

Bryce's red face turned redder. Laura's brother, George, started to rise and then sat again.

"Does anyone know something Laura did that was less than ideal?" Al asked.

"She hated ironing," Jared said.

A rumble of laughter spread through the audience.

"Laura told me something important," said the bleach-blonde woman sitting with the family in the first row. "I feel bad about betraying her confidence, even after all these years."

"Now's the time to speak up," Al said, "so we can get to the truth of the matter. Why don't you introduce yourself?"

The woman stood and faced the rows of patrons behind her. "My name's Helena Koppel. Laura was my best friend."

"And what would you like to share with us tonight?" Al sank into the chair behind the table. His face was pale, and he seemed to be having trouble breathing.

Helena turned to Bryce. "I'm sorry, Bryce, but I have to get this off my chest." She sniffed. "Maybe if I'd told the police fifteen years ago, Laura's killer would be in prison now."

"What on earth are you talking about, Helena?" Bryce demanded. "Spit it out, for God's sake."

She drew a deep breath. Why was I getting the feeling she was enjoying this?

"The night before she died, Laura called to tell me she was very unhappy."

"Nonsense!" Bryce said.

"It wasn't the first time she'd cried on my shoulder. Only this time, she said she wanted a divorce."

A braying laugh broke the stillness. It came from Ryan. "You're so full of it, Helena. My mother never told you any such thing. Only, you can't stop making yourself the center of attention, can you?"

Bursts of conversation broke out. The Fosters' lawyer looked very stern as he addressed Helena in whispers, no doubt warning her that she could be sued for saying such things about his client and his dead wife.

Al slumped in his chair.

I ran to him as his head dropped to the table. "Somebody help!"

Jared rushed over and felt Al's neck for a pulse. "I can't feel anything."

A man joined us, saying he was a doctor. He placed three fingers on Al's wrist. He raised Al's head so he could look into his eyes.

"He's gone, I'm afraid. I'll call the authorities." The doctor spoke into his cell phone.

"Someone poisoned Al," I said as tears streamed down my cheeks, "and it's all my fault."

Chapter Four

I stumbled to my feet to face the audience. My voice shook as I asked everyone to remain seated. "Al Buckley is dead. The police have been called. They'll be here soon and will want to talk to you."

Silence reigned for a moment, then the room buzzed like an angry hive of bees. People shouted, demanding more information. I was relieved to see Sally stride to the front of the room, even though her eyes bore into mine like lasers. I had the good sense to sit down.

"I'm afraid Detective Buckley has suffered a fatal heart attack," she announced. "The police will be here momentarily, but you're free to leave."

She approached me, her lips tight with anger. "You've managed to make a terrible situation worse than it is," she hissed into my ear. "The poor man died of natural causes. No one poisoned him."

Patrons couldn't exit fast enough, though they gathered in groups outside the meeting room to discuss what had just happened.

"We should stop them!" I told Sally.

"Why? I have a list of everyone here if the police want it." She kept the few curious patrons who tried to approach the table where Al sat slumped over from getting any closer.

I remained in my seat, my face in my hands, not sure what I should be doing.

"I can't believe this happened."

I looked up at Jared Foster standing before me. "Me neither," I said. "He was perfectly fine one minute, and the next . . ."

"I think you're right. Someone wanted Al dead."

I bit my lip. "Please believe me, it wasn't me, though I did buy the cookies."

A ghost of a smile hovered on Jared's lips. "I believe you. People have been chomping them by the dozen, and no one else seems the worse for it."

"Thank you."

"I'd better go and call Al's kids."

I watched him exit the room with the last of the stragglers.

Only Sally, Trish, Susan, and I remained when, minutes later, several police officers swarmed into the meeting hall. The medical examiner and tech team arrived shortly after. The ME checked over the body and then ordered it to be removed as the technicians photographed and dusted the plate and cup Al had been using, as well as the table itself. They did the same to everything on the refreshment table.

Lieutenant Mathers appeared to be in charge of the crime scene. He was a tall man with broad shoulders and shaggy blond eyebrows that gave him a perpetually quizzical look. His blue eyes were keen but kind as I expressed how shocked I'd been to see Al collapse and die in the middle of his presentation and how I'd observed Al eat a chocolate cookie that wasn't one that I'd bought at the bakery.

"Did you see anyone approach his table? Did Detective Buckley have an altercation with anyone present?" Lieutenant Mathers asked.

I described the exchange between Al and Ryan Foster and told him that Ryan had wanted us to cancel the program.

The uniformed officer who'd accompanied Lieutenant Mathers never spoke a word as he recorded my responses.

I drove home slowly, still traumatized by the evening's tragedy. Aunt Harriet and Uncle Bosco were waiting for me at the front door. Of course someone had called them. I fell into their arms and sobbed as I hadn't since I was thirteen and my dog had been run over.

"I've made you some hot chocolate with rum in it," Aunt Harriet said.

"Then get into bed and don't bother setting your alarm," Uncle Bosco chimed in. "The library will be closed until tomorrow afternoon."

The police allowed us to open the library at one on Friday, when their various teams were finished examining the meeting room. I stayed in my office and worked on the next bulletin, dreading the time I'd have to man the hospitality desk. Sure enough, during the two hours I sat there, almost every patron I assisted brought up the subject of Al's death. Of course, I remained polite and circumspect, agreeing it was a terrible shock to everyone present. Inside, I was a quivering mess. Sally had been reluctant to have Al Buckley do his presentation. I had no business advising her to go ahead with it.

I nibbled at my thumb cuticles until I drew blood as I waited for Sally's reprimand. Was she planning to fire me? Did she hold me responsible for Al's death? But she didn't show up at my office to ream me out. Angela said she was holed up in the conference room with the library board, and later in the day, Lieutenant Mathers came to speak to her.

The next few days passed slowly. I came to work on Saturday. I started the afternoon movie and then helped out at the computer station. Still no sign of Sally.

Sunday I had off from work. Lieutenant Mathers came to the house to interview me that afternoon. He asked the same questions he'd posed on Thursday evening and then questioned me closely regarding how I'd spent the short period of time when everyone was having coffee and cookies.

Did I remember which cookies I had put on his plate?

Had I noticed anyone approaching Al's table?

Had anyone appeared furtive or unusually anxious?

Sally's e-mail arrived that evening around seven: "See me first thing tomorrow in my office."

I knew it! She's going to fire me.

I went downstairs, where my aunt and uncle were watching TV in the den.

"Hear anything new about the Al Buckley case?" I asked Uncle Bosco.

"No, honey. Sorry."

Would Uncle Bosco tell me if Sally was planning to fire me? I couldn't bring myself to ask. Instead, I asked if either of them wanted tea. They both did, so I went into the kitchen, glad for something to do. I twisted and turned most of the night, wondering how, in such a short time, my position at the library had become so important to me. All I could think was that I was about to be fired.

* * *

Monday morning, I crept into Sally's office and perched on the edge of the visitor's chair.

Sally's grim expression did nothing to dispel my anxiety. "I should have canceled the program as Ryan Foster asked me to—as my common sense told me to do—and not have listened to you, an outsider with no understanding of what Laura's murder did to our town."

"I'm so sorry." My voice cracked with emotion. "I had no idea someone would want to kill Al—Detective Buckley."

Sally shot me a look of pure hostility. "He was poisoned. The poison was injected into a cookie."

I gulped in air. "I told Lieutenant Mathers I noticed Detective Buckley eating a chocolate cookie before he died. I figured someone must have brought in a batch of them, since I hadn't bought any chocolate cookies."

"There were no chocolate cookies on the table, Carrie."

My body quivered as if I'd touched a live socket. "You don't think I gave him a poisoned cookie!"

"Of course I don't! But I'm angry and upset that a presenter—someone who lived and worked in Clover Ridge—was killed in our meeting room. It's a disgrace, and frankly, it's bad publicity for the library."

Bad publicity? I opened my mouth to say that was the last thing to be concerned about but shut it just in time.

Sally was understandably distressed. After all, she was the library's director and responsible for what went on in the library. The board might hold her responsible for going ahead with a presentation that had resulted in a homicide, and she might lose her job.

"His iPad's gone missing," Sally said.

"I didn't know. The police asked me what Detective Buckley had brought with him Thursday night. I mentioned the iPad, of course."

"Well, it's gone. That's where he kept all his notes and updates regarding his book."

"Do you think he really figured out who the murderer was? He seemed very interested in hearing what people who knew the murder victim had to say about her."

"I can't imagine what was running through his head," Sally said.

"I suppose the murderer took the iPad."

Sally shuddered. "Awful to think there's a murderer running loose around town." She looked at me as though she was surprised to find me still there. "At any rate, it's time you got to work. I'm sure you have plenty to keep you occupied."

I was glad to escape to my office. As I pored through the list of possible new events for the month of March, a part of my mind couldn't stop returning to Al Buckley. I'd liked the man. Liked the fact that despite failing to find Laura Foster's murderer fifteen years ago, he'd made every effort to do so now.

I couldn't shake the image of his death—right before my eyes! Sally was right. He was dead in part because I'd insisted on holding the event. If I hadn't urged her to go ahead with the program, Al Buckley would still be alive today. Someone in that room had killed him. It could have been a member of the library staff, one of Laura's friends or neighbors, or a member of her family.

I bolted upright in my chair as I came to a decision: I'd find Al Buckley's murderer. It was the least I could do. He was a dedicated detective who had made it his life's work to find Laura Foster's killer long after he'd retired. I choked back a sob as I remembered how warm and protected I'd felt while talking to him. Al Buckley cared about people—unlike my own father, who'd spent most of my early years away from his family.

That evening after dinner, I turned down my aunt and uncle's kind invitation to accompany them to see a romantic comedy that I'd been meaning to catch at the nearby multiplex. Instead, I stretched out on my four-poster bed with my laptop computer. I Googled Laura Foster and came up with at least forty articles about her death.

It had happened the first week in February almost fifteen years ago. That night, Laura was alone in the house from eight until the time she was murdered. Bryce Foster had gone to a civic association meeting, Ryan had gone to a friend's house, and Jared had basketball practice at the high school. Ryan was the first to arrive home. He parked his car in the driveway, careful to leave room for his father's car. All the lights in the house were on. He found his mother sprawled on the living room floor. A good deal of blood was pooled around the back of her head. A ceramic Chinese vase lay on its side, two feet from his mother's body. He called the police.

The ME report said Laura Foster's death had been caused by a blow to the head. She had died between nine and ten that evening. The police said there was no sign someone had broken into the house, which led them to believe the murderer was someone Laura had known. If the murder had been premeditated, they thought, she'd opened the door to her killer, unaware of his or her homicidal intentions.

"So she knew her killer," I mused aloud. Again, that could be anyone she worked with at the library, a neighbor, or a friend. Her husband and her sons all had alibis. Jared hadn't come home until ten thirty. Bryce had left the civic association meeting early. He'd said he wanted to buy a few items at the small grocery near his home before it closed at nine thirty. And Ryan couldn't say exactly what time he had left his friend's house. After two interviews with the police, Ryan admitted that he and his friend had quarreled, and he had driven around for half an hour or so to cool his head before returning home.

Did Ryan kill his mother? I was allowing my dislike for Laura's older son to color my thinking.

The police had found no clues. The killer had wiped the vase clean of fingerprints with a dishrag that had been left near the victim's feet. No one had seen anyone enter the Foster home that night. There were no discernable tracks on the driveway to show that a visitor had parked there. The house was full of fingerprints, which was to be expected, as a couples book club meeting had been held in the Fosters' living room the Sunday before.

Everyone questioned stated that Laura Foster had been a very nice person. So why would someone want to kill her? The murder weapon was a vase, part of the Foster home decor. It could be that whoever had murdered Laura hadn't gone there intending to kill her. Perhaps he or she had wanted to talk to Laura about a pressing matter. An argument had erupted. The killer had been incensed enough to reach for an object and attack.

Or was the murderer familiar with the Foster house and knew exactly where he or she could reach for a weapon at the moment of need?

Questions about the case reeled around my brain, and I had to put them into some kind of order. I needed help with my new project and knew of two people who could be of assistance.

* * *

"You suffered a terrible shock Thursday evening. How are you feeling?" Evelyn Havers asked as I settled into my chair the following morning.

"I'm still terribly upset. It was horrible, watching Detective Buckley die as we all sat there." I shivered. "I shouldn't have urged Sally to go ahead with the program. She was thinking about canceling."

Evelyn dismissed my self-recrimination with a wave of her hand. "Don't you go thinking it's your fault, Carrie Singleton. Sally runs this show. If she didn't want the program to be presented, believe me, she would have told Al Buckley to stay home."

"But he died eating a poisoned cookie! And I feel responsible."

"A cookie you didn't buy or put on his plate."

I studied Evelyn, wondering how she got her information. And where did she keep her clothes? Today she wore a coral-colored cardigan over a white blouse and the same sensible gray skirt and white rubber-soled shoes that nurses wore.

"True, but I was the organizer. More than that, I liked the man. I liked what he was doing—exposing Laura Foster's murderer after all these years."

Evelyn pursed her lips. "He had a funny way of going about it. All those questions. Hoping for more leads and information."

"Tell me about Laura. Everyone said she was an especially nice woman."

Evelyn perched on the edge of my desk. "She was nice enough, and most people liked her. Though she had many sides, like everyone else."

"What do you mean? It sounds as though she wasn't as perfect as people claimed."

"Who claimed? Sally? She likes to whitewash every situation, especially when it comes to the library."

I cleared my throat. "Did you like Laura?"

"I did, and I'm sorry someone killed her. Why all these questions?"

"I'm curious. Al Buckley came to the library saying he had discovered her murderer after fifteen years, and then he was murdered."

"You mustn't feel responsible."

"But I do, in a way."

"That's ridiculous!"

When I said nothing, Evelyn touched my arm, sending a chill through my body. "I hope you're not planning to find out who killed him."

"I'd like to know more about Laura Foster, since I think her killer probably poisoned Al."

"Leave it to the police, girl!"

Her anger startled me. "You said you felt you were meant to help me. Maybe it was to find their killer."

She shook her head, her mouth as tight as a seam. "I don't know about that. Anyway, I don't want to talk about Laura."

Strange. "Okay. What can you tell me about Al Buckley?"

Evelyn seemed to relax. "I hardly knew him. Knew his wife, though, from church. Thelma Buckley was a nice woman. Always willing to take on the tasks no one else wanted. She was proud of her husband, proud when he made detective. But after a few years, she looked worn and worried whenever I saw her. I heard he'd been drinking. And then there was some fracas when he got involved in a bar fight. He was removed from Laura's case shortly after that. Thelma took their son and daughter and moved to North Carolina, where she was from."

I considered all that Evelyn had told me. It wasn't much, considering her usual forthcoming conversations about anything connected to the library. I suspected she knew more than she was willing to tell me about Laura's "many sides." Why not say what she knew all these years later? How could she not want Laura's murder solved? And what had caused Al Buckley to start drinking heavily after he made detective? Trish had said that her father played cards with him. She'd probably know more about his personal life.

I checked my e-mail, delighted to finally hear back from the classical quartet that Jeannie, the head of P and E in the library one town over, had raved about. They were able to come to our library the third Sunday in May, one of the dates I'd given her. I checked my calendar and saw the day was still open, so I wrote back immediately, saying we'd be glad to host them.

I received a few more responses regarding programs I wanted to present and composed e-mails to two presenters I felt obligated to drop. One was a tenor who sang arias and talked about operas. Barbara's note said he'd been a popular draw for years until last May, when his voice cracked and he repeated himself several times. Barbara had written that it was both embarrassing and sad to see the effects of aging and a failing memory. The other was a history professor at the nearby junior college who wanted to talk about an archeological trip he'd taken with his wife. His presentation nine months earlier had been boring, Barbara had written, and several patrons had walked out as he rambled on. I sighed. I didn't have much experience turning people down. I'd run the e-mails by Sally before sending them out.

I looked up and realized it was time to stop for lunch. I put on my jacket and was walking down the hall when Sally came toward me.

"They're having a memorial service for Detective Buckley tomorrow morning. Would you like to go and represent the library?"

"I would!"

"Very well. It starts at ten thirty. I'll text you the directions."

Chapter Five

As it turned out, Aunt Harriet and Uncle Bosco also planned to attend the memorial service for Al Buckley, so we set out for town hall, which was just a short walk around the corner of the Green.

"The mayor's making it his business to attend," Uncle Bosco said.

"As he should," Aunt Harriet said. "Al Buckley was an upstanding citizen and an officer of our police force."

"Too bad he had to retire before he straightened himself out."

"The important thing is he *did* straighten himself out. And recently he was on the verge of solving a cold case."

"So he claimed," Uncle Bosco said darkly.

We joined the crowd entering the white building through the double doors. Aunt Harriet and I lost Uncle Bosco when he stopped to speak to Mayor Tripp.

"Let's get seats," Aunt Harriet said. "Your uncle will join us before the service begins."

We found three seats in the center of the auditorium. I looked around, surprised by all the people who had come to pay their respects and bid farewell to retired Detective Albert Stephen Buckley. From what Trish had told me, Al was pretty much a loner after leaving the police force. I imagined most of those present were here because of his appearance at the library last Thursday night and the shocking way he'd died.

Lieutenant Mathers was among the group of police officers in their dress uniforms sitting in the back row. He noticed me and tipped his head in recognition. I gave him a small smile and then turned around. I was a bit annoyed that he hadn't told me about Al's being poisoned and his iPad disappearing when he'd questioned me a second time, though he'd told Sally. Then I told myself not to be petty. After all, Sally was the library's director and could be expected to be informed about how the investigation was progressing. But if I was going to find the murderer, I needed this information too.

I glanced at Uncle Bosco, who sank noisily into his seat between Aunt Harriet and me. "Do you know Lieutenant Mathers well?"

"John Mathers? The lieutenant who questioned you?" Uncle Bosco asked.

"Uh-huh."

"Sure do. I've known him ever since he was born. His daddy and I did our share of business together. Why do you ask, honey?"

"Soon as this ends, I'd like to ask him how the investigation's coming along."

Uncle Bosco chuckled. "I'm afraid he and his group will be the first to express their condolences to the grieving family and then be on their way. But I can always drop in at the station and make a few inquiries if you like."

"I'd like it very much. I'm so sorry Al's dead."

Aunt Harriet gently elbowed Uncle Bosco's large stomach. "Shhh. They're starting."

Sure enough, a man who appeared to be in his late thirties to early forties with a build like Al's was moving to the front of the room.

"Frank Buckley," Uncle Bosco said. "He was a good kid."

"Did you forget about the time he and Joey LaSalle climbed the water tower and scribbled all over it?" Aunt Harriet whispered.

"That was over twenty years ago. You have to be more forgiving."

Frank Buckley spoke eloquently about his father, both as a father, and as an officer of the law. He concluded to a burst of applause and then sat down. A young woman wearing a loose brown dress that nearly reached her ankles took his place.

"Jennifer's lost weight," Aunt Harriet whispered to me, loud enough for the people around us to hear. "She's a pretty girl but needs to wear more attractive clothes. But then, her mother never dressed well."

This time, Uncle Bosco jabbed Aunt Harriet's arm. "Shhh, my love."

A boy and girl—I'd guess eight and ten—came up to say how much they loved their popo and were going to miss him. The little girl added that she hoped the bad man who killed her popo would get caught and punished.

Frank returned to the podium and asked if anyone would like to say a few words. A man wearing a down vest over a red plaid shirt got to his feet and walked to the front of the hall. Trish's father, I assumed, since she was sitting beside him.

"Al Buckley was a wonderful man. I was proud to call him my friend. He spent his last year gathering evidence to solve his last murder case. I hope his killer is found—and soon."

Murmuring filled the hall as friends and spouses spoke to one another. I turned to see how the six police officers were taking this subtle nudge to action; they were talking among themselves. Silence fell. Then Jared, who had been sitting in the front row with Al's family, walked to the podium.

"Through the fifteen years since my mother's death, Al stayed in touch with me. Even after he left the police department, he never gave up trying to find out who killed my mother. I think it's safe to say the same person who killed her killed Al Buckley."

His direct gaze swept across the audience. "And I'll do my level best to find him."

I joined in the applause that lasted until Jared took his seat.

The police who were present must have decided it was time they put in a word to defend themselves.

Lieutenant Mathers strode to the front of the hall. "The Clover Ridge Police Department is doing everything in its power to find the person who murdered retired Detective Albert Buckley, one of our own. We are interviewing everyone who attended Detective Buckley's presentation at the library last Thursday night as we try to discover who is responsible for his untimely death. We ask that you contact us if you have any information related to this case."

He looked sternly at Jared. "We also ask that you not do any investigating of your own."

People raised their hands to ask the lieutenant questions. He'd answered three when Frank announced that this was a memorial for his father and not an occasion to question the police.

A priest came forward to speak about Al and lead us in prayer, and then the memorial was over. I told Aunt Harriet and Uncle Bosco I wanted to try to catch Lieutenant Mathers before I went to work, but Uncle Bosco was right. By the time I'd squeezed out of our row, the men and women in blue were gone. Trish called to me, and I waited for her and her father to reach me in the crowded aisle.

"Carrie, this is my dad. Dad, this is Carrie Singleton, my new boss at the library."

"Roy Peters. Pleased to meet you." Trish's dad stretched out his hand and we shook.

"Trish tells me you used to play cards with Al."

"Every Friday night. He was a man of great character, and he felt things deeply."

"I only met him the night he died, but I sensed he was someone you could count on."

"For sure. He lost his way there for a while. Started drinking heavily after he was injured on the job. Then he and Thelma split, and the drinking got worse. But he came back a good man, stronger than ever. Did volunteer work at the veterans' nursing home. Then he got all obsessed with the Foster murder case. Regretted how he'd failed to catch Laura's murderer and vowed to find him." Roy laughed. "Before long, he was spending his days going over his notes on the case."

I opened my mouth to ask Roy if Al had interviewed any of the suspects again when a couple squeezed past us.

"Come on, Dad," Trish said. "We're blocking traffic. Besides, I have to get home and get ready for work."

"Yes, my love," Roy said to his daughter. "Nice to meet you, Carrie."

"Nice to meet you too, Roy. I'd love to talk to you about Al someday soon. I admire the way he was investigating Laura Foster's murder after all these years."

Roy winked. "Planning on solving the murders yourself, are you?"

I felt the blood rushing to my ears. "Of course not. But I feel awful about the way he died."

"Anytime you want to talk, just give me a call. I have plenty of free time, now that I'm retired. Trish will give you my number."

I thanked Roy and followed him and Trish up the aisle.

"Carrie!" someone called behind me.

I turned around.

Jared Foster was waving his hand. "Wait up!"

I stepped into a row and waited for him to take the seat beside me. He looked handsome in his navy suit, blue shirt, and bourbon-colored tie.

"I'm glad to see you here."

"Sally asked me to come on behalf of the library, but I wanted to come. I liked Al, and I'm terribly sorry about the way he died."

"Someone murdered him!" Jared gestured at the people leaving the hall. "Look at them. Curiosity vultures—or worse. Like the drivers who rubberneck as they pass an accident."

"*Schadenfreude*," I murmured. "Taking pleasure in the misfortune of others."

"And with two murders possibly linked, how could they resist?"

"I was thinking of calling to see how you were doing. I know you were close to Al and glad he was working hard to find out who murdered your mom."

Jared swallowed. "Al's death brings it all back—something my father and brother can never understand."

"Your dad was against Al's reopening the investigation?"

"It was hard for him, especially the hostile way Ryan reacted. Dad went through so much when Mom died. He was never the same strong, confident man I remember. I think all this talk about finding my mother's killer was more painful for him than cathartic."

"Do you think Al had solid evidence to back up his assumptions? He seemed more interested in finding out what your mom's friends and neighbors had to say."

Jared laughed. "That was Al's way—always investigating and questioning to find the truth. Like a sculptor chipping away at a piece of marble to discover the beauty beneath."

How poetic.

"But to answer your question, I don't think he'd go around claiming he'd solved the case if he hadn't."

"If it was the same person who murdered your mother, he or she must have thought so too, because Al's iPad was stolen."

"Really?" Jared looked upset. "Everything he'd written—the manuscript, his notes—was on his iPad."

I suddenly realized we were the only two people in the auditorium, save for the janitor sweeping the front of the room.

I glanced at my watch. "I have to get to work. Sally's annoyed at me for insisting on having Al's presentation. I don't want to antagonize her more. And I want to extend my condolences to Al's children."

"Hey, would you like to talk about this some more over dinner? Antonio's in the next town serves the best Italian food around and carries artisanal imported beers."

"Sure."

Jared handed me his smartphone, and I clicked in my cell number.

"I'm seeing a client tonight. How about tomorrow?" he asked.

"Sounds good."

"I'll call you."

I grinned as we walked outside.

What kind of a client? I wondered. After telling Frank and his sister how sad I was about what had happened to their father, I headed to my car, pleased with the connections I'd made that morning. Though I'd missed the chance to speak to Lieutenant Mathers, I'd met Al's good friend Roy Peters and planned to talk to him in the future. Jared Foster wanted us to work together to find the person who'd murdered his mother and possibly Al Buckley—the very thing I wanted.

Jared was the one person who knew both victims well. It was possible he knew more than he realized.

Chapter Six

"Why are you checking out Jared Foster's Facebook page?" Trish asked.

I jumped up, banging my knee against the desk. "Just curious. We got to talking this morning after the service."

Trish's round face broke out in a grin. "You think he's cute."

"He's nice looking. Actually, I'm curious about Laura Foster's family. Did you know them when you were growing up?"

"I knew who they were because in Clover Ridge you know just about everyone. And when Laura was killed, we were always aware of Bryce and the two boys—what they did, where they went. It was like they were constantly on stage, with everyone watching them like a play."

"It must have been a terrible shock to them. Did the tragedy change them much?"

Trish chewed on her lower lip. "Bryce worked in finance on Wall Street before the murder. After Laura died, he walked around in a daze. He took time off but never went back. He eventually took a job managing the furniture store in the mall. Told everyone he wanted to stay closer to home."

"What about Ryan and Jared?"

"Ryan's thirty-one, three years younger than me. He's always had a mouth on him. As he got older, he became more belligerent. You heard how rude he was Thursday night. If he wasn't part of Laura's family, Sally would have ordered him out of the building."

"She'd do that?" I asked, astonished.

"Sally does lots of things that would surprise you."

"And Jared?"

Trish started to walk to her desk. She turned around. "He's twenty-nine, an accountant with the best firm in town. He was always a sweet kid. His mother's murder devastated him. And now Al, whom he thought the world of, gets poisoned after reopening her case."

"Anything else?"

"You mean, who is he dating?"

I felt my face grow warm. "I'm curious."

"As far as I know, no one right now, so the field is clear." Trish broke out into a grin. "Are you interested?"

"We're having dinner tomorrow night—to talk about the murders."

"Of course. To talk about the murders. There's no attraction."

This isn't going in the direction I wanted it to go. "Please don't tell anyone—not that it's a secret we're having a casual meal together. Only, this is a small town, and everyone knows everyone's business."

"Don't worry. I'm the soul of discretion."

"What kind of work does Ryan do?"

"If I remember correctly, he was planning to be a lawyer, but he got into a fight in his senior year of college and broke another student's jaw. He was expelled and never received his undergraduate degree. Bryce hooked him up with a few of his friends in the financial district, but it didn't work out. The last I heard, he's managing the game arcade in the mall. Another job Bryce got for him."

"He doesn't sound very stable," I said.

"Never was, never will be," was Trish's cryptic comment.

* * *

Thursday evening, I left the library at five sharp to give myself enough time to shower and change into something more casual before having dinner with Jared.

"How nice that you're going out on a date," Aunt Harriet said.

For the third time in the fifteen minutes since I'd arrived home, I gave a snort of exasperation. "As I've explained, Aunt Harriet, it's a friendly meal with a male acquaintance. Nothing more."

How frustrating that I couldn't tell her the real reason Jared and I were getting together, but our joining forces to investigate two murders would have upset her.

Aunt Harriet shot me a knowing smile. "Friendly, eh? It's good to be friendly, isn't it, Bosco?"

"Certainly, my dear." Uncle Bosco patted her arm. "It's good to start off on a friendly footing."

I gritted my teeth. "You two have it all wrong. And I think you've imbibed more than your limit."

"Our limit?" Aunt Harriet laughed. "I don't think you've ever seen us reach our limit."

"I'm going upstairs to shower."

I decided to wear black tights, a magenta tunic, and my new boots.

Aunt Harriet walked by the guest bathroom as I was brushing blush on my cheeks. "Don't you look pretty. And I've the perfect piece for you to wear."

"Please, don't bother . . ."

But she was back two minutes later with a long string of alternating silver and black onyx beads. She slipped it over my head and placed me in front of the mirror. "Lovely."

It *was* lovely. "Thank you, Aunt Harriet. I won't let anything happen to it tonight."

"I hope not, since it now belongs to you."

"You don't have to—"

"I want you to have it, Carrie. I have so many pretty things and no children to leave them to. I've given your cousins pieces of jewelry and family antiques over the years. Now I'd like you to have your share."

I hugged her tight, feeling those pesky tears starting again. Why was it that anytime someone was nice to me, I felt like bawling like a baby?

This isn't a date, I reminded myself as I dabbed blue eye shadow on my eyelids. Jared and I were putting our heads together to see if we could come up with some ideas as to who had murdered his mother and probably Al Buckley. In fact, I'd offered to meet him at the restaurant, but he said Antonio's was located off the beaten path and it was easy to miss the turnoff, so it would be wiser if he picked me up. Reluctantly, I'd agreed and made a mental note to be downstairs before seven so I could dash out when he arrived and avoid his having to exchange pleasantries with my aunt and uncle. Though I loved Aunt Harriet and Uncle Bosco dearly, I'd been living on my own for the past twelve years and wasn't used to having older, well-meaning relatives comment on my social life.

The doorbell rang at exactly seven. My heart pinged at the sight of Jared in well-fitted jeans and a black turtleneck sweater under a camel-colored blazer. We studied one another like two young kids, and then we both grinned at the same time.

"Nice to see you in casual clothes," he said.

"Nice to be in casual clothes."

Jared stepped inside and helped me on with my jacket.

"Good night," I called out, hoping my aunt and uncle would stay in the kitchen, where they were finishing their dinner.

"Good night," Aunt Harriet shouted.

"Have fun," came from Uncle Bosco.

"Thanks. Good night," Jared answered.

Was that giggling I heard as I closed the door behind me?

The moon shone our way to Jared's Lexus, which he'd parked in the driveway leading to the garage. He backed out carefully and made the necessary turns around the Green, and we were on our way.

We chatted easily about Clover Ridge and our jobs. It was as if we'd agreed to hold off any discussion about the murders until later.

"Your aunt and uncle are nice people," Jared said as we turned onto the narrow road that led to the restaurant. Sure enough, it curved around like a slithery snake. The only visible lights came from the headlights of the occasional oncoming car and from houses hidden by trees and bushes. "They've done a lot for Clover Ridge."

"Aunt Harriet and Uncle Bosco are the best, but I think it's time I found my own place."

Jared laughed. "I get that. My father and brother have no idea what the words *neat* and *orderly* mean. When I came home from college, I bought one of the newly built condos. Haven't moved since."

I grimaced. "I'd like to start off renting, but everything I see is so expensive."

"Check out the local paper and the real estate websites. Reasonable rentals, like reasonable house sales, are grabbed up immediately." He grinned. "I'll keep an eye out for you if you'd like."

"I'd appreciate that."

* * *

Antonio's was far busier than I would have thought on a Thursday evening. The front half was a pizza parlor and hopping with young families. Several people waved to Jared as we walked through to the entrance of the dining area.

The lighting there was dimmer, the only sound a guitar strumming a love song and the murmur of conversation of the four other parties already enjoying their meals. The hostess led us to a table in the back corner and handed us large menus.

Jared caught my expression of surprise. "Don't be put off by the formality of the place. The tablecloths are really paper, see?" He raised a corner and ripped it a quarter of an inch. "And the food's pizza and other basic dishes like spaghetti and meatballs and lasagna, with giant cannoli for dessert."

"I'm so relieved."

We both laughed.

I was still studying the beer and wine menu when our college-age waitress approached and lit the candle on our table. "Know what you want to drink?"

"So many choices!"

"What are you in the mood for?" Jared asked.

"Actually, I'd love a nice, full-bodied Chardonnay."

"In that case, I recommend the Kendall Grand Reserve," Jared said.

The waitress grinned and supported his choice.

He ordered a dark ale for himself. "You can taste it. See if you'd like it another time."

Another time. I liked the sound of that.

The waitress reappeared in what seemed like record time. She set down my wine and opened Jared's bottle. He shook his head when she offered to pour his ale into the insignia glass.

I took a sip. "Delicious."

Jared smiled. "Glad you like it." He took a pull on his ale and set the bottle down. "I come here often with clients. Amazing acoustics. Even when the room is full, you can hear the other person at your table. But for some reason, you can barely make out a word your neighbor's saying."

I strained to hear the conversation at the table closest to us but was unable to distinguish any words. "Amazing."

We ordered a mozzarella spinach salad to share, eggplant rollatini for me, and *frutti di mare* for Jared. An assortment of warm twists and rolls arrived. I selected a roll, spilled some olive oil on my bread plate, and tasted. "Mmm."

"Good, isn't it? This place is known for its bread," Jared said, biting into a garlic twist.

When our salad arrived, Jared dished some onto our salad plates. "Shall we begin?"

I looked at him. "Eating or analyzing the murders?"

"Both. What do they have in common? Who could have committed them?"

I considered his questions as I chewed my first forkful of salad. “I think it’s safe to say it’s likely that the same person who killed your mother killed Al.”

“The same person—if not a second person protecting the first.”

“Mmm. I never considered that.”

“I hope you’ll be able to figure out what I’ve failed to consider.”

I met his gaze and realized his eyes were hazel and not brown, as I’d previously thought. “I think we have to start with your family.”

“I agree.”

I raised my eyebrows in astonishment.

“Why are you surprised?” he asked. “I’ve gone over this a thousand times in my head, and there’s no evidence to support any one theory.”

“How did each member of your family get along with your mom?”

“I can tell you we weren’t the perfect TV family that friends and neighbors have since made us out to be. Ryan and I were in high school and trying to break out of the bubble Mom tried to create. Like Friday night family night, when the four of us did things together like eating dinner out or going to a movie. Ryan wasn’t having any of it. He’d say, ‘Where’s Dad if this is family night?’ Dad was working in the city then and came home late most nights, including Fridays.”

“Did you go out with your mom on Fridays?”

Jared shrugged. “I did for a while, but all she did was complain that Ryan and my dad weren’t with us, so I soon begged off.”

"Was Ryan always as angry as he was the night Al was murdered?"

"Not when we were little. He was a great older brother in elementary school—letting me play with his friends when they came over, things like that. He started to get moody when he was in eighth grade. He would fly off the handle for the smallest reason." Jared shook his head. "To this day, I can't figure out why."

"What about your parents' relationship?"

"It bothered Mom that Dad worked so many hours, but when Ryan brought it up, she always made excuses for him—said he had to make enough money to keep up our house and our way of living. Ryan thought she was being a pushover, accepting the late hours, and his anger was really directed at Dad. But that's changed."

"How?"

"They're the best of pals these days. Live blocks from one another, go out for dinner occasionally."

"And where do you fit in?"

"It's funny. Dad and I kind of leaned on each other the first few years after we lost Mom. But we seem to have grown apart. I think part of it is because I want to know who murdered her. Dad and Ryan would like to forget she was murdered. Neither of them liked it that I was friendly with Al."

"Do you think either of them killed your mother?"

Jared let out a deep sigh. "Neither had an alibi for the time she was murdered. Dad left his meeting before it ended, and Ryan had a fight with his friend and split."

"Why would either of them have wanted to kill your mom?"

"Neither of them would have planned to kill her, but I'd seen Ryan get angry with her if she didn't want him to go somewhere or do something. And Dad and Mom had some bang-up fights. Not often, but once in a while."

"Helena Koppel said your mom wanted to divorce your father."

Jared remained silent for a minute or two. "Helena's been known to exaggerate or even lie to be the center of attention. I don't know if my mother wanted to divorce my father. I thought everyone's parents fought occasionally. Some of my friends' fathers drank. Others ran around."

"Do you think your father had someone else? Someone in the city?"

Jared bit his lip. "I wondered about that too. I mean, working late on Friday night? Do people on Wall Street work late on Friday nights?"

Our waitress brought our entrées, and we began to eat.

"This is delicious!" I exclaimed when I swallowed my first bite of eggplant. "Want a taste?"

"Sure. And here's a shrimp for you."

We sampled each other's main dishes and gave our wholehearted approvals. We said little as we concentrated on our meals. Jared polished off his large plate of *frutti di mare*, and I was considering bringing home part of my food when Jared said, "Another thing that's interesting—Mom and Uncle George were always close. He was married and living in Westchester at the time. After his divorce, he had dinner at our house occasionally.

"Anyway, a few months before Mom was murdered, I came home from a game and heard them arguing. Uncle George wanted Mom to agree to sell this piece of property in upstate New York that they'd been left by their parents. It seemed he needed the money for a business venture. Mom wanted to hold onto the property for Ryan and me. Maybe build a summer home there. Uncle George kept shouting that she was living in a dreamworld. He needed the money for the here and now, while she wanted something that was never going to happen. Not with the way her family dynamics were playing out. She asked what he meant by that, and he refused to tell her. Finally, he seemed tired of her asking, so he said she had an absentee husband and an angry son who was bound to do something terrible one day."

"What did he say about you?"

Jared swallowed, clearly embarrassed. "'And poor Jared does his best to keep the peace at any cost. Do you think that's good for a fourteen-year-old kid? Do you?'"

"What happened after that?"

"That was the last time Uncle George came to the house—until the funeral."

"What happened to the land they were arguing over?"

"My dad agreed to sell it. Ironic, isn't it?"

"Do you think he had financial problems too?"

"Dad? Not that I knew of, but he always kept a tight lid on what he considered unnecessary expenses. He even tried to keep Ryan from going on a class trip his junior year, until Ryan nearly blew a gasket. Hmm, now I'm wondering if money was tight, and that's why Dad worked late." Jared grinned at me. "It's like you've hypnotized me, getting me to remember so many things—arguments and comments I never paid attention to." He paused to think. "Or how they added up."

"What just occurred to you?"

"I'm remembering Dad teasing Mom about working in the library part time, asking her why she wasn't getting a full-time job that paid a decent salary." He mused. "Maybe money was more of a problem than I knew at the time."

We ordered cappuccinos and cannoli, and Jared asked for the check. I offered to pay my half, but he wouldn't let me. "My treat. Next time, we'll go Dutch."

On the way home, he asked if anything he'd told me had given me ideas.

"Nothing concrete, I'm afraid. But I plan to think about it and let you know."

"Looking forward to it."

Jared dropped me off at home, bussed my cheek, and said he'd call. As he drove away, I felt a pang of disappointment because he hadn't kissed me properly. *No, Carrie!* I scolded myself. *Don't go there. Sure, Jared's good company and easy on the eyes, but don't turn this into a romance.*

I'd linked up with Jared to solve the two murders. I needed to analyze everything he'd told me that evening about his parents, his brother, and his uncle George. Any one of them might have killed Laura. And to be fair, I had to consider Jared as a possible suspect.

Which of the four family members, if any, was guilty of murdering Laura Foster?

Even if none of them was a murderer, it made me realize that even so-called normal families had their dark undercurrents.

Chapter Seven

"Someone looks happy today!"

"And good morning to you," I greeted Angela as I strode past the circulation desk Friday morning. No further comment followed, and I sighed with relief. Trish must have been true to her word about remaining mum about my dinner with Jared Foster.

"I've always loved Halloween, haven't you?"

I gave a start when I discovered Evelyn Havers walking beside me.

"All the decorations, the costumes, bobbing for apples . . ." Evelyn's laughter sounded like wind chimes. "At least, that's what we did in my day."

I looked around at the festoon of jack-o'-lanterns, skeletons, and witches adorning the walls and hanging from the ceiling. "It's turned into a fun holiday, but when I was a teenager, Halloween was an excuse for older kids to have shaving-cream fights and toss eggs at houses."

"Not here in Clover Ridge. And certainly not here in our beloved library."

"That's for sure. Sally's asked me to place more scarecrows and dried corn arrangements wherever there's empty shelf space." I entered my office.

Evelyn followed me inside.

"Did you want to tell me something?"

She blinked as if she was trying to come up with an excuse. "How are things between you and my niece?"

"Cold. Hostile. If looks could kill . . ."

"A pity, but looks can't hurt you."

"It isn't pleasant." I turned on my computer to check for urgent e-mails—namely, from Sally.

Evelyn sighed. "You're annoyed with me, and I can't blame you."

I gave her my full attention. "I'm hurt that you won't tell me what you know about Laura Foster. But I don't suppose it matters now. Jared and I are working together to find out who killed his mother and who killed Al Buckley. We're scrutinizing everyone who was important in Laura's life, starting with her family."

Evelyn grinned. "You and Jared. Now that's an interesting bit of news."

"There's nothing *interesting* about it. We've joined forces because we share the same purpose. Now if you'll excuse me, I have work to do. I have to draw up a list of supplies for the adult Halloween party next Tuesday night, and—"

"There was something I always wondered about," Evelyn said. "And I wasn't the only one."

"What was that?"

Evelyn perched on the corner of my desk. "A month or two before Laura was killed, the family lawyer came by to see her a few times. Each time they left the building, she'd say it was to have a cup of coffee." Evelyn cocked her head. "Now why would they bother to leave the library when we serve coffee here?"

"To talk privately," I said. "After all, he was her lawyer."

"Then why didn't she go to his office?" Evelyn shook her head vehemently. "I think it was for some other reason. She always looked in better spirits when she returned from their time together."

My mouth fell open. "You don't imagine. . . ."

"Heavens, nothing like that in half an hour or forty-five minutes . . . although, I suppose if they were . . ." She gave me a stern look. "That wasn't what I had in mind. I asked at the café around the corner. They actually did go out for coffee. What I'm trying to say is I think Laura and her family lawyer were romantically involved."

I shook my head. "But why do this in front of the people she worked with and then go for coffee in another public place? It doesn't make sense."

"To throw us off the trail. To make us think they were talking about some legal matter. Lawyers often see their clients outside the office. As do accountants."

"Mmm."

"Besides, I got the sense that Laura wasn't very happy at home. Ryan was a handful, and Bryce was always working. The library was a safe haven for her. A place where she could help people, and they appreciated her."

I nodded. "I know nothing about the lawyer, but the rest of it lines up with what Jared told me about his mother. She wasn't happy before she died."

"And unhappy people often do foolish things."

That said, Evelyn faded from the room.

Another suspect to add to the list. But how could I possibly find out if what Evelyn supposed was true? I mused on the possibilities as I skimmed through my e-mails. The only note from Sally was a reminder to see her before I went shopping for the Halloween party, and I was planning to do that anyway.

Why did Evelyn have a change of heart about telling me what she knew about Laura Foster? A mystery within a mystery.

I reached for a pad and pen and started jotting down appetizers I planned to buy for the Halloween party. I'd been worried patrons would be reluctant to come to a library event that included food and drink, but the sixty available slots filled in minutes, and the hospitality desk kept adding more names to the waiting list.

I was excited about the upcoming Halloween party. Patrons who signed up had agreed to come dressed as their favorite literary or movie character and had paid ten dollars to cover the cost of refreshments and prizes. The library staff was welcome—as long as they wore a costume. I was coming as a female Sherlock Holmes. Uncle Bosco had a green plaid deerstalker, and Aunt Harriet had a large green cape. I'd ordered an oversized magnifying glass online.

"Think bite-sized pieces that don't cost too much," Sally had advised. "Be sure to check all prices beforehand. The bakery makes scrumptious pumpkin breads and caramel apple cupcakes we can cut up and serve on toothpicks. Get small paper plates and napkins with Halloween patterns."

Miniquiches and pigs in the blanket made my list, along with chips and dips and cut-up veggies and two different red punches I planned to place at either end of the table. Trish and Susan had bought the decorations—with Sally's approval—and would set them up in the meeting room late Tuesday afternoon.

The party was scheduled to start at seven and end at nine. Barbara had arranged for the entertainment months ago. A magician would perform for half an hour, and then a storyteller would tell thirty minutes of ghostly, grizzly tales that had taken place in Connecticut. Then we'd have the costume parade and vote for the best male and female costume and the funniest male and female costume.

I'd planned to buy as much as I could at one of the local warehouse stores that my aunt and uncle belonged to. I'd just gone online to start checking costs before showing my list to Sally when my phone rang.

"Hi, Carrie. It's Jared."

"Hi. How are you?"

"Fine. I hope I'm not keeping you from anything important. I wanted to know if you got any vibes or came to any conclusions from what I told you last night."

I laughed. "There was so much. I'm still running through everything in my mind. But I've learned something new."

"What is it?"

Too late, I realized I'd spoken without thinking. *What if Jared asks me how I know what I'm about to tell him?* "Nothing solid, but a few people who work at the library told me your family lawyer came to see your mom a few times before she died."

"Really? Ken Talbot? He was with us the night Al died. He has gray hair. Wore a three-piece suit."

"I remember him. Why did he come?"

"Ken's an old family friend as well as our lawyer. Ryan convinced Dad that Ken had to be there in case we could sue Al for slander. I told Dad it was ridiculous, but Ryan's hysterics won out."

"Was he your dad's friend originally, or your mom's?"

Jared laughed. "Actually, Ken is Uncle George's friend—his college roommate. I wonder why he came to see Mom at the library instead of at his office."

I suddenly felt embarrassed. "The two people I spoke to seemed to think your mother and Ken Talbot had some kind of romance going."

"Really? Mom and Ken? I mean, they dated when they were very young, but they both married other people. Of course, Ken's been divorced over twenty years. Still."

"Remember what your mom's friend Helena said that night—that your mother wanted to divorce your father?"

Jared made a scoffing sound. "I find it difficult to believe anything Helena says, especially since that was the first and only time I'd ever heard that."

I exhaled noisily. "I suppose there's no way we can find out if it's true or not."

"Of course there is. We'll ask Ken."

"Really? Ask him if he had a fling with your mother, his former girlfriend?"

"Why not? It happened fifteen years ago, if it happened at all. I'll explain to Ken we're trying to solve my mother's murder. I know Ken pretty well. Despite his smooth lawyer veneer, I'll know if he's bullshitting me. Or out and out lying."

I shivered. Jared and I were about to question one of the very people who might have murdered his mother. "I'm suddenly frightened. What if he's the killer?"

"I don't think we're in any danger if we let Ken think we're asking primarily because of what Helena announced in the library before Al died."

"Good point. Do you think he'd admit to a romantic involvement?"

"I don't see why not," Jared said.

"Are older people that open?"

"It's worth a try. I'll give Ken a call, see if we can stop over there on Sunday evening around eight. I thought we'd have dinner before—that is, if you're free and would like to join me."

"I definitely want to—on both counts. I'm working Sunday, but I should be home around five thirty."

"In that case, why don't I pick you up at six thirty?"

Having our plan to look forward to made me happy enough to hum as I returned my attention to my computer and researching the cost of more Halloween items. When I finished, I walked over to Sally's office to show her my list.

Dorothy stormed out of Sally's office, a furious expression on her face.

"Hello, Dorothy," I said.

She pushed past me, slamming into my shoulder.

"Ouch!" I complained.

Sally beckoned me into her office. "I apologize for Dorothy's rudeness. I had to deliver some unpleasant news, and I'm afraid she took it badly."

"Oh," was all I said, though I was longing to know what the unpleasant news could be. *Has a patron complained about Dorothy's behavior? Is she about to be fired?*

I handed Sally my list. She studied every item, looked at my figures, and asked if I was sure my numbers were accurate.

"They are. Here are the receipts for the decorations Trish and Susan bought."

Sally looked them over, then returned them to me. "Hold onto them."

"Will do. I need to buy four prizes. If I don't see anything today, I'll buy them over the weekend."

"Don't spend more than twenty dollars on each prize. Why don't you shop for them after lunch?"

"That's what I was planning to do."

"If you need the time, take another half hour or forty-five minutes."

At noon, I walked over to the Cozy Corner Café and ordered the lunch special—spinach quiche, a salad, and a cup of coffee. As I was paying, I scanned the bulletin board I'd discovered the week before. Most of the notices were from people in need of a contractor, plumber, housekeeper, or babysitter. Workers posted business cards advertising their services. So far, I hadn't seen ads for apartment rentals, but it didn't hurt to look.

An advertisement that hadn't been up when I'd eaten here last caught my attention: "Cottage for rent. Reasonable rate for the right person." *Reasonable rate for the right person? What kind of weird ad is this?* I jotted down the phone number and walked back to the library.

I dialed the number as soon as I got to my office. It rang several times. I was about to disconnect when a male voice repeated the number to me.

"Yes, hello. I'm calling about the advertisement you posted on the Cozy Corner Café bulletin board."

There was a pause, and then the voice asked, "Can you come by to see the cottage this afternoon?"

"I'm afraid I can't leave work, but I can stop by tomorrow morning."

"As long as you can be here by ten thirty the latest."

"I suppose I can."

He rattled off the name of a road that didn't include numbers and asked if I knew where that was.

"If I remember correctly, it's a few miles north of Clover Ridge."

"Correct." He proceeded to give me directions to his home. "Any questions?"

"No, I know exactly where you are."

"If you say so. Please call if you get lost. I need to leave here no later than noon."

"I won't get—" I began, but he'd already clicked off.

Chapter Eight

Exhilaration surged through me as I drove the five blocks to the supermarket on Mercer Street. Instead of mentally running down the list of items I planned to buy, I daydreamed about the cottage I'd be looking at the next morning. Of course, it was bound to be too expensive for me to rent, but it sounded like a fairy tale come true. The landlord was seriously rude, but I needn't have anything to do with him except send him the rent once a month. The rent! A dose of reality reminded me that visiting the cottage was about all I could look forward to, but I could give my imagination free rein until then.

The supermarket wasn't very busy, and I was able to collect everything I'd planned to buy for the Halloween party. As I wheeled my wagon up and down the aisles, I considered what would make good prizes for the winners of the costume contest. Wine was one possibility, but not everyone drank wine. Gift certificates were another possibility. If only there were electronic gadgets for twenty dollars. I'd have to check that out online.

When I returned to the library, I rang for a custodian to help me carry in the bags of party refreshments.

Max was a big, burly man in his fifties. He had a round, bald head and wore glasses. "I'll get the wagon and bring everything inside," he told me. "Are you keeping it all downstairs in the utility room?"

"Yes, please."

"Shouldn't take me more than ten minutes. I'll set the bags on the big table. You can sort it all later." He gave me a broad grin, showing the gap between his two front teeth. "I'm sure looking forward to this party. So is my missus."

I grinned back at him. "What are you coming as?"

"Not telling. Let it be a surprise."

As usual, Max was good to his word. I found the six bags of groceries on the table in the utility room, which was off to the side of the meeting room. I placed the perishables in the refrigerator and small freezer. By the time I finished, they were so solidly packed, not another item could fit in either one.

The room had no cupboards or pantry, so I left the nonperishable items in the bags. Now that I was involved in many events that included food, I couldn't wait for the library's expansion to begin. We were getting a good-sized kitchen with new appliances and a much larger meeting room, among other improvements. Uncle Bosco was largely responsible for the expansion and had worked diligently to push the vote through. Of course, he'd contributed a lot of his own money to sweeten the deal. I didn't look forward to the actual construction, but the results would be wonderful.

"What's all this?"

Startled, I looked up as Dorothy Hawkins stepped into the room.

"Is this for the Halloween party?" She peered into a paper bag.

"Yes." I moved closer to the table so she had to step back. "Why do you ask?"

Dorothy shrugged. "Just curious."

"I hope you know better than to touch anything I've bought for the party."

She sniffed. "I wouldn't dream of it." She turned on her heels and left.

What was she doing down here? Would she sabotage the party?

I went upstairs to tell Sally I'd bought the supplies for the party and that they were in the utility room. I handed her the receipt.

"Very good." She scrutinized it and returned it to me. "You spent less than we'd figured."

"The candy and a few other items were on sale. Er . . . do we have a key to the utility room? With so much food down there, I think we should lock the door."

Sally laughed. "This isn't the big city, Carrie. No one's going to steal our party refreshments. Close the door and forget about it."

"I closed the door, but I'd feel better if it were locked."

Sally sighed. "The truth is, we lost the key a few years ago and never bothered to fit the door with a new lock. We've never had a problem with theft." She turned her chair, a sign it was time for me to leave.

I was desperate. I didn't trust Dorothy. I felt certain she'd do something spiteful to ruin the party. If anything happened to the refreshments, no patron would eat another morsel of food in the Clover Ridge Public Library.

"Dorothy was down there as I was leaving. She wanted to know if the supplies were for the Halloween party."

Sally's face hardened as she turned to glare at me. "And you're suggesting that Dorothy Hawkins, who has worked at this library for twelve years, is going to do something nasty to the party refreshments?"

I swallowed. "I don't know."

"You don't know. Well, I know Dorothy would never do anything to jeopardize the reputation of our library. So if there's nothing more you want to say, I have work to do."

I woke up early Saturday morning; showered; put on jeans, one of my new sweaters, and my new boots; and hurried downstairs. On weekends, Aunt Harriet usually made pancakes. This morning, they were apple-and-walnut multigrain pancakes topped with cheddar cheese and maple syrup that her sister had collected from her trees in Vermont.

Uncle Bosco glanced up from the sports section he'd been frowning at to ask me what plans I had for the day.

"I thought I'd look at a few more apartments." I remained deliberately vague. Though they would never pressure me, I knew Aunt Harriet and Uncle Bosco wanted me to continue living with them—at least for another few months.

I picked up the classified ads section. The same ads from the past two weeks were there. No takers, of course. Who would want them? I felt a pang when I noticed the ad for the cottage.

"Interested in renting a country cottage with every convenience?"

Every convenience? The ad in the café hadn't said that. Nor had it mentioned that it stood on a property of ten acres and had views of the river. This ad didn't say the rent was reasonable for the right person, but the phone number was the same one I'd called. My heart plummeted to my boots. Someone was bound to grab this jewel—someone who could afford it.

"Well, I'm off." Uncle Bosco stood and kissed Aunt Harriet's cheek. "I have a council meeting this morning, but I'll be home no later than two."

"Make sure that you are," Aunt Harriet said. "You'll need to nap before we go over to Randy and Julia's." She turned to me. "It's both their children's birthdays, so we're celebrating with an early dinner at five." She shot me a meaningful look. "You were invited."

"I know. Sorry, I have work to do, but thank them for me."

Uncle Bosco fixed his gaze on me. "You're twenty-nine now, Carrie. Time to get past your cousin's teasing when you were kids."

Teasing? Was that a euphemism for torturing a younger cousin going through the worst time of her life? It was the summer I'd turned seven. My father had taken off "to work," and I hadn't seen him in months. My mother had to stay in the city to work, and she'd kept Jordan with her for some reason. Of course, I cried a lot and moped around. Randy, who lived a few miles from the farm and was there practically every day, never missed an opportunity to call me "crybaby," "mopey dopey," and worse.

"Off you go," Aunt Harriet said to Uncle Bosco. "Remember, you've had your breakfast and don't have room for another."

"Yes, dear," he said meekly, but all three of us knew he'd probably have more than a cup of coffee at the council meeting.

We heard the front door close.

"Maybe you'll come with us another time." Aunt Harriet set a plate of three huge pancakes before me.

"Maybe."

I poured syrup over the pancakes and then proceeded to devour them. I downed the last of my coffee and set out for my ten thirty appointment.

It was another sunny late October day. I drove slowly out of town, drinking in the sight of trees arrayed in yellow, gold, and brown. Soon all the leaves would fall to the ground, but for now, they created a scene more beautiful than any painting.

I obeyed the woman in my GPS and drove north on the main road for eight miles, then turned as directed onto a long driveway bordered by evergreens. I gasped when I pulled in front of the white house. House! It was a three-story mansion with a screened-in porch on one side, a three-car garage on the other, and green shutters on every window.

I was still gaping when someone said, "Hello, I'm Dylan Avery. I assume you're here to see the cottage."

The man beside my car window was in his midthirties. Tall and well-muscled in his forest-green rugby shirt and khakis, he would have been handsome if not for his grim expression.

"You startled me! Yes, I've come to see the cottage. My name's Carrie Singleton."

He backed up as I stepped out of the car. As we shook hands, I gazed up at his unsmiling face and into his gray eyes. He had a cowlick over the center of his forehead that he'd almost succeeded in forcing into submission. He seemed to be studying me too, and not the way men usually did, but as if I were a horse or a dog he was considering buying.

"Shall we?" He gestured to the path that continued past the mansion, cutting through a meadow as it veered to the right. He walked so fast, I found myself running to keep up.

"Could you please slow down?"

He spun around, and we almost collided. "Of course, if that's what you want."

If that's what I want? I was a potential renter breaking in new boots, not a cantering pony.

We walked side by side without speaking. Had this once been farmland? The path stopped in front of a cottage.

"Oh!" I quickly covered my mouth. Too late, I remembered the first rule of negotiation: don't act too interested or you'll give the seller an edge.

"Nice, isn't it?" Dylan said.

Nice didn't cover it any which way. The cottage was a one-story replica of the mansion, without the garage or the screened-in porch.

He unlocked the front door, and I followed him into the small hall. The place had a musty odor, as if no one had lived here in many months.

"It could use a good airing," he mumbled as though to himself. "Look around. The furniture can remain or be removed. It's up to the renter."

The kitchen was to the right of the hall. I was pleased to see the appliances looked new. I stared out of the large picture window. Twenty feet from the sweep of unkempt lawn was the river.

"It *is* close to the river," I said.

"Of course. I put that in the ad. One ad, anyway." His amused expression surprised me.

I crossed the hall to peer in at the dining room, which was large enough to hold a breakfront and a table with six chairs. "In my experience," I told him, "most people exaggerate or lie outright when describing the place they want to rent."

"I never lie. Ahead is the living room."

It was furnished with a contemporary sofa, a lounge chair, and an upholstered chair, all in muted gold and blues. The chairs faced a large flat-screen TV. The three large windows faced the river.

"Equipped with Wi-Fi and a Blu-ray player," Dylan said. "Want to see the bedrooms?"

"Of course," I said, but I didn't move from the river view. Suddenly I was curious about the property. "Did your family live here?"

"Years ago. The place is mine now. I had the cottage redone and updated."

When? And why is no one renting it now? I was growing more and more curious about the previous tenants. Or was my curiosity more about the man standing beside me?

The bathroom and two bedrooms were down a narrow hall past the living room. The master bedroom had French doors that opened up onto a terrace that overlooked the river. The bathroom was compact but well designed, with updated fixtures. The other room had a twin bed, low bureau, and desk.

"You could use this room as a study or a guest room when a friend stays over."

I could if I had a friend to invite over. And I could barbecue out on the terrace if I barbecued. But drinking a glass of wine on the terrace as I gaze at the river is doable. I shook my head to clear my brain. Time for a reality check.

"What rent are you asking?" I cleared my throat. "The amount wasn't mentioned in either ad."

Dylan pursed his lips. "Given its condition and location, I'd say twelve hundred dollars a month is a fair price."

I did some quick figures in my head. Fair price or not, it was a bit steep for someone with only a few hundred dollars in the bank. I reentered the master bedroom and gazed out at the river. Such a peaceful view. For some reason, it struck a nostalgic chord, as if I'd seen this view before. The oddest sensation came over me. I felt as if I'd come home.

I'd rent the cottage regardless of the cost. Uncle Bosco would advance me a loan. He'd be happy to lend me the money so I could live someplace nice.

My moment of joy evaporated when I remembered what owing money had done to my family. I wouldn't overextend myself. I couldn't.

"I'm sorry," I said. "The rent's too high for my budget."

"How much is too much?"

"Excuse me?" I stared at Dylan, wondering if he was mocking me.

He met my gaze straight on. "I imagine you have a job."

"Of course I have a job!"

"But not one that pays a very good salary."

"It will. Eventually. I've recently been promoted. I'm head of programs and events at the library."

"Congratulations." He clasped his hands together and gazed at them, deep in thought. After a second or two, he looked up. "What would be a comfortable amount to pay each month?"

"Eight hundred would leave me with enough left over to buy what I need." I pursed my lips. "Two-thirds of your asking price."

"How about we compromise. A thousand even. I should add that includes heat and electricity."

I considered. I wanted the cottage. I'd pay what I had to. So what if I ate mac and cheese every night and spent my weekends watching TV instead of going out?

"I suppose I can swing it."

Dylan studied my face. "But not comfortably."

"Not really." I thought of the ad he'd posted on the bulletin board in the café. "You did write 'a reasonable rate for the right person' in the Cozy Corner Café ad."

"So I did." He circled the room and came to stand beside me once again. "Okay, I'll agree to eight hundred a month—"

"Really? Thank you so much! You could get three times that amount."

"Please let me finish." The grim expression was back in place.

"Certainly. Sorry."

"The cottage is important to me, and I want someone living in it who will take care of it. I feel I can trust you to do that."

"Oh, you can!" I gushed.

"I have one small request. If you agree, I'll get the rental agreement to you ASAP, and you'll be free to move in as soon as you like."

A tremor ran through my body. Here was the catch. Dylan probably ran an illegal business out here where no one could spy on him, and he expected me to help him out. Sure, he figured now he had a patsy—someone who wanted the cottage desperately but couldn't afford to rent it.

Dylan smiled, and suddenly he looked familiar. "Don't look so frightened, Carrie. I'm not about to ask you to pass counterfeit money or forge checks. I'm away a good deal of the time. I need to know if you'll agree to pick up my mail twice a week and send it to me. Since I'm never in one place too long, I'll call or text you my address so you'll know where to send it."

I released a gust of air. "Sure, I can do that."

He extended his hand and I shook it, feeling a tingling that went clear to my toes.

"In that case, we have a deal. And November's rent is on me."

Chapter Nine

Back in my car, I made sure all the windows were closed and then let out a rousing cheer. The cottage was mine! I could move in tomorrow if I wished. All I needed to do was pack up my clothes, toiletries, laptop, and books. But I decided to wait until next weekend—mainly for Uncle Bosco and Aunt Harriet's sake. They'd grown used to having me living with them and would be sad to see me go.

I drove to the nearby mall to buy a few items I needed and then ate an early lunch. I had the strongest urge to stop by the library to check on the party supplies. I didn't like the idea that Dorothy knew they were unprotected in the utility room. After the few tricks she'd pulled and the way she continued to glare at me, I knew she still held me responsible for her not getting the P and E position. But Sally had discounted my concerns, so there was nothing more I could do.

Aunt Harriet and Uncle Bosco were enjoying tea and cookies in the den when I arrived home, close to two. They didn't see me pause in the doorway as they discussed whether to install a new kitchen floor. Aunt Harriet was all for it, but

Uncle Bosco insisted it was unnecessary; the job would make a mess and therefore be more work for her.

"Now, if you'd like a new oven, I'd go for that," he said.

"Finally!" Aunt Harriet exclaimed. "I've been telling you for weeks the oven thermostat is way off. And one of the burners on the stove doesn't work."

Uncle Bosco reached over to pat her hand. "My dear, we'll go looking on Monday."

"Thank you, Bosco." She lifted his hand and kissed it.

I felt a pang in my chest. Would a man ever love me the way Uncle Bosco loved Aunt Harriet?

I entered the den, hugged them both, and then sat on the sofa. "I've found a place to live. It's the most adorable cottage with views of the river. And the rent is reasonable."

Uncle Bosco frowned. "Really? Where is this cottage with river views? Who owns it?"

"It's on an estate about eight miles from town. Someone named Dylan Avery owns it."

"I don't know if renting that cottage is a wise idea," Aunt Harriet said. "It's rather far from town."

"Far? It's a ten-minute ride from here."

"Your aunt is thinking of your drive once winter sets in." Uncle Bosco let out a laugh that was supposed to come off as jolly but sounded rather mournful instead. "We get a lot of snow. It sounds like the cottage is quite a distance down a private road. Who will be plowing you out?"

"I'm sure Dylan will take care of it." I wasn't sure of any such thing. I'd never thought to bring up the subject of snow removal. But I would before signing the rental contract. For the first time since college, my life was on the right track and I intended to keep it that way.

"If it's the money you're concerned about, I'd be happy to loan you enough for a down payment on a nice place. Like one of Joe Sheridan's condos," Uncle Bosco said.

"The condos are on the main road," Aunt Harriet added. "Nothing to worry about in bad weather." She tsk-tsked. "I hate to think of you living in so isolated a location."

"Dylan's house is close by." Then I remembered he'd be away a good deal of the time.

Aunt Harriet shook her head. "Carrie, dear, we're concerned about your welfare. I don't think taking that cottage is a good idea."

To change the subject, I asked, "Did you know the Avery family? Dylan mentioned his relatives owned the property before, so I assume they've been living here for years."

Uncle Bosco's face darkened. "We knew them, all right. Dylan's father was one of the reasons your granddad and I had to sell the farm."

Aunt Harriet put a hand on his arm. "Let's not get into old history. What's done is done. Fretting about it isn't good for your blood pressure."

Uncle Bosco pursed his lips but remained silent.

"What do you know about Dylan?" I asked.

"Not much. He left Clover Ridge to go to college and only moved back a year or two ago. He seems like a nice enough young man."

"With money to burn," Uncle Bosco grumbled. "Probably money that came to him at our expense."

I opened my mouth to ask another question, but Aunt Harriet stopped me with a shake of her head. End of discussion—at least for now.

* * *

That evening, Aunt Harriet and Uncle Bosco returned from visiting my cousin Randy and his family in high spirits. They regaled me with stories about the children's antics.

"Mark is so athletic," Uncle Bosco said. "He reminds me of Jordan at that age."

Jordan! A shock ran through my body whenever someone said my brother's name. My mind went blank as my aunt took up her own story until I heard another name—one that astonished me.

"What did you say the little girl's name is?" I asked when Aunt Harriet paused for breath.

"Tacey. She turns four tomorrow. Mark was eight yesterday."

She has to be the little girl who tried to give Evelyn cookies. "What an unusual name."

"It's an old English-Welsh name. We had a few Taceys in our family," Uncle Bosco said.

I listened closely as they related more anecdotes, thinking how interesting it was that my first cousin's daughter and I were the only people who could see Evelyn Havers's ghost.

"Maybe I'll visit Randy's family the next time you go."

"That would make me very happy." Uncle Bosco gave me a broad smile.

* * *

The library didn't open until noon on Sundays, so I made the most of my leisurely breakfast. This morning's treat was buttermilk pancakes topped with blueberries. "I'm going to miss this." I swallowed my last bite.

"Don't be silly," Aunt Harriet said. "You're always welcome to come for breakfast. Or anytime you like. You know that."

"Thank you."

She stood behind me and hugged me. "Your Uncle Bosco and I are going to miss seeing you every day."

I turned, intending to smile, but instead, my eyes filled with tears. "You both have been so very good to me."

"And now it's time for you to have your own place," Aunt Harriet said briskly. "We get that."

"Speak for yourself, Harriet." Uncle Bosco rose from his chair.

"Bosco! Where are you going?" my aunt called after him as he strode out of the kitchen.

He turned on the TV in the den. Aunt Harriet and I looked at one another.

"Don't mind him," she said softly. "He's gotten used to having you around."

Outside, the sky was gray with the threat of rain. I drove to the library, glad to have a destination on this gloomy day. My only obligation was to introduce the husband-and-wife team scheduled to sing show tunes from two until three thirty. Barbara had told me they were a big draw, which meant the sixty seats in the meeting room would fill up quickly.

Sally was waiting for me outside my office, a stack of papers in her arms.

"Oh. Hi."

"You sound surprised to see me," she said. "I do come in on weekends, same as everyone else."

Not quite like everyone else. Sally set her own hours when it came to making an appearance on weekends, but I was learning when to remain mum.

I unlocked the door, and she followed me into my office.

"Anyway, with all that's gone on the past two weeks, I forgot to give you this earlier."

"What is it?"

She thrust the papers at me. "Your financial report of this month's expenses is due November first. Barbara's covered all expenses for when she was still here, but you need to fill in what you've spent this month since you've taken over as head of P and E."

Dazed, I leafed through the printouts.

"I brought your department's September expense sheet so you can see how it's done."

Why are there so many columns? "I'm not sure—"

"Let me explain." Sally perched on the edge of my desk and held out that month's stapled-together sheets for me to see. "We'll need the receipts for the Halloween party supplies."

I handed Sally the manila folder that held all the papers related to the party. She pulled out the long receipt from the supermarket and proceeded to tell me which numbers went where. I nodded until she turned the page.

"Here are the subtotals, and here"—she turned another page—"you need to fill in a description of each item—size of each purchase, how many items are in a box, if they come in a box. The words at the top of the columns explain what is wanted.

"And here"—she pointed with her finger—"is where you put in your method of payment—charge card, check, or cash. Be sure to include your charge card's last five digits or your check number. And that of your assistants, since you say they bought the decorations."

I suddenly remembered. "I don't have a detailed receipt from the bakery where I bought the cookies for Detective Buckley's program."

"*You don't*?" Sally's forehead wrinkled like a Shar-Pei's.

"It just lists the amount I spent. But I remember the three types of cookies I bought."

"That's good." She turned to leave. "Since I'm giving this to you late, I'll let you hand it in Wednesday at noon instead of first thing in the morning."

"Thank you." Then I remembered. "Since the Halloween party's the night before, could I please have a little more time?"

"In that case, hand it in at two and not a minute later."

I sank into my chair, my good mood completely gone. How was I going to get this done and done correctly? All those details!

I studied the top expense sheet and then looked at my receipt from the supermarket. I could barely make out what the abbreviations stood for. Perhaps I'd better go downstairs to the utility room and match what was there against the list.

My pulse quickened as I headed for the stairs. I hadn't been in the library since Friday. But Dorothy had been scheduled to work yesterday. What if she . . . ? I raced down the last five steps, eager to see if she'd sabotaged the Halloween refreshments.

Thank goodness the meeting room was empty! Max had set up the chairs for the two o'clock performance. I flew to the small room and pulled open the refrigerator and freezer doors. Everything seemed to be there. A quick glance into the six bags showed me they'd been untouched as well. Whew! I let out a gasp of air and pulled over a chair to begin my inventory.

Too late, I realized I should have brought along a few sheets of paper to write down everything before filling in the forms. I grinned as I remembered the old copy machine down here that the staff used when the big one upstairs wasn't available. I made two copies of the five pages and pulled a chair over to the table to get started. I looked at what Barbara had written for October. Then I tried to make heads or tails of the September expense sheets.

My anxiety level jumped to near panic. I was never great with bookkeeping. Though I'd had enough sense to save every receipt for any item I'd purchased for the library, I had no idea I'd have to do this type of report each month. Barbara must have forgotten to explain it to me. And Sally certainly hadn't when she told me about my responsibilities and obligations as head of programs and events. Had she deliberately left this so late because she wanted me to fail? Then she could tell the library board she'd hired me under protest, and she was right about me after all.

Or maybe she was still upset with me because Al had died in her library.

I glanced at the clock. Half an hour had passed, and I hadn't made much headway. People would start filling the room at one thirty. I had two hours. Monday and Tuesday, I had other obligations and the party, and . . .

I let out a huge sigh and buried my face in my hands.

"Can I be of assistance?"

I jumped up and burst out laughing when I saw Evelyn standing in the doorway.

"I sure hope so. Sally's just given me a financial report to fill out. It's due Wednesday. I have programs to take care of and the party Tuesday night."

A chilled breeze rippled along the side of my neck as Evelyn examined the forms. I closed the door. I didn't want anyone who might come downstairs early to wonder why I was talking to myself. "Maybe if I sleep here, I'll get this done in time."

"Don't be despondent, Carrie. I'll help you fill it out if you like."

"You will?"

"Of course. I used to do the reports for a few of the heads."

"Really? You used to do them?"

Evelyn snorted. "I said I did. Why do you doubt me?"

"Because Sally said I'm supposed to fill it out."

"And she first gave it to you today?"

I nodded.

"Interesting."

Evelyn had a strange look on her face. She seemed angry and upset at the same time. I was about to ask if she thought Sally was deliberately acting against me when she said, "Why don't we go upstairs and work on this in your office?"

An hour later, a good deal of the October financial report was complete. We'd started with the receipt for the cookies for Al's program and then moved on to my Friday purchases. Evelyn manned the receipts. She told me what to write and where to write it. She was barely visible when we agreed to stop.

"You look exhausted. We should have stopped sooner."

"I'll be fine," she said. "We had to make headway on this immediately."

"Thank you so much."

"My dear, I hope this shows you I'm on your side."

I grinned. "Indeed it does."

She was fading when I remembered what I wanted to tell her. "I found out this morning that little Tacey who can see you is my cousin Randy's daughter."

Evelyn's smile was visible. "For some reason, that doesn't surprise me."

Chapter Ten

"You look terrific!" Jared exclaimed as I stepped into his car.

My cheeks grew warm, and I was glad it was too dark for him to see that I was blushing. This was more like a date than two people out to catch a murderer. "It's a wonder what a shower and fresh clothes will do for a girl."

"Not every girl." He patted my hand.

I leaned back and luxuriated in anticipation of the evening ahead. "Did Mr. Talbot agree to see us?"

"Absolutely. I told Ken we'd be there between eight and eight thirty. I thought we'd have a pub meal tonight, since we don't have that much time."

"Fine with me."

Jared laughed. "Are you always so agreeable?"

"Are you kidding? I can be as ornery as the next one, but tonight's your show."

"I'm curious to hear what Ken has to tell us. I think he suspects why we're coming to talk to him."

That said, he changed the subject and asked me how my day went.

"Today's program was a big hit. Every seat in the meeting room was taken."

Jared told me he'd stayed home most of the day doing work. "Sometimes it seems I'll never catch up on all the paperwork."

I nodded grimly. "I know exactly how that feels."

The Pub Crawler was located on a side street on the edge of town. It was filled to capacity with young couples and families with children. As soon as the middle-aged woman handling seating arrangements spotted Jared, she greeted him with a hug and smile and led us to a booth for two.

"I see you have pull here," I joked, glad we didn't have to join the ten or twelve people waiting to be seated.

"I believe in reservations."

"And it's good to know the manager."

"That too. Especially since Molly's my neighbor."

A young woman who looked remarkably like Molly handed us large menus.

"Hi, Jared." She gave me the once-over. "Glad to see you've brought a friend."

"Carrie, this is Gemma, Molly's daughter."

"Pleased to meet you," I said.

Gemma answered with a broad grin. "Me too. The meatloaf's real good tonight. So is the chicken pot pie. We're running out of pies, so let me know if you guys want to order it." She winked. "I saved a few for my fave customers."

"Give us a minute to decide. Meanwhile, I'll have a pint of the dark ale you have on tap."

"Carrie?"

I opted for a Beck's lager.

"Be right back."

I studied the menu, impressed by the extent of its offerings: a pork chop with cranberry stuffing, a quesadilla with steak tidbits, all sorts of salads. The burger and wrap lists were extensive. When Gemma returned with our beers, I ordered a burger with guacamole and mushrooms, and Jared ordered a bowl of chili and a side salad.

We drank our beers and chatted about the restaurants in Clover Ridge. I asked Jared how he liked being an accountant.

He grinned. "I know it sounds like the most boring job there is, but I've always been good at figures, and I like dealing with people on a one-on-one basis. Most of my work is in and around Clover Ridge, but I'm beginning to get clients a good distance away. Frankly, I like the idea of traveling to break up the week."

My burger came out exactly as I'd requested—between medium and medium rare. Even the bun was tasty. Jared offered me a spoonful of his chili, and that was delicious too.

"I can see why this place is so popular," I said.

Gemma stopped by our booth as we finished eating. "Would you guys like some dessert?"

She opened her mouth to reel off a list of choices when Jared said, "I don't think so tonight." He turned to me. "Ken expects us for coffee or tea, and it's ten to eight."

"Is it?" I asked. "I lost all track of time."

"I'll take that as a compliment." To Gemma, he said, "Just the check, please."

"Coming right up."

Jared reached for his wallet and pulled out a charge card.

I felt a twinge of anxiety. *Are we friends on a common mission or out on a date?*

"Jared, I can pay for my own meal."

"Of course you can, but I'd like this to be my treat, if you'll let me."

"Okay, but I'm not sure—I mean, I thought we were two people getting together to solve two murders . . ."

"We're two people getting to know one another," he finished for me. "Why not agree it's both and leave it at that?"

I nodded. "Okay."

Why was I so jumpy about getting involved? Did I actually believe he was a possible murder suspect or was it something else? "As long as we take it slow."

"As slow as you like."

Once we were outside, Jared reached for my hand, and we walked to the car. He put on a station of soft rock music, and we said little as we drove off into the darkness. I was very aware of the change in our relationship. Half of me liked the idea of having a guy caring for me. The other half was terrified. I wasn't good at relationships, and I didn't want to screw up my friendship with Jared.

As we drove along, I recognized the road. "I know where we are! The cottage I'm renting is coming up on the right."

Jared stared at me. "You found a place to rent? Why didn't you say so?"

"It must have slipped my mind."

"I noticed an ad for a cottage in the paper—one with a river view. But I figured it would be expensive, so I didn't bother to tell you."

I was sorry I'd brought up the subject of the cottage. It was almost as though I wanted to keep it a secret. Which was silly, considering I'd be living there, and people would be visiting me. "Well, it turned out not to be as expensive as I'd thought."

"When are you moving in?"

"Next Saturday morning. That gives me the rest of the weekend to settle in. The place is furnished, which makes things easy. Still, I'll be making my own meals, so I have to stock up on food and basic supplies."

"I'd be happy to help you move," Jared said.

"Thanks, but I don't have that much stuff. Just my clothes, some toiletries, my computer, and a few cartons of books. If there's not enough room in my car for my books, I can always pick them up later on."

"But with two cars at your disposal, you should be able to bring over everything in one trip."

I hesitated. I was used to doing things for myself and by myself. "Jared, I appreciate your offer, but you don't have to take me under your wing."

He laughed. "I'm just offering to help. Moving can be trying and exhausting, especially when you plan a big shopping trip afterward."

"True. Shopping for food and supplies is not my favorite activity."

"I'm a great shopper," he said, "but if you'd rather do it on your own . . ."

I thought about it. Moving in and then buying everything from eggs to Band-Aids could take hours. And there was something sad about doing it all alone.

"When you put it that way, I can't refuse."

Jared reached over to rub the back of his hand along my cheek. "You're helping me find my mother's killer. The least I can do is help you move."

"In that case, thank you." *Am I doing the right thing, or are things happening too quickly?* As we passed the private lane that led to Dylan's property, I tried to see if there were lights on in the big house, but the shrubs and trees that grew along the road gave nothing away.

We drove past a few farms and a general store. Soon more houses appeared on both sides of the road. We turned right onto a narrow street for a mile or so and then turned left into what appeared to be a gated community. Jared gave his name to the man in the booth, who made a call. A minute later, the bar in front of us lifted, allowing us to proceed to Ken's home.

"It's very pretty in here," I said.

"And very expensive. I always love visiting Ken."

"You've known him a long time?"

"For as long as I can remember."

Jared pulled up in front of a modern-looking home, the front of which was beautifully landscaped with a pond and low shrubs. Tall trees grew on either side of the house.

We walked past a Lexus SUV parked in the center of the two-car driveway.

"I wonder who's here," Jared said.

He rang the bell, and the front door opened. Our host stood there, clearly happy to see Jared.

"Jared, my boy! Come in, come in!" Ken Talbot embraced Jared in a bear hug. He shook my hand and hugged me briefly. "Carrie, nice to see you again. This time under pleasant circumstances."

"Thanks for having us, Mr. Talbot."

"Please, call me Ken." He helped me off with my coat. "May I offer you something to drink? A glass of wine? Imported beer?"

"A beer would be great," Jared said.

"I'll have a glass of seltzer, if you have it," I said.

"I do. Coming right up. Please make yourself comfortable in the living room." Ken disappeared into what I imagined was the kitchen.

Jared took my hand, and together we walked into the living room. A blonde woman in her fifties perched on the sofa, her crossed legs revealing high boots over black leggings and a forest-green knitted tunic. She was elegant, stylish, and looked vaguely familiar.

Jared squeezed my fingers so hard, I had to bite my lip not to cry out. "Hello, Helena. I can't say it's nice to see you."

Of course! Helena Koppel. Jared's mother's best friend. What is she doing here?

Helena let out a silvery laugh as she set her glass of white wine on the cocktail table before her. "Jared, my dear, is that any way to greet your Aunt Helena?"

Jared's face had turned beet red. "You lied about my mother in front of everyone in the library! My father almost had a heart attack because of you!"

"I'm sorry, but I was telling the truth."

"I don't believe you!"

"Your mother wanted to leave your father. Did you not know she was unhappy?"

Instead of answering, Jared sank into one of the wingback chairs.

To break the uncomfortable silence, I extended my hand to Helena. "I'm Carrie Singleton."

"I remember you. You're the young woman who introduced Al that evening at the library. Such a tragedy. Nice to see you again, Carrie."

Her grip was surprisingly strong for a woman no taller than five foot three.

I sat in the other wingback chair as Ken joined us. He handed Jared a bottle of beer and me a glass of seltzer and placed two coasters on the cocktail table.

"Helena called me from her car half an hour ago. She said she was in the area, so I invited her to stop by for a drink."

"Here again, Helena? What brings you back to Clover Ridge?" Jared took a long draw of his beer.

His comment startled me until I realized he was very upset. I couldn't blame him after Helena's shocking announcement that his mother had wanted a divorce. Helena struck me as an attention seeker and troublemaker. But I had to admit, I was eager to hear what she had to say.

Helena grinned. "I believe I've found my perfect new home. One of Joe Sheridan's condos. It has two bedrooms, a den, a deck, three skylights, and an active clubhouse with an indoor pool. I put in a bid and should know in a day or two if it's been accepted."

Jared made a choking sound. "You're moving back?"

"I started checking out communities as soon as I had a buyer for my house. Coming back here two weeks ago, I realized I'd be most comfortable living in Clover Ridge. There are some wonderful new restaurants and plenty of activities for retirees like me."

"What did you retire from?" Jared asked. "I don't remember your ever holding a job."

That silvery laugh again. "Silly boy, I often worked in Lloyd's office."

"Really? Your husband was an architect. Did you help him design houses?"

Silence. I tried to meet Jared's gaze, but he steadfastly kept his eyes on the Persian carpet at our feet.

"At any rate, I must be going." Helena drained what was left of her wine and stood. "Good-bye, Jared. Nice to see you again, Carrie."

"I'll get your coat." Ken walked her to the hall closet.

"Thank God she's leaving," Jared muttered.

Ken helped Helena into her mink. The door closed behind her, and Ken returned to us.

"I'm sorry Helena's presence was so unpleasant for you, Jared." He sank into his leather recliner. "When I told her you'd be coming over, she said she'd love to see you, and so I assumed things were okay between you two."

Jared expelled a burst of air. "That's Helena all over. Exaggerating. Telling lies. Whatever it takes to grab the limelight."

"Still, she's an old family friend." Ken sipped the drink he'd left on the small table beside his chair.

"She had no business saying what she did in front of half the town."

"You're absolutely right," Ken said.

Jared didn't seem able to let the subject of Helena Koppel rest. "At my parents' parties, she always drew attention to herself—dancing provocatively, belting out a song. Poor Lloyd had a lot to put up with. And look how she was dressed tonight—like someone half her age."

"Helena mentioned she'd recently ended a long-term relationship," Ken said. "I think she's lonely, which is why she's moving back to Clover Ridge."

Jared eyed him warily. "Don't tell me you're beginning to fall for her."

Ken laughed as if Jared had said the most amusing thing possible. "There's small chance of that. I have a significant other in my life."

I got what Ken was saying. When I met his glance, he merely nodded. Jared frowned, oblivious to what I'd just learned and had no intention of sharing with anyone, including Jared. In ways, Jared was like an overgrown kid who had yet to learn about the complexities of life.

"I'm glad she didn't stay. Carrie and I need to talk to you," Jared said.

"I'm well aware of that. I told her we had business to attend to. Shall we go into my office? Bring your drinks if you like. We'll have coffee and cake afterward."

Jared had finished his beer, but I brought along what was left of my seltzer to a room beyond the living room. It was clearly an attorney's office: built-in bookcases filled with law books and tall file cabinets stood against a wall. Ken walked around the mahogany desk that took up a quarter of the room to sit in his leather chair, while Jared and I took seats facing him.

Jared wasted no time telling Ken why we were there: "Various library employees said you came to the library to speak to my mother on several occasions a month or two before she was murdered. They think you and she might have been romantically involved."

Ken stretched his arms overhead. "Jared, years before, when we were in college, your mom and I dated for a few months."

"I know that," Jared said impatiently. "I'm talking about years later. When you were both married."

"Your mom and I remained good friends, and I became your family lawyer, but in no way were we romantically involved."

Jared looked puzzled. "Then why did you go to the library to talk to her? If she needed legal advice, why didn't she go to your office?"

"Because my office manager at the time was one of Laura's friends. Betsy was a wonderful worker, but she had a tendency to gossip, at least about the people who came to see me professionally." Ken frowned. "But I gather the library staff was just as eager to chatter about my coming there to see Laura."

Jared bit his lip. "Why did she want to talk to you? Don't tell me Helena's telling the truth, that my mom was unhappy."

Ken leaned back and sighed. "I'm afraid it's true. Bryce worked late most nights and wasn't available to her or you boys. She needed him for her own sake and for help with you and Ryan. Especially Ryan. He was angry and beginning to act out. He needed his father's input, but Bryce was too busy working overtime so he could give you all the life you were used to living."

"Was my father having an affair?" Jared asked.

"I doubt he had the time or interest for any such thing."

"Was Laura having an affair?" I asked.

Jared glared at me.

"I'm sorry, but we have to consider everything," I said. "If your mother had a lover, there's a chance he murdered her."

"I don't know if she had someone or not," Ken said. "The subject never arose during any of our discussions, and I never posed the question. Laura wanted to know what her financial status would be if she left Bryce. How I thought the split would affect you and Ryan. If I thought she would get custody of you boys, if there'd be enough money to keep the house. I asked to see your family's last two tax returns and a list of monthly expenses. She brought them the next time we went out for coffee."

"What did you tell her?" I asked.

Ken released a huge sigh. "That things would be tough for all of you if she were to leave Bryce. With the size of the mortgage they were carrying, there was no way she could hold onto the house. And she'd have had to get a well-paying job if she hoped to find a decent house to rent in Clover Ridge or any of the nearby towns."

Jared slumped into his chair. "I had no idea. I thought my parents were just going through a rough patch."

"Ryan knew something was wrong," Ken said. "He used to call your uncle George. Unfortunately, there was nothing George could offer him by way of good advice."

Jared nodded. "I remember how angry Ryan was then. He picked fights with everyone—me, Mom, his friends."

"He must have felt so frustrated," I said, "sensing the distance between your parents and your mother's unhappiness and not being able to do anything to help the situation."

"What did my mom do when you told her we'd be poor if she and Dad split?" Jared asked.

"She started to cry. She asked if we could meet one time more. I agreed, more to be a sympathetic friend than because I could tell her anything different."

"How was she the third time?" I asked.

"Sad but resolved. She told me she was prepared to stay with Bryce—at least until you boys graduated high school. After that, maybe there'd be a better life for her."

Jared nodded but said nothing. After a minute, he stood. "Thanks, Ken, for sharing this with me. I wish I'd known what she was going through so I could have been more . . . caring or something."

"I think she was doing her best to keep her feelings from you and Ryan."

I got to my feet too. "Ken, did Laura say anything to you that might lead you to believe she was afraid of someone in her immediate circle?"

"Not afraid, no. But the last time, as we were leaving the café, she gave me a bittersweet smile and said it was ironic how life often played out like a soap opera."

Chapter Eleven

"I wonder what Mom meant by that," Jared said as we climbed into his car.

"I can't imagine." Had she been involved in an affair gone sour? "We know she was unhappy and wanted to divorce your father. Just as Helena said the night Al was poisoned."

I hoped Jared wasn't going to explode and was relieved when he nodded in agreement.

"Mom confided in both Ken and Helena. Much as I hate to have anything to do with her, we should question Helena about the last few months before the murder."

"Good idea—as long as you're prepared to hear news you probably won't like."

Jared snorted. "Lately, that's the only kind of news I've been hearing. No one likes to find out his parents were unhappy."

But he must have known that. Or had he managed to block it from his mind? I hesitated but then ventured to say what I'd been thinking. "You might want to ask your dad what he was experiencing the months before your mom died."

"Believe me, I tried that a few times. Dad said he was working hard because the money wasn't coming in as it had in previous years. He admitted he should have paid more attention to Mom, Ryan, and me, but that was it." Jared grimaced. "My father's not one to talk about feelings."

"Maybe Helena can tell you more."

"Good idea. I'll get her cell phone number from Ken tomorrow."

Ten minutes later, we arrived at my aunt and uncle's home. Jared took my hand in both of his. "I'm glad you came with me to Ken's tonight. It helped having you beside me to ask pertinent questions."

"I'm glad I could be of service. And thank you for dinner."

"You're more than welcome."

Jared reached over and put his arms around me. I breathed in the heady fragrance of his aftershave as his lips found mine. Our kiss touched off sensations I hadn't experienced in a long time. Too soon, it was over. I opened my eyes and we smiled at one another.

"Taking it slow," Jared said in a teasing manner. "I'll call you as soon as I speak to Helena."

* * *

"Have a nice time?" Aunt Harriet called to me from the den as I walked in the house.

"Very nice. See you in the morning."

As I changed into my nightgown and got ready for bed, I reviewed everything I'd learned about Laura's life and the people around her just before her murder.

For one thing, Ken had made it clear that he was gay. It must have been something he'd recently discovered or acknowledged because he'd dated Laura when they were young, and he'd been married. Jared hadn't picked up on Ken's disclosure, which made me realize he was obtuse when it came to nuances and relationships. Sure, he was young when his mother had been going through an emotional crisis, but his brother had sensed her unhappiness. Jared was smart, but he wasn't people smart.

Ken was a lovely man. I believed what he'd told us tonight was an accurate account of his conversations with Laura. She was a caring mother who had considered her sons' standard of living and refused to act rashly.

Helena, on the other hand, was something else. I chuckled because I'd noticed all the work she'd had done on her face. Her eyelids and neck were as smooth as a baby's behind. How had she and Laura become best friends? But that was a silly question. The most unlikely people were often drawn into a friendship or romance. And one didn't always fall for the right sort of person. I drifted into sleep thinking of a few old boyfriends and of Dylan, my landlord.

* * *

On Monday morning, I woke up with my head crammed with arrangements for the Halloween party. A twinge of anxiety jolted through me as I walked across the Green. I still hadn't bought the four gift cards I needed for the best costume winners. I cheered up when I realized I could do this online. All I needed was the library's credit card, and that meant getting it from Sally. I was a bit nervous as I walked to her office. Sally hadn't been very happy with me lately.

As I approached her door, I heard loud voices. Through the glass pane, I saw Sally leaning over her desk as she berated Dorothy.

"What would you have me do? Fire her? Murder her?"

I couldn't make out Dorothy's answer, but whatever she said angered Sally even more. The heat rose to my ears. They were arguing about me.

"I gave her those sheets to fill out, the ones you can't complete without my help. Once Carrie learns every director has trouble with them, I'll get flack from her. She'll go to her uncle, and then I'll be in trouble."

I tiptoed away, hoping Sally wouldn't look up and see me through the glass. I was frightened by the lengths to which Dorothy would go to get my job. I'd get the charge card later. Now I had to go down to the utility room to check on the refreshments for the party.

I examined every bag carefully. None of the packages seemed to have been disturbed or opened. The refrigerated and frozen foods were exactly as I'd arranged them. I breathed a sigh of relief. After Trish and Susan decorated the meeting room, I'd ask Sally to lock the door for everyone's sake.

In my office, I worked on the forms Sally had given me. There were still many blank spaces to be filled in. But having heard what she'd told Dorothy, I no longer felt pressured to finish them by Wednesday.

"I see you're getting the hang of it." Evelyn manifested at my side.

"I am, and I'm not worried about getting them done on time."

"Really?" Evelyn cocked her head. "Why is that?"

I told her what I'd overheard Sally say to Dorothy.

Evelyn's face grew grim. "That spiteful, spiteful girl."

I snorted. "That *girl*, as you've put it, is still holding a grudge because I'm head of programs and events and she isn't. Somehow she's managed to get Sally to hassle me with these financial forms."

"I'm glad Sally had the good sense to read her the riot act."

I gnawed on my lip before expressing what was bothering me the most. "I hope she doesn't sabotage the party tomorrow night."

Evelyn waved a nearly transparent hand in the air. "Don't be silly. Dorothy's not foolish enough to disrupt the Halloween party. She knows it would reflect poorly on the library."

"And especially on me." But I didn't want to argue with Evelyn. "I'd love to chat, but I'd better get back to work."

"Let me help you." Evelyn sat in a chair beside me and glanced at the figures on the sheet before me.

I was glad my door was solid wood and no one could glance in and wonder what they were seeing. We worked this way for half an hour. Evelyn was a big help, and I appreciated her assistance.

I told Evelyn I'd found a place to live. I also told her Jared and I had gone to see Ken and found out what Laura had discussed with him a short time before her death.

"That's quite a busy weekend you had!" Evelyn said.

"I'm planning to move into the cottage on Saturday. Jared offered to help me."

"He's a nice young man, though I'm afraid his brother's a bit of a hellion."

"He is nice. He was relieved to learn his mother hadn't been having an affair with Ken but upset because she wanted to divorce his father."

"And who could blame him? No child wants to find out his parents were unhappy."

"Ken said Ryan was aware that Laura was unhappy. He called his uncle George to talk about it."

"And what did Helena Koppel have to say? She knew Laura wanted a divorce."

"Helena left before we spoke to Ken. She's moving back to Clover Ridge, which upsets Jared to no end."

It was a few moments before Evelyn spoke. "So you haven't learned anything new that points to Laura's killer?"

"Do you think Laura had a lover who killed her for some reason?"

"It's possible, I suppose, but there's no evidence of that. From what Ken told you, I'd say Laura was mainly concerned about her sons and how their lives would be worse if she were to divorce Bryce."

I nodded. "I suppose you're right, but Jared's going to ask Helena if she knows if there was another man in his mother's life."

"She'd be the one who would know. I think we can finish this up in another half hour. Want to give it a try?"

I grinned. "I sure would."

* * *

At noon, I walked over to Sally's office, the stack of financial forms in my arms. We'd managed to finish them all. I was secretly pleased that I'd figured out how to fill them out. With Evelyn's help, of course.

Sally was wearing her coat and was in the process of locking her office door. "Oh, Carrie. I was just on my way to lunch. Can this wait?"

"I don't know." I thrust out the pile of papers in front of me. "These are the financial reports you wanted me to complete. I wanted to get them to you ASAP."

Her eyes widened. "You completed them all?"

"I did."

"The way I told you to?"

"Exactly as you told me to." I held her gaze.

I must have managed to let Sally know I was on to her bad behavior, because she gave a little laugh as she broke eye contact. "Well, in that case, why don't you bring them inside, and I'll review them when I'm back from lunch."

"As you like." I followed her inside. "And may I please have the library's credit card?"

"Why?" she demanded before I could explain.

"Because I want to buy Amazon gift cards for the four winners of tomorrow night's costume contest." I suddenly remembered. "I didn't add that expense to the October report. I couldn't."

"No matter. Give me the paperwork ASAP, and I'll take care of it."

"You will?"

Astonished, I tried to read her expression, but she was opening a file cabinet to retrieve the charge card, which she handed to me. "Please return it as soon as you've completed the purchase. Don't forget to print out the receipt."

"I will." I exited the office as quickly as I could and watched her hurry off to the library's rear exit. Sally might have read Dorothy the riot act, as Evelyn had put it, but she still had no fondness for me.

Back in my office, I bought four twenty-dollar gift cards for the costume winners and arranged to have them e-mailed directly to me. I was printing out the receipt when Ginny, one of the aides, delivered the sandwich and bottle of Snapple I'd ordered from the café. I ate my turkey and guacamole on rye quickly because Trish and Susan would be there any minute to decorate the meeting room for the Halloween party.

They arrived in good spirits, chatting and laughing as they gathered up the skeletons, witches, and jack-o'-lanterns they'd bought the week before. Armed with various kinds of tapes and two staple guns, I followed them downstairs to supervise their work—at least for a while.

I told them my idea of how I thought the place should be decorated, and they got started while I went to check on the food in the utility room. Everything seemed to be as I'd left it hours earlier. I opened up a bag of chocolate candies and offered a few pieces to Trish and Susan. They happily accepted. For a while, I watched them fasten cardboard figures to the walls and hang jack-o'-lanterns from the ceiling amid orange and black streamers of crepe paper. I was surprised to see Trish defer to Susan as to where various objects should be placed. *Good for her.* I was glad Susan had a gift she could be proud of.

I went upstairs to my office, thinking I'd better return the charge card to Sally before she had a fit. I'd left it beside my computer and hadn't bothered to lock the door because I wasn't planning to stay downstairs with Trish and Susan more than ten minutes.

It's not here! I looked through the papers on my desk, on the floor, behind the computer screen. No sign of the card. I checked my pocketbook, which I'd stashed in the closet. No sign of the card.

Ten frantic minutes later, I had to admit the card was gone. Someone had taken it. And that someone was Dorothy.

That is, I *thought* that someone was Dorothy, but I couldn't be sure. My office was in the back of the library, where most patrons didn't go, but that didn't mean that someone looking to steal something hadn't been lurking. And even if I thought it was Dorothy, I couldn't very well say that to Sally. She'd made that very clear to me. No matter how much Dorothy annoyed her, Dorothy was her best friend, and she wouldn't tolerate hearing one bad word against her.

I walked slowly to Sally's office, hoping she'd be out. No such luck. She hung up her phone and stared at me as she beckoned me inside.

"Sally, I don't know how to say this, but the library charge card is missing."

"What do you mean it's missing? I gave it to you an hour ago."

"I know, and I'm sorry."

Sally blinked furiously. "Did you go outside and drop it somewhere?"

"No, I left it on my desk beside my computer. I went to supervise Trish and Susan while they decorated the meeting room and then came upstairs. When I returned to my office, the card was gone." I cleared my throat. "Someone must have taken it."

"Taken it? You left your office door unlocked?" Her voice rose with each word.

"Yes, I'm afraid that's what happened."

"Happened!" she shrieked. "You did it! You were responsible for the card."

"I know, and I'm sorry. I'll call the card company. Just give me the account number—"

"I most certainly will not give you the account number. I'll take care of this now!"

I was dismissed. Shoulders hunched, I trudged back to my office. Sally was furious with me. What was worse, I had no idea if the gift cards I'd ordered would come through. And since I hadn't locked my office door, I couldn't very well ask her to lock the meeting room. I locked myself in my office and wrapped my arms around my head. *I will not cry. I will not cry.*

The tears came, despite my commands.

Chapter Twelve

I pulled myself together and ran through my program for the Halloween party, trying not to think about the missing charge card. I gave a loud cheer when the gift cards arrived via e-mail.

To keep my mind occupied, I looked over the week's schedule and was happy to see that most of the programs were weekly or monthly series with seasoned presenters. The Thursday-night movie was safely locked in my desk.

I was scouring Barbara's collection of possible new programs and not finding anything appealing when my cell phone's jingle played.

"Hi, Carrie," Jared said. "How are you?"

"Fine." I told him about the missing charge card.

"That's awful. You're sure it didn't fall on the floor? Sometimes that happens."

"I've looked all over. The card disappeared, and Sally's furious."

"Do you think someone took it?"

"Yes, and I know who it is, but Sally won't hear a word against her."

"Wow! Maybe you should tell your Uncle Bosco about this. The board should—"

"I won't do that. I'll find a way to deal with this person on my own."

"If you say so." Jared sounded skeptical.

"Did you manage to get Helena's cell number from Ken?"

"I did." His voice went flat. "I called her."

Bad news. "What did she tell you?"

"That my mother was having an affair, but Helena didn't know who he was, since my mother wouldn't say."

"I'm so sorry, Jared."

"You can imagine how I feel. First I learn my mother wanted to divorce my father, then I find out she was seeing someone on the sly. All this going on while I went about my little life, worried about a math test or not getting enough playing time in a basketball game. I should have known what was really going on."

"Don't do this to yourself. Even if you'd known part of the truth, what could you have done? Your brother knew, and all it did was make him angry. We can't control our parents."

"You sound like you know this for a fact."

"Don't I." I drew in a deep breath. "My dad spent more time away from us than with us. He was a thief."

Jared laughed. "You're kidding!"

"Do I sound like I'm kidding?"

"Sorry. I didn't mean to make you angry."

"And I didn't mean to snap at you, but it's true. And my mother wasn't very good at mothering, especially after my brother died."

"You had a brother who died?"

"Jordan. He was four years older than me. I can't believe I'm telling you all this, and over the phone."

"I suppose you wanted to. After what I told you about my mom."

"I guess I did."

Silence. I was grateful that Jared didn't start spouting all kinds of pop psychological jargon to try to make me feel better.

"Well, I'd better let you get back to work," he finally said. "Remember, I'm going to help you move on Saturday."

"Thank you. I could really use your help."

I felt oddly at peace after our talk. I hated to think about my dysfunctional family. I think part of me was eager to engross myself in Jared's family's problems because it helped me realize that other families weren't always as perfect as they appeared on the surface. I'd seen Laura as a caring mother who wanted the best for her children, but learning she'd had a lover put a different spin on things.

Who was he? Had Al discovered his identity, and when he threatened to reveal it to the world, had the lover murdered Al?

But if Laura had a lover, why was she so worried about money? Was her lover poor? Unwilling to marry her and take on her teenaged sons?

Or was he married, and when Laura told him she wanted to divorce Bryce, he decided to kill her instead?

Or had Bryce found out about Laura's lover and killed her in a fit of jealous anger?

My mind whirled with various possibilities. I set aside the box of potential new programs and events and decided to go down to the meeting room to see how my assistants were getting along.

Trish and Susan were stuffing the packaging debris in the garbage pail.

"You did a wonderful job," I told them.

And they had. The room was festive and colorful without looking garish. After all, the party was for adults. Trish saw me eying a glass vase filled with artificial pussy willows and orange flowers.

"Susan's idea," she said. "It's the table's centerpiece."

"Brilliant," I said.

Susan beamed.

I walked around, admiring their results, then we headed for the staircase. When we reached the main level, Gayle Morrison, the children's library assistant, approached.

"Come with me! You're invited to the children's Halloween party."

We followed her to the children's room. It was crowded with children aged four to eight dressed as fairies and princesses, Darth Vader and Batman, and various other figures. The costumes were well made and must have cost quite a bit of money—certainly more than the homemade costumes I had worn when I was a kid. Their parents stood against one wall, watching Marion Marshall, the children's librarian, lead them in a game.

"Have some punch and cookies," Gayle offered.

"Don't mind if I do." Trish followed her to the table set up with Halloween goodies.

We drank red punch and nibbled on spider cookies as we watched the children's antics. I was about to say it was time to go when a slender woman with long brown hair left the parents' group and walked over to me.

"You're Carrie Singleton, aren't you?"

What did I do now? "Yes, I am."

She extended her hand. "I'm Julia, Randy's wife."

"Oh! Nice to meet you." Startled, I shook her hand with more energy than I'd meant to.

A little girl in a princess dress came running over to Julia. "Mommy, Mark is bothering me."

Julia stroked her daughter's head. "Stay with your friends and leave the big boys alone."

"Quentin and Rory don't mind. Only Mark says I'm bothering them."

"Tacey, this is your cousin Carrie. Say hello."

Big blue eyes looked me up and down. "Hello."

"Hi, Tacey. Nice to meet you."

"Are you really my cousin?"

"Yes, I am. Your daddy's my first cousin."

"Then why don't you come to my house?"

Heat rose to my ears. "I'd be happy to—soon."

"Cousin Carrie has an important job in the library. She's very busy," Julia said.

"Do you know Miss Evelyn?"

"Um." I didn't have the slightest idea how to answer.

But I needn't have worried. Julia shot me an apologetic smile. "Evelyn is Tacey's make-believe friend who lives at the library."

"She's not make-believe, Mommy," Tacey said. "She's real."

"I really must get back to work." I glanced at Trish and Susan, who had stepped back when Julia came to speak to me.

"I'd love to have you visit us," Julia said.

"Thank you. That would be lovely," I answered.

"Who's Evelyn?" Susan asked as we walked toward my office.

"The only Evelyn I know of used to work in the library," Trish said. "She died a few years ago."

I reached into my pocket for the key and unlocked my office door.

"Oh!" I exclaimed as I stepped inside.

Lying on the floor was the charge card that had disappeared earlier in the day.

Chapter Thirteen

I handed the charge card and printed receipt to Sally. She looked at the card, turned it over a few times, and let out a disparaging sound. "Where did you find it? On the floor behind your desk?"

"Someone slipped it under my door while I was downstairs checking on the decorations."

"Good thing I hadn't canceled it yet. I'll call the card company to make sure no one has used it in the past hour."

I nodded and left as quickly as I could.

With the Halloween party under control, I thought it would be a good idea to resume working on the March–April newsletter I'd begun a few weeks earlier. I got out a copy of the January–February issue to use as my framework and whatever notices I'd collected so far for the new edition. Then I shot off e-mails to the various departments asking for a heads-up regarding special events they had planned for March and April. I sent one to Sally as well.

Trish, Susan, and I spent a peaceful afternoon working in harmony. At five, we left for home. Trish offered me a lift, but I chose to walk across the Green in the dying light of day. I couldn't shake the fear that Dorothy was planning to ruin the Halloween party somehow.

I joined Aunt Harriet and Uncle Bosco in the den, where they were enjoying their usual glass of wine. Uncle Bosco got up to pour me a glass, and I sipped it eagerly.

"Rough day?" he asked.

"Just hectic." I didn't want to bring up the subject of the missing charge card or the fact that Dorothy Hawkins was pulling all sorts of tricks to make me look bad. Then I remembered. "I met Julia and Tacey at the children's Halloween party. Julia wants me to visit them. I said I would."

"Lovely!" Aunt Harriet beamed at me. "I think you two will become fast friends."

I breathed in the delightful aroma of our dinner. "What have you prepared for us tonight?"

"Mushroom soup, followed by candied baked chicken, noodles, and roasted veggies."

I grinned. "Sounds wonderful. Can't wait to taste it all."

Aunt Harriet stood. "In that case, I'll see to our dinner. Make sure nothing's burning. It should all be ready in ten minutes or so."

When she left, Uncle Bosco said, "I ran into John Mathers today."

My pulse quickened. "Really? Lieutenant Mathers in charge of Al's homicide?"

"The very man. I had business in town hall. So did he."

"Did you ask him about the case? What did he say?"

Uncle Bosco chuckled. "I don't mean to make light of poor Al Buckley's murder, but you're as excited as a little kid getting a treat."

I shrugged. "I'm simply curious. I hope the police have made some headway finding Al's killer."

"Unfortunately, there aren't many leads. John's pretty sure whoever poisoned Al was trying to shut him up about the Laura Foster case. He's planning to question her family and friends again."

"That makes sense. Did the police find any notes Al might have made about the Laura Foster case?"

"No, unfortunately. He kept everything on his iPad."

"Which was stolen the night he was killed."

Uncle Bosco leaned forward and squinted at me. "You've gotten pretty friendly with Laura's younger boy, haven't you?"

"Jared. Yes, we've become friends."

When Uncle Bosco didn't respond, I gasped. "You don't think Jared killed his mother and Al Buckley!"

Uncle Bosco reached across the coffee table to pat my shoulder. "I worry about you, Carrie. I don't want you mixed up in a family involved in two homicides. You've been running around like a mad hare these past few years, and now that you've finally settled down in a good job, you choose the oddest people as your friends."

I felt as though I'd been slapped. "Jared's a very nice person. Really, he is." I stood. "I think I'll see if Aunt Harriet can use some help."

"Don't go yet." The plaintive note in his voice stopped me. I sank back into my chair.

"I'm sorry I upset you. It's just—your aunt and I have gotten so used to having you living here. We're going to miss you."

I gave a little laugh. "I'm only moving a few miles away. And I'll be at the library every day if you ever need to see me."

"I know. I'm just a silly old man."

"You're *not* a silly old man." I put my arms around him. "You're the dearest relative I have in all the world. I don't know what would have become of me if I hadn't come to live with you and Aunt Harriet back in May. Everything was so bleak then. I had nothing to look forward to."

Uncle Bosco patted my arm. "You did right to come home to Clover Ridge."

Home? Do I consider Clover Ridge my home?

"Dinner's ready!" Aunt Harriet called.

"Be right there."

Dinner was as wonderful as I knew it would be. When we finished eating, I helped Aunt Harriet clear the table. While she loaded the dishwasher, I placed the leftovers in containers and stacked them in the refrigerator. We chatted about the Halloween party and my upcoming move as we worked.

After she put away her apron, Aunt Harriet said, "You know you're welcome to have dinner here with us any night you like."

"Thank you, Aunt Harriet." I hugged her. "My library hours are crazy. I'll probably eat out or bring in food more often than not."

"It's time you started making your own dinners, my girl. Which is why I've printed up the recipes of some of your favorite dishes with easy, fail-safe directions."

She handed me a pack of five-by-seven cards, each neatly printed in her careful handwriting. I flipped through them: meatballs, chicken dishes, various soups and vegetable dishes. Even her apple-walnut pancakes.

"I left out desserts," Aunt Harriet said. "Figured you could come here for those. Or I could make enough for you to take home with you."

I had trouble swallowing the lump in my throat. "Thank you. This is the nicest present I've ever received."

"A packet of recipes? Pshaw." Harriet waved her hand to make light of it, but I could see how happy she was that I appreciated her gift. "They're usually handed down from mother to daughter."

"Not my mother," I said. "I don't think she ever made us a meal that wasn't frozen or didn't come out of a can."

Harriet sank into a kitchen chair. "Have you heard from her lately?"

"Nope." I looked at her, wondering why she was asking. My aunt and uncle knew I hated talking about my parents. "Haven't spoken to Brianna, as she likes to be called now, since I called asking if I could stay with her and Tom and was told their Hollywood life was too hectic for me to come."

"And your dad?"

I shrugged. "He sent me a card last Christmas. I have no idea where he is."

"A pity. They should know you're here in Clover Ridge working at a wonderful job."

The faint sound of my cell phone playing its jingle saved me from commenting. I took the stairs two at a time and managed to pull my phone out of my pocketbook on the fourth ring.

"Hello?" I said breathlessly, wondering if Jared had learned something new about the murders.

"I was about to give up," a male voice said. "Sorry I made you run to answer your phone."

"Who is this?" I asked. My heartbeat sped up, because suddenly I knew.

"Dylan Avery, your landlord."

The touch of humor in his voice made me smile. "Hello, Dylan. How are you?"

"Fine. I just found out I'm flying out west on business tomorrow. I'd like to go over a few items—have you sign the lease and give you the key to the cottage—before I leave. Could you meet me this evening or tomorrow morning? I know you work, but if you prefer tomorrow, I could make it as early as six thirty."

A thrill surged through my body. Dylan Avery wanted to see me! I shook my head to clear it of fanciful thoughts. We were getting together to take care of business, nothing else.

"Tonight will be fine," I said. "Where do you suggest we meet?"

"My lawyer's office is a few blocks from your aunt and uncle's house. Why don't I pick you up in, say, fifteen, twenty minutes?"

"Sounds good."

"And Carrie, no need to bring your checkbook. I won't be taking a security deposit from you."

"That's a relief." I hadn't given it much thought.

I put on fresh lipstick and a bit of blue eye shadow and mascara and then changed into a pair of new black leggings and a red velour tunic. Then I went downstairs to the den to tell my aunt and uncle I'd be going out.

"You look lovely," Aunt Harriet said. "Where are you off to?"

"To sign my lease. Dylan is leaving town tomorrow and wants to give me the keys to the cottage, et cetera."

"Now's a strange time to sign a lease," Uncle Bosco grumbled.

"Good night. Sleep well." I blew them each a kiss.

I shrugged into my jacket, glad I'd soon be living in my own place. As much as I loved my aunt and uncle, I was beginning to feel smothered by their comments and questions.

I waited in the kitchen almost half an hour until a black BMW pulled in front of the house. I hurried out into the chill October air and down the concrete stairs to the street. Dylan reached across the seat to open the passenger door for me.

"Nice wheels," I said as I stepped inside.

We took off swiftly and smoothly.

"Sorry for the delay. Last-minute business calls took more time than I thought."

We drove along Main Street and turned left on Walnut. Dylan pulled into the driveway and parked in the rear of a yellow-brick four-story building with a large oval window on the top floor. The parking lot was empty except for two other cars.

"Ken's not here, but he lets me use his office when I need to set up a business meeting at odd times."

"Ken? Is your lawyer Ken Talbot?"

"You know him?"

The surprise in his voice made me smile. I had a feeling very little surprised Dylan Avery. "I do."

"Of course," he said wryly. "All Clover Ridge residents tend to know one another."

I was about to point out that I wasn't a Clover Ridge resident but realized that was no longer true.

We climbed out of the car. Dylan unlocked the rear door of the building and led me to an office on the top floor. It was the one with the large window.

"This is lovely," I said as I studied the few pieces of antique Chinese furniture and the paintings on the walls.

"So you've never been here before?" Dylan asked.

"No. I've only been to Ken's house."

"Really?" was his dry comment.

"Really."

I didn't know why I was playing at being mysterious—except that I was enjoying myself. Probably because from the little I knew of him, Dylan Avery was used to having all the answers.

He led me into a smaller room with leather chairs around an oval table, which was bare except for a manila folder and a few pens. Dylan picked up the folder and skimmed the papers inside.

"Ah, here it is. All in order. Have a seat." He gestured to the chair beside the one in front of the folder.

"This is your lease." He handed me one of the two stapled packets of pages. "It states your monthly rent, the fact that you can break the lease at any time, and your financial obligations if you deliberately damage anything in the cottage."

"Oh!" I exclaimed. "I'll be very careful with everything."

"The lease states 'deliberate,' not 'accidental.'"

"And you'd know the difference?"

"Of course."

Weird, I thought but nodded in agreement. "I'd like to read through this, if you don't mind."

"Certainly. I'll be in the next room. Please sign both copies and tell me when you're done." His cell phone was ringing as he got to his feet.

There were only four pages, so I had no problem getting through them in a matter of minutes. I signed both copies, saw that Dylan had already done so, and went to find him. He was standing in a corner of the other room with his back to me, engrossed in conversation.

"I want to examine them, make sure they're authentic, before we act. Not a word to anyone, including your cop friends, or you'll scare them off." Silence. "You heard me: no police." Another silence, then, "My ETA's twelve fifty-three PM. You can meet me at the airport or wait till I catch a cab to your office. We'll talk then."

Dylan spun around so quickly, I jumped back in alarm.

"Sorry to have frightened you. I had to take that call. Now I'm shutting off my phone so we'll have no more disturbances tonight."

He shot me a smile so tender, all I could do was nod. Dylan Avery was a man of many moods. I was intrigued by his mysterious phone call, but he owed me no explanation.

"All read and signed?" he asked as we returned to the room where I'd left the copies of the lease.

"Read and signed."

He examined the last page of both copies. "Terrific. Keep your copy. I'll leave mine in the folder for Ken to hold. When are you planning to move in?"

"Saturday morning. I have a few questions, especially since you're leaving town and I don't know when you'll be coming back."

Dylan glanced at his watch. *A Rolex*, I thought, though I couldn't be sure. "It's eight fifty-three. How would you like to have a cup of coffee in the Cozy Corner Café and go over whatever's on your mind?"

"I'd like that."

We drove to the café and managed to park right in front. The place was all but deserted, with only a few booths occupied.

"The café clears out after dinner," Dylan said.

Sal, the bald-headed owner, led us to a corner booth. "I saved you a piece of apple pie," he told Dylan.

"Thanks, Sal, but first, I'll have a cheeseburger with the works. And coffee."

"And for you, miss? Know what you'd like?"

I glanced over at the covered bin of pastries on the counter. "Coffee and a piece of Russian coffee cake, please."

"Coming right up."

When he left, I asked, "Do you always eat dinner this late?"

"No. Tonight turned out to be more hectic than expected."

I forced myself to concentrate on the important questions I needed to ask him.

"I'm concerned about getting to work during the winter months, when snow covers the road to the cottage. Especially since you won't be there much of the time."

Dylan handed me a folded sheet of paper. "I have a caretaker who looks after the property. Name is Jack Norris. Here are his numbers. Call him day or night, whenever you have a problem—a leaky faucet, the heat won't work, the road needs plowing. He's totally reliable."

That's a relief.

Dylan explained the heating system to me, where the fuse box was located, along with other household matters. He answered my questions calmly and patiently. There was no sign of the grumpy man I'd first spoken to on the phone.

Sal brought over our coffees, my dessert, and Dylan's cheeseburger. From the way he devoured it, he must have been ravenously hungry.

"Sorry," he apologized. "I forgot to eat lunch. Haven't had a thing since breakfast."

He ate his apple pie more slowly but finished every crumb on his plate. We both welcomed a coffee refill.

I finished my large piece of cake because it was delicious. *I'd better not eat too many sweets at tomorrow's party.* When I looked up, I realized that Dylan had been waiting to tell me something important.

"Yes?"

"As I told you, I'm often away for long periods at a time, and I'm usually on the move." He cocked his head at me. "You did say you were willing to collect my mail twice a week."

"Of course. It's the least I can do, given your generous terms of my lease."

"Very good. I'll give you a key to my house, since the mail is delivered directly through the slot in the front door."

Trust a thief's daughter? "I'll be happy to send you your mail, but giving me the key to your home is kind of weird. I mean, you hardly know me."

Dylan burst out laughing. "Oh, I know you all right, Miss Carolinda Singleton. Though you wrote *Carrie* on the lease."

My cheeks were burning. "I hate that name. I've been using Carrie since I was fourteen. Made it my legal name when I turned twenty-one." I glared at him. "How did you know?"

"I used to play with your brother, Jordan, when the two of you came to spend summers on the farm."

My brother. The farm. That's why Dylan seemed familiar. Powerful emotions churned up inside me. "Jordan's dead."

"I know. I'm sorry."

We sat there quietly. I thought of my older brother, who had been killed in a car accident ten years ago.

"We met the summer you were four and I was eight," Dylan said softly. "Jordan and I were playing ball in one of the meadows. You ran over and insisted we had to let you play."

"Did you let me?" I asked.

"Are you kidding? We tried to explain you were too young, which made you mad. Finally, your mom came and took you away."

"I don't . . ." Suddenly I remembered crying as my mother walked me back to the house, promising me a piece of blueberry pie.

"And that's why you trust me to take in your mail? Because you met me a few times when we were kids?"

"And because I'm a good judge of character."

Dylan reached inside the breast pocket of his blazer and handed me an envelope. "Here's the key to my front door and some cash to cover mailing charges and envelopes. Call and let me know what's come in, and I'll tell you which items to forward and where. You'll let me know when you run out of cash."

I nodded. "How long will you be away?"

His expression turned grim. "I can't say, but I'll come home as soon as I'm no longer needed."

"What kind of work do you do?" I asked.

"I'm an investigator for an insurance firm. I've been tracking expensive gems that were stolen years ago and are now coming on the market."

Chapter Fourteen

Since I'd be working late on Tuesday night, I didn't have to be at the library until one thirty. I'd planned to sleep late but woke up at seven ready to start the day. I sang as I showered. Everything in my life seemed as bright as the late October sun shining outside. I had a job I was beginning to love, an event I couldn't wait to begin, a sort of good friend in Jared, and a wonderful cottage I'd be moving into in four days.

Aunt Harriet was clearing Uncle Bosco's breakfast dishes when I joined her in the kitchen. I bussed her cheek. She set a cup of steaming hot coffee before me.

"That was quite a long lease-signing session last night." She smiled. "Your uncle and I were fast asleep when you came in."

"Dylan and I stopped for coffee at the Cozy Corner Café. He's leaving on a business trip today and had several things to tell me about the cottage. He has a handyman who plows the road when it snows and makes repairs at the cottage."

"That's a mercy. Would you like cereal or toast this morning?"

"Two slices of multigrain toast, please, with orange marmalade."

"Coming right up."

I reached for the newspaper Uncle Bosco had left at the other end of the table. I glanced at the headlines, decided I didn't want to read about terrorist attacks or the fighting in the Middle East, and put it down.

"I didn't realize Dylan and Jordan were friends when they were young."

Aunt Harriet set the bottle of marmalade on the table and nodded. "They were the best of friends. Our family was on good terms with the Averys."

"So what happened?"

"A few years of poor crops. The farm not able to carry itself. Your uncle went to the bank to ask for a loan, and Cal Avery wouldn't give it to him. Told Bosco the Singleton farm hadn't been paying its way the past three years, and there was no sign from above that it would start doing so anytime soon."

"Was the farm not making a profit?"

Aunt Harriet sighed as she sank into a chair. "We were getting deeper and deeper in debt. Don't tell your uncle, but I think we were very lucky to get a buyer when we did. The couple who bought it had other ideas about farming, one that included turning my home into a B and B. It hurt at first, but I grew to love this house."

"And Uncle Bosco's as busy as can be, running Clover Ridge affairs."

Aunt Harriet laughed. "Without having to get up at five in the morning to see to the livestock and what-have-you."

We heard a pop, and I went to get my toast. I was spreading marmalade on the two slices when Aunt Harriet said, "It looks like you have two beaus interested in you, darlin'."

The knife clattered to the table. I adored my aunt, but I wasn't ready to talk about my personal life.

"I do not! Jared's a—a friend." *He certainly isn't my boyfriend.* "And Dylan, if that's who you mean, is my landlord."

"Who buys you coffee and keeps you out till all hours."

"Not all hours. I'm sure I was home by eleven."

"If you say so."

I spent the morning sorting through my clothes and books. Aunt Harriet's words circled my brain like an earworm as my discard pile grew higher and wider. I didn't have two beaus, as she'd called them. I liked Jared and enjoyed the time I spent with him going out to dinner and working on our common goal. But some of his reactions made me wonder if he'd ever fully mature. Maybe the horror of his mother's murder when he was in his teens would keep him a perennial youth.

As for Dylan, I laughed out loud. No one could accuse Dylan of being anything but a mature man, but he wasn't interested in me. He was only being nice to me because he'd been my brother's childhood friend. We had Jordan in common, which was probably the reason he was willing to rent me the cottage dirt cheap.

Still, I couldn't help remembering how warm and friendly he'd been the night before after his abrupt manner the first time we spoke. Which was the real Dylan? He was an investigator for an insurance company, a job that took him all over the country—all over the world, for all I knew. It sounded exciting . . . and romantic.

I told myself to stop fantasizing and look at the facts. Sure, Dylan was handsome and lived in an amazing house. His job was probably dangerous, since he dealt with criminals. *Criminals use guns and other weapons.* I shook my head to keep from going off on *that* tangent.

I needed some cartons for my books and discards, so I went looking for Aunt Harriet.

She led me into the garage. "Let me know if you need linens or towels."

"I will, but I think the cottage has everything. Except for food, of course. I'm going food shopping with Jared after he helps me move in."

"Jared's turning out to be a very good friend."

I ignored her broad grin and carried the cartons to my room.

I packed my books in two of the cartons and filled the others with my Goth clothes. I'd have to buy more jeans and leggings and tunics that didn't have skulls and crossbones on them. I giggled to realize I was changing my style, and it didn't bother me one bit.

That done, I gathered up my Sherlock Holmes costume: the oversized magnifying glass I'd ordered online, Uncle Bosco's plaid deerstalker cap, Aunt Harriet's green cape, the meerschaum pipe I'd borrowed from Angela's boyfriend, and of course, my own wonderful new boots!

At twelve thirty, I grabbed a quick lunch and then dressed for the Halloween party. I stuck the pipe in my mouth and went to find Aunt Harriet and Uncle Bosco. They were watching television in the den.

"You look wonderful!" Uncle Bosco said. "Just like Basil Rathbone."

"Who?"

My aunt and uncle burst out laughing.

"What's so funny?" I asked.

"Basil Rathbone played Holmes in several movies around the time of World War Two," Aunt Harriet explained.

"That was a long time ago," I said. "The only Sherlocks I know are Benedict Cumberbatch and Johnny Lee Miller."

"Both television series portraying a modern Sherlock," Uncle Bosco scoffed.

"Robert Downey Jr. played Sherlock in two movies," I pointed out. "Will you be stopping by the library tonight?"

"Wouldn't miss it." Uncle Bosco leaned forward so I could kiss his forehead.

I drove to the library parking lot and walked toward the back entrance. I felt the Halloween spirit all around me as I entered the building. My e-mails had worked! Every librarian and aide I greeted was in costume. And what a variety there was. Marion Marshall, the children's librarian, was a beautiful Snow White. Scott Thompson, our electronic specialist, made a dashing Captain Jack Sparrow. I spotted Alice in Wonderland, Superman, and several princesses.

"Your hard work paid off, Carrie. This is the best Halloween celebration we've had in ages." Evelyn was keeping pace beside me.

I stifled a giggle when I saw she had on a long black dress and a pointy witch's hat instead of her usual conservative apparel.

Unfortunately, she noticed. "What's so funny? Halloween's one of my favorite holidays. I always loved dressing up." Her eyes took on a dreamy look. "When we were younger, my husband and I hosted a Halloween costume party every year."

"Sorry."

"I'm going to walk around to check out the costumes." Evelyn took off.

Several e-mails waited for me on my computer. Most were from presenters wanting to do a library program. Two wanted to make changes to their existing programs. Sally had instructed me to find out about changes well beforehand so I could post a bulletin in hopes of avoiding complaints from disgruntled patrons.

The last e-mail was from Sally. "See me" was all it said. I locked my door and went to her office.

Sally wasn't there, so I stopped by the circulation desk to say hello to Angela. I laughed when I saw her getup. She was dressed the way I used to look: a wig of purple spiky hair, earrings brushing her shoulders, a black tunic with a skull and crossbones over black velvet tights and clunky brown boots. If I didn't know better, I'd think she'd rummaged through the cartons I'd just filled with my throwaways.

"Look familiar?" She winked.

"Very."

We both laughed.

A finger poked my shoulder. "Did you get my e-mail?"

I spun around. Sally's blazing face was as red as her Orphan Annie mop of curls.

"Yes, I went to your office, but you weren't there."

"And it didn't occur to you to return to your office so I'd know where to find you?"

"No. I'm sorry. I . . ."

Sally strode off with me in tow.

What's the problem now?

It turned out there wasn't any problem. Just Sally letting off steam. By the time we were sitting across from one another in her office, she'd calmed down.

"Sorry," she mumbled. "There was a situation with some teenagers outside the library. They had spray paint and were about to deface the front of the building when a police officer happened to pass by."

I waited.

"Actually, I wanted to tell you how nice it is to see the staff in costume. I know it was your doing, along with the terrific decorations throughout the library."

I heaved a big sigh of relief. "Thanks. Trish and Susan worked hard on this event."

"And your financial report's in amazingly good shape." She gave a little laugh. "Much better than what people who have been here for years have been handing in."

"I'm glad."

Sally gave me one of her rare smiles. "Everyone's looking forward to the party tonight. A reporter from the local paper will be coming to write an article about it."

"Really?"

She placed both hands on her desk. "That's about it. See you later, Carrie."

I shouldn't have, but as I left Sally's office, I couldn't resist glancing across the room at the reference desk. Dorothy, in her Wonder Woman costume, was staring at me, a malicious grin on her face.

Chapter Fifteen

Trish and Susan arrived at five. We oohed and ahhed over each other's costumes. Trish came as a flapper, no doubt inspired by *Downton Abbey*, and Susan wore an elegant green gown and wig of beautiful brown hair.

"Scarlett O'Hara!" Trish and I shouted at the same time.

Susan blushed with delight. The girl was surprising me in more ways than one.

We carried the bags of Halloween paper plates, cups, napkins, and plastic cutlery down to the meeting room. The custodians had arranged the chairs in rows facing the front of the room as I'd requested.

"The decorations look awesome," I said. "You gals did a terrific job—here and upstairs. Sally sang your praises."

Which she had, in a way.

They grinned and high-fived each other. Their happiness made me glad, and I realized how important it was to let my assistants know I valued them and counted on their support. I'd never thought about this, but then, I'd never been charge of anyone before.

We listened to the CDs of spooky music that Trish had brought and chose our favorites to play during the two hours of the party. We included the CDs of "Danse Macabre" and "Night on Bald Mountain" I'd borrowed from the library's collection.

We set out the paper goods and some of the refreshments on the long table along the back wall. I thought we'd wait until a little before seven before turning on the oven for the hors d'oeuvres that required heating. I filled the enormous coffeemaker with coffee and water. Max and Pete, our two custodians, came downstairs to see what help we needed. I told them I needed boiled water for tea and asked them to please put a large garbage pail at each end of the table.

The magician and the storyteller arrived, talking up a storm. They knew one another and had often performed in tandem. The magician was a bit upset because he didn't have a room of his own where he could set up his props. I told him the utility room was his to use as long as he understood we'd be coming in and out as needed. He agreed reluctantly and went to unload his suitcases. Trish winked at me. I grinned back at her.

I'm doing it! I'm becoming a department head in the full sense of the term.

At six forty-five, I joined Sally at the door and greeted patrons as she checked off names. A few people tried to fake their way in, but Sally was adamant. "Sorry, but if your name isn't on the list, I'm afraid you can't join the party."

When it happened a third time and a husband tried to join his wife, I added, "We're expanding the library next year, which means more people will be able to attend our events."

Sally shot me a dirty look. But when the fourth person tried to enter without a ticket, she quoted the line. I turned away so she wouldn't see my grin.

I'm learning the tricks of my job.

At ten after seven, I introduced the magician. Though he wasn't very tall and was rather chubby, he had such presence, a silence fell over the crowd. While his routine was run-of-the-mill, he performed every minute of his half hour and then took his bows.

I allowed a break for conversation and refreshments and then introduced the storyteller. Trish dimmed the lights. Though Natasha spoke softly, she knew how to project her voice so that everyone in the room could hear her. Still, we all leaned forward for fear of missing one word of her riveting tales.

Eerie and peculiar they were—of boys wandering into the woods never to return, of a ghost that haunted a brothel. I heard sighs when she brought the last story to its sad ending.

When the lights were on again, I announced that the costume parade would begin in twenty minutes, and all those participating were to line up against the sidewall. I checked on the coffee and dessert situation and asked Susan to come with me to the utility room to help carry out more cookies and platters of cake.

"This is such fun," she said.

"I'm glad you're enjoying yourself."

Trish came to join us. "We need more milk and hot water."

"I'll get them," I said.

"I will." Trish gave me a meaningful look. "You go out there and mingle."

The meeting room buzzed with chatter. Sally was speaking to a young man wearing a cap. Somehow I knew he was the reporter from the local paper.

I'll mingle, all right. I went over to them. "Hello," I greeted him in my friendliest tone. "Are you enjoying our Halloween party? I'm Carrie Singleton, the head of programs and events."

"Ah!" His attention strayed from Sally to me. "I'm Terry Egan. I was hoping to speak to you. This year's party really pops. Can't wait to see the costume parade."

I answered his questions as Sally drifted away. Then I tried to excused myself to see to a few things.

"May I first snap a photo for tomorrow's edition?"

"Of course." I beckoned to Trish and Susan, who were on their way to replenish the refreshment table. "I hope you don't mind including my two assistants."

His eyes lit up when he caught sight of Susan. "Certainly not. The more the merrier."

I allowed Terry to shoot a few pictures and left him chatting with Trish and Susan. I smiled as patrons came up to me, telling me what a wonderful time they were having.

A man in a bear suit nodded at me. "Carrie, I want you to know I'm having a ball."

"I'm glad."

The man lifted the bear head and tucked it under his arm. "It's me, Roy Peters. Trish's dad."

"Oh." I started to laugh. "I didn't recognize you."

"Trish tells me you're doing wonders here in the library."

"Did she?" I felt a stab of pleasure. "Actually, Barbara chose the magician and the storyteller. I think they were terrific."

"They sure were, but I'm talking about the costumes and decorations. The food. The entire party atmosphere. Trish loves the way you include her and Susan whenever you can."

"The truth is, I need their help."

Roy's expression turned somber. "Too bad your first event turned into a tragedy." He shook his head. "I miss Al sorely, and not just because we're one man short in our poker games and still looking for the right replacement."

"I only met him that night, but he made me feel safe and cared for. Silly, isn't it?"

"Not silly at all."

Suddenly I was curious. "What made Al start drinking all those years ago?"

Roy grimaced. "One night, he and his partner were chasing after a suspect in a bad part of town. From nowhere, someone threw a metal rod down on Al's back. Caused him awful pain. Whatever he tried brought no relief, so he started to drink. And he was no pretty drunk. Which was why Thelma finally left him."

"What made him clean up his act?"

"One of the fellas invited Al to fill in at our poker game on the condition that he didn't drink that night. We got friendly. I convinced him to go to AA and see my pain management doctor. Dr. Bailey tried several ways to deal with his pain. Finally, acupuncture worked."

Someone touched my arm. Aunt Harriet was holding a plate of spider cookies. "Carrie, your party's a big success!"

"When did you get here? And where's Uncle Bosco?"

"We arrived a few minutes ago. Your uncle's lined up to take part in the costume parade."

I giggled. "Really? What is he wearing?"

Aunt Harriet winked. "You'll see. It's to be a surprise."

Max and Pete had removed several chairs and were turning those remaining to face a wide center aisle, while Sally kept order among the patrons lined up for the costume parade. *Time to get the show under way!*

Three of the four judges—Angela, Marion Marshall, and the head of the computer department—were already seated at their table. I hurried across the room to relieve Sally so she could take her place as the fourth judge. I'd progressed no more than a couple of feet when an older woman dressed as a bee approached to tell me what a wonderful time she was having. I smiled and said I was glad and moved on. A few more people stopped me to say how much they were enjoying the party. Suddenly, I no longer felt obliged to rush them along.

My job is to be in constant communication with the library's patrons. I need to know what they like and don't like in order to set up programs and events they'll enjoy.

"You think you're so smart, don't you?"

I snapped out of my daydreaming and met the angry glare of Wonder Woman, whom I'd been trying to avoid all evening.

"What do you want, Dorothy? Why do you always have to cause trouble?"

"I want you out of here!"

"Well, that's not going to happen."

Her sly smile made my stomach turn. "We'll see about that."

Shaken, I finally reached Sally and told her to take her place with the other judges.

"What's wrong, Carrie? You look as if you've seen a ghost."

A ghost's niece. "Nothing."

Sally smiled. "Relax. The Halloween party is a huge success."

"I'm glad. We're ready to start the parade. As soon as you join the other judges, I'll give the intro and then give Trish the signal to start the music for the parade."

I forced myself to erase Dorothy from my mind and not dwell on all the possibilities of how she could ruin this, the final segment of the party.

Would she pull a fire alarm?

Shut down the lights?

Set off a stink bomb?

I asked the first person in line—a lion with a glorious mane and tail—to wait until I gave the signal to begin and then went to stand before the judges' table.

"Good evening, my fellow ghouls and ghosts. I hope you're having a wonderful time."

The applause and cheers were deafening.

"We're about to begin the Clover Ridge Library Halloween costume parade." I nodded to Trish to start the music at the lowest volume possible. "We have four judges to award the best male and female costumes and the funniest male and female costumes. Each contestant will have a solo moment, and the judges will take your applause into consideration when they make their choices."

"What if we can't tell if the person is male or female?" a wise guy called out.

"Do your best." There was laughter. "It's the judges' responsibility to decide."

I nodded to the lion to begin, slowing him down as he came toward me. I instructed Trish to raise the volume and

Susan to switch on the strobe light and then took my seat to watch the parade.

"Psst, Carrie," a fat man in a red suit stage-whispered as he passed me.

My mouth fell open at the sight of Uncle Bosco in full Santa Claus regalia. Then I grinned at him—at all the contestants in their marvelous array of costumes. It looked like this time, Dorothy's threats against me were no more than posturing.

Chapter Sixteen

The party ended at nine fifteen. I thanked everyone for coming, thanked Trish and Susan and the judges for their work, and asked the four contest winners to stay a moment to give me their e-mail addresses so I could send them their prizes. Several patrons made a point of hugging me good night and promising to attend more library programs in the near future. I told my aunt and uncle I'd be home in half an hour or so, after I saw to the leftovers. Both Trish and Susan offered to stay with me, but I shooed them home after I told them once again what a wonderful job they'd done. I was exhausted but exhilarated. The party had been a success.

There wasn't much food left, so I told Max and Pete to take what they liked. I yawned as I lifted the huge coffee urn to wash it out in the utility room.

"We'll see to that, Carrie," Max said. "Go on home."

"Are you sure?" I asked.

He laughed. "Of course. Let us do our job."

"In that case, good night." I headed for the door. I was happy to leave, as I was scheduled to be back at the library first thing in the morning.

Only a few dim lights were on upstairs in the main area of the library. The bookshelves cast shadows, making me uneasy. What if someone was lurking behind one of them, waiting to hit me over the head? Maybe Laura and Al's murderer was waiting to attack me for trying to discover his or her identity.

"I say, that was one hell of a party!"

I jumped, then shook my head in exasperation when Evelyn manifested. "You didn't have to scare me like that."

"Sorry, but it *is* Halloween, Carrie. The time for ghouls and ghosts, as you said."

"What are you doing here?"

"You were too busy to notice me bobbing around, listening to comments. I wanted to tell you that tonight was an important event."

"It was? I'm glad everyone seemed to have a good time."

"Now you're the library's darling. Let's keep it that way."

"How do I do that?"

Evelyn grinned. "By connecting to the patrons. Talk to them. Give them programs they love. You'll have a few duds, but that's to be expected." She started to fade. "See you soon, Carrie!"

Too late, I realized I wanted to speak to her about Dorothy.

I pushed open the back door to the parking lot, glad for the four bright beams lighting my way. The car beeped as my door unlocked. I was about to slide in when I let out a groan of dismay. The window on the passenger's side had been smashed in, spraying shards of glass all over the front seat.

Dorothy did this! My fury rose like a volcano about to spill over with boiling lava. I slammed the door shut and started walking home. As I crossed the Green, I plotted all sorts of revenge on Dorothy Hawkins. Aunt Harriet and Uncle Bosco were in the kitchen drinking tea. They turned to me, their faces glowing with pride.

"That was one wonderful Halloween party!" Uncle Bosco was now in his pajamas and bathrobe. "Patrons came up to me saying what a wonderful job my grand-niece is doing."

"What's wrong, Carrie?" Aunt Harriet asked.

"Someone smashed a window of my car."

"That's terrible!" Uncle Bosco exclaimed. "Sally told me some teenaged boys were about to deface the front of the library in the early evening. Maybe they vandalized a few cars in the parking lot too."

"I wonder." Aunt Harriet watched me closely. "Carrie, do you have any idea who might have done something like this?"

Of course I do! I wanted to shout. Instead, I shook my head. I couldn't involve my aunt and uncle. That would only give Dorothy more fuel for her crusade against me. I had to resolve this on my own.

"Leave me the key. I'll have someone from Bailey's Garage pick it up in the morning and make sure they fix the window ASAP. You'll need your car for your move out to the cottage."

I handed Uncle Bosco my car key and planted a kiss on his forehead. "Thanks for taking care of it. I'm going to bed."

* * *

News of my smashed window was already circulating around the library when I came to work the following morning.

"Sorry about your car," Angela said.

"Was there damage to other cars?" I asked.

"Not that I've heard."

We exchanged knowing glances. While I hadn't complained to Angela about Dorothy's behavior, she'd seen a few of her actions for herself. I liked Angela. She was smart, and she was sassy.

"Want to go out for lunch today?" I asked.

She grinned. "Love to. The café around the corner?"

I shook my head. "Someplace we can talk quietly."

Her eyes lit up with interest. "What about that new Indian restaurant on Mercer? Their food's terrific, and I love their curved booths. They're never busy at lunchtime."

"Awesome. Can you leave at twelve thirty?"

"I'll wait for you here, and we can walk over."

Sally stopped by my office to tell me again what a big success the party had been. "Terry's article will be in Friday's paper."

"That's nice."

She shot me a puzzled look, but I refused to pretend I was happy when I was furious with Dorothy. "Well, I thought I'd let you know."

"I appreciate it, Sally," I called as she left.

I sat at my desk, mulling over the Dorothy situation. Confronting her wouldn't help. She'd only deny it. Sally refused to hear a bad word against her bosom buddy, and I refused to bring Uncle Bosco into it. Retaliation would only make things worse.

I forced myself to check through my e-mails. The many messages from patrons complimenting me on the Halloween party got me out of the doldrums. I had to do something about the Dorothy problem, but my job was my priority. As Evelyn put it, I had to relate to the library's patrons and provide programs they'd enjoy.

An idea suddenly occurred to me: I could have local chefs give cooking demonstrations at the library. The patrons would love it, and the chefs would have an opportunity to promote their restaurants and sell their cookbooks, if they'd written any. I switched tabs and Googled restaurants in Clover Ridge and neighboring towns. I pulled out a legal pad and began jotting down names and phone numbers. It was probably too early to call them, but Trish could start phoning them this afternoon.

"Hello, Carrie. How are you this morning?"

I glanced up. Evelyn perched on the edge of the chair across from my desk.

"Not very good. Someone smashed my car window last night, and I think that someone is your niece, Dorothy. She threatened me at the party."

Evelyn's face took on a strange expression. "She did?"

"She told me she wanted me out of here, and then my car was vandalized. No other car was touched. Only mine."

Evelyn bit her lip. "Did you tell your uncle?"

"No, but I'm tempted to, especially since Sally won't hear a word against her best friend."

"I tried to stop her," Evelyn said, "but she couldn't hear me. I'm sorry, Carrie."

"You saw her break my car window?"

"Alas, I did. I tried to grab her arm, but she never saw me or felt my presence."

"Oh." Instead of upsetting me, Evelyn's confession brought me solace. I was glad to know she'd tried to stop her niece. Though I couldn't call on her as a witness, I now knew for certain that Dorothy was guilty.

"She's out of control!" Evelyn cried. "I can only hope and pray that she didn't—"

"Didn't *what*?" I coaxed.

But Evelyn refused to say. I'd never seen her so upset. She muttered "The foolish girl" again and again under her breath.

"What time did Dorothy do this?" I asked. "And what were you doing in the parking lot? I've never seen you anywhere but inside the library."

"I can't talk about it!" Evelyn's hands fluttered to her face. For the first time, I realized that, ghost or not, she was almost as old as my aunt and uncle.

A moment later, she was gone, leaving me with several questions that required answers.

* * *

"I know Dorothy smashed my car window, but I've no way of proving it," I said when Angela and I were seated in a semicircular booth. The restaurant was perhaps a quarter full. Tasteful art decorated the pale-pink walls. Human-sized statues of Hindu gods and goddesses stood in the far corners of the room.

"She's a nasty piece of work. And shrewd. Very shrewd," Angela said. "You'll need evidence to prove it to Sally."

Our waiter approached to ask what we'd like to drink. I ordered a mango lassi. Angela shot me a quizzical glance, and I explained it was a mango-yogurt drink. She ordered one too.

We decided to go for the buffet, which was set out in metal chafing dishes along one of the sidewalls. I picked up a plate and promised myself that I would *not* overeat. I needed to stay alert this afternoon in order to do my work and keep an eye on Dorothy.

I skipped the mulligatawny soup and checked out the various chicken, lamb, and vegetable offerings. I put two small mounds of basmati rice on my plate, over which I ladled chicken tandoori and chicken tikka masala. I served myself dollops of palak paneer—yummy cheese cooked with spinach—and a lentil dish mixed with onions and peas. I passed up the salad and returned to our table.

Angela joined me a few minutes later, her dish piled high with a bit of everything except dessert.

She giggled. "Thought I'd try everything while I'm here."

I glanced at her tall, slender figure. "Why not?"

When our naan arrived, I dipped it in one of the sauces our waiter had placed on our table. "Delicious. Light and fluffy."

"I'm glad you agreed to come here," Angela said. "So many of my friends say they don't like Indian food because they don't like curry. It's hardly in most dishes. Besides, I like curry."

"Me too." Wanting to return to the subject on my mind, I asked, "How do you know Dorothy's a nasty piece of work?"

"Are you kidding? Everyone on staff knows to keep out of her way. They warned me when I started working at the library. The only person who could control Dorothy was her aunt, Evelyn. She worked at the library." A faraway look came into Angela's eyes. "Everyone liked Evelyn. I did too, though she died a few months after I started working there. Poor thing, she slipped and fell one night getting into her car. They didn't find her until the following morning."

"How awful. Why did Dorothy listen to her aunt?"

"The way I heard it, Dorothy's mother spoiled her, but her aunt expected her to behave. She respected Evelyn and wanted to please her."

"I'm glad someone managed to make her behave."

"I had my own Dorothy experience the first week on the job." Angela paused to sip her mango lassi. "Mmm, this is yummy."

"What happened?"

"She came over to the circulation desk where Fran and I were working and said that since things were slow at the desk, surely Fran could work alone an hour or so while I did some research for a patron. I refused. Dorothy fumed and fussed, then settled down. Or so I thought. A few days later, when we were backed up with more than the usual amount of returns, she told Sally I wasn't reshelving books and tapes after they'd been checked in."

"What did you do?"

"I told Sally the situation, then I tackled Dorothy." Angela's grin was devilish. "I said two could play at her game. To prove it, I had four pizzas delivered to her at the library. Dorothy is the one person on earth who hates pizza. For all her bluster, she hates dealing with problems. She finally called the pizzeria and said it was a mistake, but she knew it was me and never messed with me again."

I frowned. "I thought the rubber spider would have stopped her from coming after me."

"Dorothy hates spiders, but your offense is huge in her eyes. She wants to be head of P and E, and you took it away from her."

"I didn't take it away from her."

Angela rolled her eyes. "I know that. You know that. Sally knows it, as does the rest of the world. But Dorothy's stuck in her own mind-set. She thinks the position was meant for her and her alone."

"Sally seems to think well of Dorothy."

"Ha!" Angela found that amusing. "I think Sally's well aware of Dorothy's shenanigans and wants to stay on her good side. Dorothy doesn't get along with most people, and that included Laura Foster."

"What happened?"

"I wasn't here then, but Marion Marshall told me that Laura was hired to work in reference. Because she was cheerful and patient, patrons started requesting her instead of Dorothy." Angela chuckled. "Sometimes three or four people would be sitting around, waiting for their turn with Laura. Dorothy was beside herself. This time, she knew enough not to complain to Sally. Instead, she took it out on Laura. It got so unpleasant for Laura, she finally asked Sally to move her to a different department. Sally said she could work in the other departments occasionally, but if she wanted her job, she had to stay in reference because she was needed there."

"Did they get into any serious blowups?"

Angela glanced up as she thought. "A few. The worst was a few days before Laura was murdered." When she caught my expression, her mouth fell open in disbelief. "You don't think *Dorothy* killed Laura, do you?"

"It never occurred to me. But then, I never knew Dorothy bullied Laura and had a reason to want her gone."

"The police got wind of the quarrel and questioned Dorothy. In fact, Al Buckley came into the library to interview her. I don't know what took place—nobody does—but for the next few days, Dorothy walked around with a terrified expression on her face."

"Do you think Dorothy could have killed Laura?" I asked Angela.

"If we're assuming that the same person killed Laura and Al, then Dorothy's off the hook. Since she wasn't at Al's presentation, there's no way she could have poisoned him."

Painful as it was, I forced myself to remember that evening. "You're right. I don't remember seeing her then."

"That afternoon, Dorothy told me she wouldn't waste her time listening to a cop who'd been drunk on the job the first time he investigated the case. I made a point of looking for her to see if she meant what she'd said."

"The police didn't charge her for Laura's death."

"No, but she was one of the very few people who didn't like Laura. Both patrons and staff members still tell me what a wonderful person she was."

"Really?" I said.

"You sound surprised."

Evelyn had implied that Laura wasn't quite the wonderful person everyone raved about, but I couldn't very well tell that to Angela.

Before I could think of a plausible answer, Angela glanced at her watch. "Jeez, all this jabbering, and we've ten minutes to eat some dessert and get back to the library on time."

We served ourselves generous portions of gulab jamun—fried milk-based dumplings in honey syrup—and ate every last crumb. We paid the bill and agreed we'd come again soon.

Jared called as we were walking back to the library. I said I'd call him when I got to my office.

Angela's eyes gleamed with mischief. "And who was that?"

I shrugged. "A friend."

"Jared Foster, per chance?"

I stared at her. "Yes, as a matter of fact. How did you know?"

She grinned. "A friend saw you guys at Antonio's."

Are there spies everywhere in Clover Ridge? "We're not *dating*."

"Uh-huh."

I wasn't about to tell Angela that Jared and I were trying to find out who killed his mother and Al. Still, she might know something about the people involved.

"We met the night Al Buckley came to speak at the library. Al introduced me to Jared. The two had remained friendly since Laura's murder. I called Jared afterward to see how he was doing."

Angels shook her head. "What a horrible business. First, Laura Foster's murdered. When Al claims he knows who did it, he's poisoned under our noses."

"Did you know Al?"

"When my older brother Tommy was in high school, he never missed a chance to raise hell and get into trouble with the law. More often than not, Al Buckley brought him home instead of arresting him. My parents were always grateful for that."

"Where's Tommy now?"

"Out in Hollywood making films. Kind of like Tarantino's, only bloodier."

I laughed. "I'm glad he found his outlet."

"Al sensed Tommy was meant for better things, though personally, I don't think Tommy's movies are anything to rave about," she confided as we entered the library.

Chapter Seventeen

Back in my office, I greeted Trish and then went downstairs to introduce myself to the psychic who had a monthly program and drew a large crowd. She was charming and exuded an air of compassion and good humor. I was tempted to stay but thought I'd better get back to work.

I replayed my conversation with Angela. Of course Dorothy had disliked Laura. She disliked anyone she couldn't control or outdo. But that didn't mean she had killed her. If she had, she'd have made it her business to attend Al Buckley's talk to find out what evidence he'd uncovered. On the other hand, she might have chosen to avoid the possibility of a public accusation. Regardless, she hadn't come to the program, so she couldn't have poisoned Al. And if she hadn't poisoned Al, she hadn't murdered Laura.

My focus jumped to Evelyn and how horrified she'd been by her niece's act of vandalism. A sense of excitement filled me as my thoughts led me down a completely different avenue.

Evelyn had been nothing but helpful to me when it came to library procedures, but she'd remained inexplicably silent whenever the subject of Laura Foster arose. The only piece of information she'd offered was that Ken Talbot had come to see Laura a few times. And that had proved to be a dead end.

I suddenly understood! Evelyn was terrified that her niece—the nasty, malicious Dorothy—had murdered Laura Foster and maybe even Al Buckley. Evelyn loved Dorothy, but she didn't much like her. Dorothy was her sister's daughter—her own flesh and blood—and Evelyn couldn't bring herself to point a finger at her.

What if I could convince her that Dorothy wasn't the murderer? Then perhaps Evelyn would be willing to help me solve the two homicides.

Trish was working on the next newsletter. She greeted me with a smile. "Sally was by. She'd like you to man the hospitality desk for a few hours."

"Thanks. Will do."

I enjoyed sitting at the hospitality desk, signing up patrons for courses and helping them with general questions. Three women were waiting to sign up for next month's series of yoga classes. I took their names and checks and then called Jared back.

"How are you, Carrie? It's been bedlam here in the office. I feel as if we haven't spoken in ages."

"A lot's been happening here too."

"How did the party go?"

"I think it's safe to call it a success. I believe everyone who came had a great time."

"So what's the problem?"

I laughed. "You can hear it in my voice? Someone broke my car window last night, and I know who did it. Dorothy Hawkins."

"That awful woman! My mother hated having to work with her. She would have quit if not for the pay."

"I heard she made your mother's life miserable."

"Yeah!" Jared laughed. "That's why Ryan and I played a trick on her."

"What did you do?"

"Mom came home every night with a new Dorothy story about what she had to put up with. So Ryan had this idea to pretend to be ghosts. We found a pipe in the basement that made our voices sound weird. One night, we went to Dorothy's house and jimmied up a window when she was alone in the den watching TV. We pretended to be dead people and said we saw the awful things she did. We took turns threatening her with what we'd do if she didn't change her ways. She shrieked and screamed. When her husband came downstairs to see what was wrong, we ran away."

"Was she nicer to your mother after that?"

"For a few days. Then things got worse."

"I suppose she realized it was a prank and not ghosts at all. Maybe she figured it was you and your brother and thought your mom put you up to it."

"Which she didn't. Poor Mom. By the way, Helena bought a condo, but not in my community, thank God. Turns out, she snagged 'a steal,' as she put it, in Devon Woods. The owner remodeled the entire unit and then died suddenly. Her children wanted to sell ASAP."

"Lucky Helena. Those condos usually sell for close to a million dollars. How did you find all this out?"

"My dad mentioned it. She called him to say she was moving back."

"What nerve, calling your father after her awful announcement about your parents' marriage."

Jared laughed. "That's Helena. She thinks she can say anything she likes, and the funny thing is, she gets away with it. As for Dad, he never could hold a grudge. Of course, my brother's angry at him for speaking to her."

"How is Ryan?" I asked.

"Better than usual. He started dating someone a few weeks ago, and I think he really likes this girl. His temper is much improved."

We hung up, saying we'd talk again in a day or two. It occurred to me that the effects of the boys' prank and my fake spider had worn off in a few days. On the other hand, Dorothy was terrified of ghosts.

At three thirty, Sally stopped by the hospitality desk and said she'd take over. I returned to my office, where Trish was still working on the newsletter. I wished I had a way to contact Evelyn. Maybe once I convinced her that Dorothy hadn't killed Laura, she'd be more helpful and tell me more about Laura and what she was like just before she died.

* * *

Uncle Bosco called me on Thursday to say that my car window would be fixed by five that afternoon.

"Would you like me to drive you to the garage so you can pick it up?" he asked.

"Sure, that would be great. I'm happy they were able to fix it so quickly."

Uncle Bosco laughed. "I've been doing business with Jim Bailey as long as we both can remember. He was happy to do me the favor."

I swallowed. "Did he say how much it will cost? I have a pretty big deductible."

"Carrie, dear, don't give it a thought. I'm taking care of it."

"No. I can't let you—"

"Consider it a parting gift from Aunt Harriet and me. Which reminds me, we'd like to take you to dinner tonight—at Spotters, if that pleases you."

For a moment, I couldn't speak. Spotters was the new upscale chophouse fifteen minutes from Clover Ridge. It was highly touted by food critics as the best steak house in the area. Sally had mentioned that her husband had made reservations there for her birthday in May.

"I'd love to eat there. How did you get a reservation? Even during the week . . ." I started to laugh because I should have known better. Uncle Bosco could get pretty much anything he liked in and around Clover Ridge.

I said good-bye to Uncle Bosco, luxuriating in the warm glow of his care. For the first time in my life, an adult—someone older than me—was looking after me. Making sure I was enjoying some of the goodies in life.

But was it right that Uncle Bosco could get pretty much whatever he wanted? I agonized over this as I answered e-mails and stopped by classes and programs in progress. He served on many committees in town. He contributed to projects like the library's renovation. Did that entitle him to privileges?

I couldn't help wondering if Uncle Bosco had pressured Sally to offer me the position of head of P and E. I had the unsettling thought that maybe Dorothy was right, and the only reason I had the job and she didn't was because my uncle was on the library board.

Chapter Eighteen

Evelyn was waiting for me in my office when I arrived at the library on Friday morning.

"Am I glad to see you!" I said. "I've been wanting to talk to you about Dorothy."

"I know." There was no sign of her usual good cheer. I wondered why.

"How did you know?"

"I can sense it."

"In that case, why didn't you come sooner?"

Evelyn nibbled her lip. "I'm a coward. I dread hearing about more awful things Dorothy has done."

"You care about Dorothy and wish you could help make her a better person."

"I do." When she lifted her head, I saw sorrow in her eyes.

"Your niece is a piece of work, but she's not a murderer."

"How do you know?"

"Since she didn't kill Al, she didn't kill Laura."

Evelyn shot me a look of pure skepticism. "That sounds like cockeyed logic to me."

"Dorothy wasn't here the evening Al gave his presentation, so she couldn't have poisoned him."

"Are you sure?"

"Positive."

"And Laura?" Evelyn's voice was fretful. "How that foolish girl envied Laura because all the patrons liked her and wanted her to help them. I told Dorothy they would like her as well if she smiled and spoke in a pleasant manner, but she thought she knew better because she was the librarian, and I was only an aide. She said her job was to answer questions and look up information. She wasn't being paid to be an entertainer as well."

I snorted. "What an attitude. Was she always this sour?"

Evelyn released a deep sigh. "Dorothy was a difficult child—envious of her siblings and her classmates. I had no children of my own and often helped my sister care for her three. I was closest to Dorothy. For all her shenanigans, she tugged at my heartstrings."

Evelyn's smile was bittersweet as she gazed into the past. "I was the one person she turned to. She listened to her Aunt Ev. I could manage to calm her when she would have one of her outbursts and get her to see reason."

"Too bad her disposition never improved."

"Dorothy had a few rough patches as an adult, which embittered her more. She made no friends, except Sally. Most of her coworkers run from her, and with good reason. I can only imagine how she treats her husband and wonder why he stays with her."

"I'm sorry she's been upsetting you."

"I was so afraid she'd killed Laura and too terrified to ask if she had. The police heard of her argument with Laura just before Laura was murdered and questioned Dorothy several times. She walked around pale and nervous for weeks afterward. I never knew if she was innocent or if they simply didn't have enough evidence to charge her."

"Well, now you can rest easy."

Evelyn thrust back her shoulders. "No, I can't. I don't like the way she's treated you from the first day you came to work in the library. Instead of making you her friend, she's envious because you're young and pretty and your uncle is held in high esteem by everyone in town. I'm grateful to you for not telling him what nasty things she's been doing to you. Smashing the window was the limit!"

I threw up my hands. "What can I do to stop her?"

Suddenly Evelyn's demeanor changed. She broke out in a grin, and a minute later, she was giggling. "Tell her that her Aunt Ev is watching her every move and is deeply disappointed."

I shivered as Evelyn leaned over the desk to whisper in my ear. A minute later, I was giggling with her.

"I'm exhausted." She started to fade. "I'll be back soon to find out how everything went."

Five minutes later, someone knocked on my door. Before I could say "Come in," Sally stepped into my office. She looked flustered.

"Hi, Sally. Is everything all right?"

"Why shouldn't everything be all right?"

I shrugged. "Just wondering."

"It's the opposite, in fact."

I stared at her as she stood on the other side of my desk. "Why don't you have a seat?"

She dropped into a chair. "I wanted you to know I've been getting phone calls."

"Yes?"

"Some were from patrons telling me how much they enjoyed the Halloween party."

"I'm glad. I thought it went well."

"Everyone who called wanted me to know how much they like having you as our new head of programs and events."

"Really?" I felt myself grinning. "I'm happy to hear that. I am trying to do a good job."

"I know you are."

"But?"

"There is no 'but'!" Sally shot back at me.

"You don't seem happy with me. If I've done something you don't like, I wish you'd tell me."

Was that fear I saw flicker across her face? "I think you're doing a good job, Carrie. Believe me, I have nothing but good things to say about you. And that's what I told the board yesterday."

"I'm glad to know that." I looked directly into her eyes and held her gaze. "Then why do I get the feeling you don't approve of me? Is it because my uncle is on the board, and he was the one who proposed you hire me for this position?"

Sally looked away. She shook her head vehemently. "I thought that at first, but you proved you were right for the job."

"Is it Dorothy? I know she doesn't like me."

"Of course not!" Sally shot to her feet. "I must get back to work. I said what I came to say."

I watched her leave, pleased with her good report but still in the dark as to why she didn't like me. Was Dorothy holding something over her, something Sally didn't want the rest of us to know?

I spent the rest of the morning adding to my list of chefs who worked within a thirty-mile radius. I composed an e-mail asking if he or she would be willing to give a cooking demonstration at the library. I required that the menu—listing three or four dishes to be prepared in amounts large enough for forty attendees to sample—be sent to me three months before the demonstration. The menus could be seasonal: cookies and candies for Valentine's Day, something green for St. Patrick's Day, or holiday desserts for Easter and Passover. The meals could be ethnic or simply the chef's favorites.

Angela tapped me on the shoulder, startling me. "I thought we were meeting at the back door at noon."

I glanced at my watch. It was seven minutes past twelve. "Sorry. I got caught up in my latest project."

When I told Angela what I'd been doing, she was full of enthusiasm. "That's a terrific idea."

"If the chefs are willing to come. It's wonderful publicity for their restaurants."

"Every business—every art and creative institution and organization—requires publicity and promotion," Angela said.

I laughed. "I'm beginning to realize there's a business side to everything."

"Even the library."

We had a pleasant time chatting over our sandwiches and sodas at the Cozy Corner Café.

As we walked back to the library, Angela said, "I'm glad we've become friends. Before, I had the feeling you weren't planning to stay in Clover Ridge. I didn't want to get too close and then lose you."

"You were right. I almost didn't take the position, but my aunt and uncle convinced me to give it a try."

"And you're doing one hell of a job," Angela said. "Now, if only you could do something about the Dorothy problem."

I grinned. "I may have come up with a solution after all."

We stopped in the ladies' room. Angela left while I was rummaging through my pocketbook in search of my hairbrush. A minute later, the door opened, but I didn't bother to look up until whoever had entered was halfway into one of the four stalls.

Dorothy! I grinned as I prepared my attack.

She frowned as she walked to a sink.

"Hello, Dorothy."

No answer.

"I know you're the one who smashed my car window."

"Prove it," she snarled.

"Your Aunt Ev saw you do it."

Dorothy scrubbed her hands without looking at me. "You're crazy. My aunt's dead. She died six years ago."

"I know. But she often visits the library, and I'm one of the few people who can see her. She saw you smash the window. I expect you to pay for it. Three hundred and fifty dollars will do it."

"I'm not paying you anything."

"Evelyn's very disappointed in your behavior," I said, amazed at how calm I sounded. "She hoped you would have outgrown your childish tantrums by now."

"You're lying." Dorothy let out a derisive snicker. "You can add that to your list of offenses."

"What offenses are you talking about?"

"Stealing the job that should have been mine! You only got it because your uncle's on the library board."

"Do you really believe that for a minute?"

"Of course! I'm an excellent reference librarian. Ask anyone."

"That doesn't qualify you for programs and events. Even if your best friend's the library's director."

That hit home.

Dorothy's face expressed anger and pain. "Sally had to give it to you. Because of your uncle."

"I have the right qualifications."

That stopped her, but only for a minute. "I would have done a great job."

"Sally tells me I'm doing a great job."

Dorothy's expression was murderous as she strode toward the door. I ran around her and blocked her from leaving.

"I want your sabotaging to stop. And I expect you to pay for my car window."

"Get out of my way." She tried to shove me, but I held my ground.

"Evelyn told me to tell you it's time to stop believing the grass is always greener in someone else's life."

Dorothy dropped her hand and stared at me. "What did you say?"

"She told me you stole Cathy Perkins's crayons in second grade because they were nicer than yours. Then you tossed them in the garbage."

Dorothy's mouth fell open.

"And you told Billy Evers that Marigold Truman had a disease because he'd invited her to the junior dance."

Now her eyes bulged with fear. "No one but Aunt Ev knows that. How did you find out?"

"She told me."

Dorothy's head dropped to her chest. "How could she?" she whispered.

"Because she's disgusted with what you've been doing to me. For the longest time, she was afraid you'd murdered Laura Foster."

"But I didn't!"

"That's what I told her."

"How did you—?" Dorothy jumped away from the door as someone pushed it open and entered the bathroom. Marion and I exchanged greetings. I held the door for Dorothy and followed her out.

"I think we understand each other."

Without waiting for her answer, I hurried to my office.

Chapter Nineteen

Jared dropped my heaviest suitcase on my new bedroom floor and then went to gaze out the window at the river beyond. He let out a whistle. "What a view! How did you manage to snag this cottage?"

"I know the owner." This was as true a statement as any.

"I'd give anything to live in a place like this." His eyes went from the low bureau lit by an antique lamp with a copper base to the pair of watercolors on the wall next to the closet. "And you say it comes furnished? Do you mind my asking what rent you're paying?"

"Dylan's giving me a special rate. He's an old friend of the family."

Jared's eyes popped open in astonishment. "You're not talking about Dylan Avery, are you?"

"Yes, why?"

"Wow!" Jared paced the floor, seemingly oblivious to me and our surroundings. "I've never spoken to him, since he's a few years older than Ryan, but everyone knew the hotshot quarterback of Clover Ridge High. He was supposed to go to one of the major football universities on scholarship, but it

turned out he didn't go to any of them. No one knew where he went after graduation. It was like he fell off the face of the earth.

"Then a few years ago, his parents died in a car accident while on vacation out west. Dylan came back to Clover Ridge—some people said from Europe—and moved into the family home on the river. Is it close by?"

"Not far."

"Hey!" Jared pointed a finger at me. "He lives in the white mansion we passed on the way here, right?"

I hesitated. "Yes."

"It's impressive. But why the mystery?"

Though Dylan had never said so specifically, I sensed that he didn't want people knowing he was an investigator for an insurance company. I didn't want to hurt Jared's feelings, so I put the onus on Dylan. "Dylan's kind of a private person. He travels around a lot."

"Did he say what kind of business he's in?"

I shook my head.

Jared's eyes lit up with excitement. "I heard he works for the FBI on all sorts of exciting cases." He sounded like a ten-year-old talking about his favorite baseball player.

"I wouldn't know."

"I don't suppose he'd tell you if he was in the FBI."

I glanced at my watch. "Let's unload the rest of my things. We still have a huge shopping trip ahead of us—if you're still game."

"Of course I'm game. In fact, I drew up a list of staples you'll want to keep on hand."

"So did I." I grinned. "We can compare notes."

Jared retrieved my other suitcase from the back seat of my car, along with the plant Aunt Harriet had insisted I needed.

I grabbed a carton of books I'd stashed in his car and followed him back inside. Ten minutes later, all my possessions were inside my new home.

"Let's have some coffee before we set out for the supermarket," I said.

"Good idea."

I'd packed coffee, milk, and a bag of brownies in a small carton. I filled the coffeemaker and then joined Jared at the kitchen table. I watched him devour two brownies before opening a subject weighing on my mind.

"We haven't made any progress in our investigation. Any ideas what to do next?"

"No, though I'd love to know the identity of my mother's lover." He cringed at the word. "She might have told him if someone was threatening her."

"I understand the police questioned Dorothy Hawkins about her death."

"They did, once they got wind of how Dorothy was treating Mom, and got nowhere. She claimed she was home with her husband that night, and he backed her up. They didn't find any evidence that she'd been to my house, so they couldn't hold her."

"Dorothy wasn't at Al's presentation, so I think we can assume she didn't kill him either."

Jared frowned. "Maybe her lover killed her."

"Maybe he did."

We finished our coffee and brownies and climbed into Jared's car.

"I almost forgot. My uncle George came to spend the weekend with Ken. He invited Ryan and me out to dinner tomorrow evening. Ryan's bringing his girlfriend. I'd love to have you come too."

I was about to claim I had too much to do and then thought better of it. Here was my chance to question three people who had been close to Laura.

"Sure, Jared. I'd like that."

"Great!" His face lit up with pleasure. "I'll let George know and get back to you after I find out which restaurant and the time."

We headed back toward Clover Ridge. I pulled out my to-buy list and read it aloud. Jared handed me a paper with his suggestions. I selected a few and jotted them down.

We went through the supermarket and then stopped at the drugstore to buy first-aid items like Band-Aids and bacitracin. Then we paid a visit to the local hardware store to pick up a few flashlights and basic tools. Our last stop was a liquor store, where I bought a few bottles of Chardonnay, my favorite wine. I was exhausted when I climbed back into the car.

Jared helped me unpack and then kissed me good-bye. "I'll leave you to settle into your new home."

"Thanks. You've been a great help."

He grinned. "That's what friends are for. See you tomorrow."

When he was gone, I walked through every room to claim it as my own. I opened my laptop on the small desk in the second bedroom and read my e-mail. That done, I went into the living room and gazed out at the river.

The cottage was lovely, but it was also very isolated. It was only five, and the evening loomed ahead of me. I wished Dylan were home, simply to know someone was close-by. Was this why the rent was so cheap? Because no one wanted to live this far from town without a neighbor for miles?

Don't be silly. You'll get used to it.

My phone rang, sending a jolt along my spine.

It was Uncle Bosco. "Hi, there. How are you settling in?"

"All right, I suppose. Jared helped me move everything in. Then we went shopping."

I must have sounded forlorn because he chuckled. "And now you're feeling abandoned."

"Well . . ."

"Your aunt and I don't want to intrude, but if you'd like company—"

"I'd love company!"

"In that case, we'll come right over. I suppose you haven't had your dinner yet."

"No, though I have plenty of food here."

"I'm sure you do, but we'll stop in town and bring dinner. Italian or Chinese?"

"Chinese, I think."

"Chinese it is. Give me your address. I'll put it in my GPS."

I gave him my address, along with general directions in case they got lost.

"Sounds easy enough. See you in about an hour, Carrie."

I hurried to the kitchen to set the table. There were two sets of dishes in the cabinets. I chose the more casual set—lovely pottery dishes with a colorful pattern. I found crystal wineglasses over the dishwasher.

It would be a while before Aunt Harriet and Uncle Bosco arrived, even if they didn't get lost. They were older, and everything they did took more time. I switched on the outside lights and went into my bedroom to start unpacking my clothes while I waited.

I analyzed my feelings toward Jared as I folded my underwear and nightgowns in the drawers of the double dresser and hung my blouses and pants in the closet. I *liked* him, and I certainly appreciated his help today, but I could never be in a serious relationship with him. His psychological development had been stunted—and no wonder. His mother had been murdered, his father had been distant, and his older brother was a hothead. I gave a bark of laughter. His family was even more dysfunctional than mine. I wasn't attracted to him. Still, he'd proven to be a good friend in so many ways. We were both determined to solve the two homicides. He'd invited me to dinner tomorrow night, where I hoped to learn more about the last days of Laura's life.

I uncorked a chilled bottle of Chardonnay and sipped. Delicious! A few minutes later, my aunt and uncle arrived, laden with packages.

"I see you didn't get lost." I kissed them.

"I used my GPS," Uncle Bosco said. "Besides, I remembered coming out here to a big bash the Averys threw—what was it, Harriet, fifteen years ago?"

"More like twenty, dear."

Uncle Bosco placed the bag holding our dinner on the kitchen counter. Aunt Harriet set down a bottle of wine and one of her cakes beside it. I gave them a quick tour of the cottage. We stood in the living room, gazing out the window.

"It's too dark to see the view, but the river's right outside."

"Lovely—and so beautifully decorated." Aunt Harriet rubbed the fabric on the arm of the sofa. "If only it weren't so isolated."

"Harriet!" Uncle Bosco said in his warning voice.

"Well, Dylan's here some of the time." *But not now.* "And his handyman has a cottage nearby."

Uncle Bosco came to join us after checking the doors and windows. "The locks are strong and of good quality."

"I can always get a dog for protection," I joked.

"That might be a good idea," Aunt Harriet said.

"Let's eat," Uncle Bosco said, "before everything's ice cold."

We ate our soup and then shared the three main courses we always ordered: chicken with broccoli, shrimp in lobster sauce, and duck with vegetables. We finished the Chardonnay, and I brewed a pot of decaf coffee.

Aunt Harriet's cake was a lovely pumpkin bundt cake filled with nuts, dried cranberries, and chocolate chips. There was enough for the next few weeks. I planned to cut it up and freeze it in small portions.

We moved to the living room. Uncle Bosco dropped into the leather lounge chair. Minutes later, he was snoring. Aunt Harriet and I looked at each other and giggled.

"I'm so glad you decided to come by tonight," I told her.

"We almost didn't call. We thought Jared would still be here, and we didn't want to intrude."

I waved my hand. "There was no intruding. I'll see Jared tomorrow night. His uncle George is in town visiting Ken Talbot. He's invited his nephews to dinner. Since Ryan's bringing his girlfriend, Jared asked me to come along."

"That Ryan." Aunt Harriet frowned. "He gave his parents a rough time. Always getting into trouble. I suppose he's settled down, since we haven't heard very much about him in recent years."

"What kind of trouble?"

"Breaking car windows. Climbing up to the water tower to paint all kinds of nasty signs. It's amazing he didn't end up in reform school."

"Really?" I was shocked. "From what Jared said, I thought he was upset because his parents weren't getting along."

"Could be the reason, but he showed signs of it early on—stealing candy from Candies and Sweets."

"He was very belligerent toward Al Buckley the night Al gave his presentation."

Aunt Harriet chortled. "That's because Al brought him down to the station more than once."

"I had no idea. Jared's not like that at all."

She smiled. "He was the good child." She scrutinized my face. "Are you two . . . ?"

"We're just friends."

Uncle Bosco roused himself with a loud clearing of his throat.

"Good morning," I said. "Have a nice snooze?"

"I wasn't sleeping. I was thinking."

"We know, my dear," Aunt Harriet said.

"And I was thinking," he said louder, "that this cottage would make the perfect setting for your thirtieth birthday party."

"Birthday party?" I echoed. "I wasn't planning any such thing."

"Of course you weren't. Only egotists throw themselves a party."

"My birthday's next month. I really don't have the time to arrange a party."

Aunt Harriet waved away my objection. "Carrie, dear, you won't have to do a thing. Your uncle and I will bring in the food and drink. Your job is to invite whomever you'd like and decorate the place to your heart's content."

"I don't have that many people to invite."

"Of course you do!" she insisted. "Your friends from the library will come. And Jared, of course. And that Avery boy."

If he's around.

"It would be nice to invite your cousins," Aunt Harriet said.

"Not *all* of them!" I said.

"I had Randy and Julia in mind."

"And their children," I added.

Aunt Harriet looked at me sideways. "Certainly, if you like."

I found myself warming to the idea of a party. Aunt Harriet asked for a pen and paper to jot down ideas. I worked on my guest list.

"Why don't we make it a joint birthday-housewarming party?" I suggested. "I'll create an electronic invitation."

"Excellent idea!" Aunt Harriet said.

I made a mental note to design an e-invitation the next day. "Do you have Julia and Randy's e-mail address?" I asked.

Uncle Bosco reached into his pocket for his smartphone. "Here it is." He rattled off the address, and I copied it down.

When it was time for them to leave, I hugged them fiercely. I didn't bother to brush away the tears that filled my eyes. "You're both so good to me. No one's ever been this good to me."

"That's 'cause we love you, honeybun." Uncle Bosco's voice was hoarse with emotion.

"You're the daughter we never had," Aunt Harriet said.

"Now, remember to lock up after us," Uncle Bosco said as I helped him into his jacket.

"Bosco, she's not a child. She knows what to do."

I smiled as they climbed into their car. How lucky I was to have returned to Clover Ridge and to them.

I was loading the dishwasher when Jared called.

"I'll pick you up tomorrow at five. Uncle George wants to have an early dinner before driving home."

I told him about my aunt and uncle's visit and our plans for my thirtieth birthday party.

"A party! What a great idea. Leave the decorations to me."

We chatted a bit and said good night. I cleared the coffee and dessert dishes from the kitchen table and then wandered into every room. *This is mine! This is mine!* I'd never had an entire house to myself. I ended up in the bathroom, where I washed my face and brushed my teeth, and then got into a nightgown and into bed.

I was reading and feeling drowsy when the housephone on the nightstand rang. Startled, I lifted the receiver.

"Hello, Dylan here. I hope it's not too late to call."

"No, it's fine." *Better than fine.*

"Sounds like you're half-asleep."

"Kind of. It was a hectic day."

"Sorry I couldn't get away to call sooner. Do you have everything you need? Remember to call Jack Norris if you need anything. My housekeeper, Mrs. C, comes on Tuesdays. Leave her a note if you have something that requires special attention. Like a few blouses that might need ironing."

Ironing? "Mrs. C cleans the cottage every week?"

"She'll change the bedding and towels and do a load or two of wash, if you like. Please pick up my mail Tuesday evening and send it to me on Wednesday." He gave me an address and had me read it back to him.

I heard voices in the background.

"I have to go, Carrie. Sleep well."

"Good night, Dylan."

I was smiling as I turned out the lamp. I'd just lived the most perfect day of my life.

Chapter Twenty

Where am I? I looked around, my heart thudding like a drum, until I realized the darkened room was my bedroom, and I was comfortably ensconced in a well-padded bed under a soft comforter. I stretched my limbs, enjoying the smell of freshly laundered linens. It was a bit past six AM, when I usually turned over and went back to sleep. Instead, I went to the window and pulled open the curtains and blinds to let in the early morning sunlight. My eyes caught sight of the river flowing gently by. I went to the bathroom and then changed into a warm-up suit and sneakers and raced out of the house as if a mad dog were pursuing me.

I jogged along the river for half an hour and then, suddenly famished, turned and retraced my steps. An old tan SUV was parked beside my car. I opened the front door slowly. "Hello. Who's there?"

A wizened elf of a man with leathery skin who could have been anywhere from sixty-five to eighty emerged from the guest bathroom.

"Jack Norris here. Sorry if I frightened you. Dylan asked me to look in on you first thing, see if you need anything.

I knocked, but when you didn't answer, I thought I'd best come in and make sure everything's workin'. Turns out, the toilet in the guest bathroom keeps runnin'. I'll see to it soon as I'm able."

Various responses, from "Seven in the morning isn't the time to come by" to "If no one answers, come back later," came to mind. Instead, I put out my hand.

"I'm Carrie Singleton. Nice to meet you, Jack."

He had a strong grip.

"Bosco's niece." He made it sound like an accusation.

"That's right."

He jerked his head toward my bathroom. "I tightened the faucet in the sink. Anything else need fixin'?"

"I haven't used the washing machine, dryer, or dishwasher."

"They're all new. Should be okay, but let me know if there's a problem."

"Will do."

He scratched his head as he appeared to think this over. "In that case, I'm off. I'll be back to fix the toilet."

"Thanks, Jack."

I shot him a smile and was surprised when he gave me one in return.

It transformed his face. "Welcome, Miss Carrie. I think you'll like livin' in the cottage."

I made myself a breakfast of coffee and a toasted croissant, then sat down at my laptop to create the party invitation. An hour later, I was pleased with my result: a picture of a lime-green house with colorful balloons and stars around it. I wrote, "Housewarming/Birthday Party, Saturday, December 11, from five to nine," and the location. I typed in the e-mail addresses and sent the invitations on their way.

The day passed quickly. At four fifteen, I showered and dressed for dinner in my new gray pants, a burgundy-colored turtleneck, and my treasured boots. Jared came for me at five.

"Where are we eating tonight?"

"Due Amici, an Italian restaurant not far from here. Uncle George likes to eat there whenever he's in the area. And since he's paying . . . Actually, the food's quite good."

"Great. I love Italian food."

"I think everyone does."

Jared helped me on with my jacket, and we walked out to his car.

He wasn't kidding about the restaurant being nearby. We hadn't driven more than ten minutes when he turned into a driveway beside a well-lit building the size of a small house. Butterflies flitted around in my stomach as we approached the side entrance. I hardly knew these people. Ken was nice, and I imagined George was too. But Ryan was a hothead, and I had no idea what his girlfriend was like.

I reminded myself that tonight's dinner was the perfect opportunity to find out more about Laura.

The maître d' led us to a round table in a corner of the room, where Ken and George sat with two glasses of wine and an open bottle before them. They were deep in conversation.

"Hey, look who's here!" Ken stood and patted Jared on the shoulder. He greeted me with a hug and a kiss, which immediately put me at ease.

"You remember Carrie, don't you, George? She was our hostess at the library the night poor Al Buckley met his end."

George took my hand in both of his. "Of course I do."

"Nice to see you again," I said.

"Have a seat," Ken said.

I sat next to him while Jared and his uncle traded insults the way men fond of one another often did. Eventually, Jared sat beside me.

"Would you like some red wine," George asked, "or would you prefer something else?"

"Red's fine with me," I said.

"Me too," Jared said.

Ken poured wine into our empty glasses, and the four of us clinked and sipped. The wine had a nice, rich flavor.

"Where's Ryan?" Jared asked.

"They'll be here eventually," his uncle answered. "He called to say he was delayed, then he had to pick up Gillian on the far side of town."

"And we're supposed to wait?" Jared asked.

I stared, taken aback by the bitterness in his voice.

Jared patted my hand. "Sorry, Carrie, but my brother does this all the time."

"So he does," George agreed mildly. "Which is why I told him to get here when he could but that we'd be ordering at five thirty, because I have a long ride ahead of me."

"That must have pissed him off," Jared said.

"Of course it did. Ryan said he might as well not come, but I told him I hoped to see him. He promised to be here as close to six as he could make it."

I was glad Ryan would be late. I remembered his hostile manner toward Al that night. Now I knew it was because Al had previously caught him doing all kinds of vandalism and worse. From what I'd just heard, Ryan was his own worst enemy. The less time I had to spend in his company, the better.

The four of us sipped our wine and chatted about a variety of subjects. George asked me how I liked living in Clover

Ridge. I told him I loved working at the library and that I'd just moved into a new rental.

"It's a cottage on the Avery property," Jared added.

"Good for you!" Ken winked at me. He already knew I was renting the cottage, since he had a copy of the lease in his office. I was pleased he didn't mention that Dylan was his client and glad I'd sent him an invitation to my party.

George whistled. "That's some gorgeous piece of property. Right on the river, isn't it?"

Ken laughed. "I bet you'd love to buy it and build condos along the shore."

George frowned as he nodded in agreement. "Wouldn't I ever? But I'd never have the cash to do any such thing."

Our waitress approached the table, said her name was Michele, and asked if we were ready to order.

"I'm afraid not." George glanced at the pile of menus we hadn't bothered to open. "Though we might start with a large antipasto, if everyone's agreed."

We all nodded, and Ken distributed the menus. Michele recited the evening's specials and said she'd be back in a few minutes with our salad and to take the rest of our order.

Jared and I decided to share an order of eggplant rollatini and seafood marinara. Ken poured more wine.

"Looks like we need another bottle," George said, gesturing to our waitress.

Michele opened a second bottle and poured. We talked about various subjects as we ate and drank. George and Ken were excellent conversationalists, relating one humorous anecdote after the other. I was thoroughly enjoying myself, and all traces of my shyness dissolved.

Michele was just setting down our main courses when a male voice said, “I see you’re having a wonderful time without us.”

We all turned to see Ryan, who wore an aggrieved expression. For some reason, I felt as if I’d been caught doing something illicit.

“We were beginning to wonder if you were really coming,” Jared said.

“Your brotherly concern is touching.” Ryan pulled his pretty companion closer. “Everyone, this is Gillian.”

Her lips tightened at his rough handling and then formed a smile. “Hello. Nice to meet you all. Sorry we’re late.”

“Gillian, this is my uncle George; his college roommate, Ken Talbot; my brother, Jared; and his friend . . .”

“Carrie Singleton,” I said.

“Right.” Ryan led Gillian around the table so she was sitting next to Jared. He took the seat between Gillian and his uncle.

Silence fell. Michele appeared and asked the newcomers what they’d like to eat. Ryan ordered for both of them.

“Would you like some salad?” I offered.

“We can manage, thanks.” Ryan reached for the bowl and spooned salad onto their plates. He glared at the bread basket. “You didn’t leave very much bread for us.”

“Ask for more. You can have as much as you like,” George said. “Wine?”

“I’ll have a real drink.” Ryan raised his hand and snapped his fingers.

I gasped, horrified, but no one else seemed to notice.

“I’ll have some wine, please,” Gillian said.

Michele returned and took Ryan's order of a double scotch, and George asked for more bread.

When his drink arrived, Ryan gulped it down. It seemed to steady him. He smiled at his uncle. "For as long as I can remember, you've always loved this place."

"Why not? Their food is consistently good."

"Which is quite a surprise, given its history." Ryan turned to me. "Carrie, do you know what *Due Amici* means?"

"Two friends."

"Good girl." Ryan smiled. He was very handsome when he smiled.

I smiled back and then caught sight of Gillian's frown.

"Two friends, Silvio and Tonio, opened this restaurant in the forties. Isn't that right, Uncle George?"

"It is."

"By the eighties, their sons, Rudy and Tony, were running the place—almost as well as their fathers. Rudy took care of the business end, while Tony and his son, Alessandro, did the buying and cooking. Rudy had a heart attack, which was when his daughter, Mia, took over the DeVito half of the business."

"I don't think we have to—" Ken began when Ryan interrupted him.

"I think we do. I think Carrie and Gillian need to know the history of Due Amici to get full enjoyment of their dinner."

This story didn't have a happy ending, I was sure of it. I felt a sense of foreboding, but I was curious and more than a little excited. "Then what happened?"

"Mia was beautiful and full of life. She had a lot of new ideas for the restaurant. Different tablecloths. A singer on Thursday nights. Tony wasn't happy about the changes, but

Alessandro was inspired. He started offering new dishes for the first time in years. Mia became the hostess, and business picked up.

"Tony and Alessandro had a falling out. Alessandro said he'd open his own restaurant. Tony was furious—at his son for leaving and at Mia for interfering. Rudy tried to reason with his friend, but Tony was devastated to think his life's work was being tossed aside all because of a young girl.

"Mia decided she had to try to explain things to Tony. That one had to move forward with the times. That she and Alessandro were in love and planning to marry. But she never got that far. Tony was so incensed by what he considered to be her meddling, he reached for the knife on the cutting board and stabbed her in the heart."

I gasped. "How tragic."

"So sad," Gillian murmured.

"Poor Rudy died of a heart attack, and Tony's in prison for the rest of his life."

"Does Alessandro own Due Amici now?"

"He sold the place to a cousin and moved to California."

I didn't have much appetite after hearing that story and asked to have my meal wrapped to take home. The others conversed quietly as they ate. George asked Ryan about his job. Ryan shrugged and said it was okay. His tone made me wonder if he even still had a job.

We ordered several desserts for the table, and my appetite returned. I ate half a cannoli, a slice of Italian cheesecake, and a serving of tiramisu with my cappuccino.

Jared hadn't said much since his first comment to Ryan, and I couldn't blame him. Ryan was one nasty dude, desperately in need of a course in anger management. He fed Gillian a forkful of cake. She seemed to be enjoying herself, though I'd gotten the definite impression she'd been furious with him when they first arrived. Sure, Ryan was good-looking, but looks wore thin when the guy came with a chip on his shoulder. And Ryan was weighed down with cement blocks on both shoulders.

He caught me staring at him and winked. Flustered, I turned away.

"Tell me, Carrie, how is your investigation going?" he asked.

"What investigation?" For a moment, I didn't know what he was referring to.

His grin grew wider. "Come on. You can tell me. After all, it's my mother's death you're looking into. You and my baby brother."

"That's enough, Ryan." Jared's face had turned a mottled red.

I wasn't sure if he was angry, embarrassed, or both. "We haven't learned anything recently," I admitted, "but I'd think you'd want her murderer brought to justice."

"Justice, ha! A fat lot of good that will do us."

"Who do you think killed her, Ryan?" Jared said.

"Now that we know she had someone on the side, I bet my money on him."

I scowled at Jared, furious he'd shared this information with Ryan. I quickly realized I had no right to be angry. Ryan was his brother and entitled to know of any new developments we uncovered.

"I think it's time to change topics," George said. "This kind of conversation isn't going to get us anywhere."

"She was pretty friendly with Lou Devon," Ryan said, ignoring his uncle.

"Our next-door neighbor? Come on, Ryan. He's a geek and has that stupid laugh."

Ryan shrugged. "He was over all the time."

"Only if something broke and Mom couldn't fix it. Like when the hose in the upstairs toilet got loose and spouted water all over the floor."

"I found them talking at the kitchen table plenty of times."

"Doesn't sound very romantic to me." Ken turned to George. "It's getting late. I think you should start heading home."

We took turns thanking George and wishing him a safe trip home. I was surprised to see Jared and Ryan walking side by side to the exit.

"Underneath it all, they love one another," Gillian said.

I gave a start. I hadn't realized she was standing next to me. "I think you're right. It's terrible what they went through—losing their mother that way."

"It was one of the first things Ryan told me after we met. I suppose that's why he watches all those real-life murder cases on TV. He doesn't have much hope the police will ever find his mother's murderer."

"I wonder who Al Buckley, the detective on the case, finally decided was responsible."

"Ryan thinks he had no idea and was using his so-called presentation to gather information."

"I got the feeling Al was looking for proof to confirm his suspicions."

"He found out for sure she was very unhappy," Gillian said.

"Helena didn't say so then, but she told Jared that his mother was having an affair."

"I know, but with whom?"

We looked at one another—two curious women.

"Hey, why don't the four of us go out together sometime?" she said.

I smiled. "Sounds good to me."

Chapter Twenty-One

The drive to work took twelve minutes. I parked and entered the library through the back door. Since I had a few minutes to spare, I stopped in the staff ladies' room.

Angela was there, beaming at me. "I got your invite. Count Steve and me in. I can't wait to see your cottage."

My cottage. For the first time ever, I had a home I loved and a friend where I worked. "Hey, why don't you come over for dinner one night this week? I make a mean mac and cheese."

"Love to. I'll bring the wine."

We settled on Thursday evening. I used the lavatory, poured myself a cup of coffee, and unlocked my office door just as the minute hand on the large clock moved to twelve.

I spent the next quarter of an hour going through e-mails that had arrived over the weekend. A few were from chefs asking if the library owned any of the cooking supplies they'd need for their demonstrations. They all said they'd bring their own utensils—from knives to measuring cups, graters to frying pans—but they required a hot plate with two, preferably four, burners; a cutting board; and a demo table with a mirror that tilted and allowed the audience to see what they were doing.

One chef wondered if it would be all right if he diced the ingredients at home to save time. Another asked if he could preprepare the food the audience would be eating because, though he planned to demonstrate every step of the preparation, the actual cooking time was two hours. I decided yes in both cases, since TV cooking shows allowed it.

All the chefs would receive the same remuneration. From this, they had to buy and pay for the necessary ingredients. I had to figure out how much to charge the patrons before I could put something in the newsletter.

Sally was the only person who could help me with this. I locked my office and knocked on her door.

"Come in," she shouted and then resumed arguing with someone on the phone. "Sorry about that," she apologized when she'd finished her conversation. "I brought my car in for repairs. They quoted me one price, then called to say it's one hundred and fifty dollars more."

"That's happened to me more than once."

She smiled suddenly. "I got your invitation. Bob and I would love to come to your party."

Bob? Of course. Sally was married. She wore a wedding ring, though I'd never heard her mention her husband's name before.

"I'm glad you can make it. And I'll finally get to meet your husband."

"He's looking forward to meeting you too."

"Oh." I'd debated before adding Sally's name to my guest list and finally decided it was a wise move, since she was my boss. Now I was glad I'd included her.

"I need your input." I told her about my plans to have chefs come and give food demonstrations at the library.

Sally pursed her lips as she listened.

At first, I thought she was annoyed with me for not running the idea past her. "I hope you don't think it's too much or too complicated for us to handle," I said.

"No, I don't. In fact, I think it's a wonderful idea. We have some available funds for new programs. Why don't we drive over to the restaurant supply store in Merrivale and see what they sell along these lines."

"I could ask the chefs who responded to tell me what pots and pans they'll require."

"Of course we can't buy everything they'd like us to have on hand."

That settled, we discussed what to pay the chefs—given that they'd be providing the ingredients—and what we should charge our patrons for the program.

"We don't want it to be too expensive," Sally said. "How many patrons should we allow for each demonstration?"

"Forty, I think." I was flattered she wanted my opinion.

"I think so too. Why don't you contact the chefs who responded, request a menu of the three or four dishes they plan to prepare, and ask how much they think the ingredients will cost for forty samples."

I hummed as I returned to my office. I unlocked the door, and it wasn't until I'd closed it behind me that I noticed the envelope on the floor. Puzzled, I bent to retrieve it. Inside was a note with one word—"Here!"—and a check for three hundred fifty dollars.

Thrilled, I called Uncle Bosco to tell him that I could pay him back at least some of the cost not covered by my insurance for the broken car window.

"Where did you get that windfall?" he asked.

"From the person who broke the window."

Uncle Bosco laughed. "I suppose you won't tell me who the culprit is."

"Of course not."

"I want you to keep the money, Carrie, and buy something nice for yourself."

I tried to argue that he and Aunt Harriet were doing too much for me, but he stopped me before I got very far.

"Honey, having you here in Clover Ridge is a blessing to us. We're happy to do what we can to make your life easier."

"But you're paying for my birthday party and always treating me to dinner."

"Did you ever consider that it gives us pleasure, and we do it for the sheer fun of it?"

"I guess not."

"Your aunt and I are enjoying ourselves more than we have in years. So please, let us go on doing things with you and for you as long as we can."

Tears sprang to my eyes. "Thank you, Uncle Bosco. No one's ever done this much for me. Ever."

"Don't I know it, honey. Talk to you later."

It was hard settling down to work after that. All the good things happening in my life kept churning around in my mind. I had loving relatives, a home, and a friend. My boss liked my plans for my department. And I'd convinced Dorothy, the library's Cruella de Vil, to pay for the window she'd broken. Jared and I were no further along in our investigation, but maybe that was about to change.

I called Jocko Wright, the first chef who'd agreed to come to the library. Jocko was the sous chef at Spotters, the wonderful restaurant Uncle Bosco had taken me to the week before. No one picked up when I called, so I left a message asking him to call when he got to work.

I felt Evelyn's presence as she reached for the check I'd left on my desk. "I see Dorothy's paid you for the window she smashed."

"She did it for your sake, Evelyn."

"I'm glad she owned up to her misdeed. I wish I could give her a good talking-to. Tell her to stop being such a destructive sourpuss."

I laughed. "I think everyone in the library would love to see her lighten up and let go of her grudges."

"How do you like living in the Avery cottage?"

I filled Evelyn in on the move, my aunt and uncle's visit, and their offer to host my birthday party. Then I told her about the previous night's dinner and how Ryan thought Laura might have been having an affair with their neighbor Lou Devon.

Evelyn giggled. "I doubt that very much. Lou Devon's completely devoted to his wife and his computer."

"Jared didn't think much of that idea either. Laura *was* having an affair, but no one knows who the mystery man might be."

"Helena Koppel was her best friend. If Laura confided in anyone, it would have been her."

"That's what Jared thought. But when he asked Helena if she knew who the man was, she told him his mother never revealed his name."

"He was probably married," Evelyn said. "Why else would she be so secretive?"

We were making progress by examining what we knew and didn't know and following the leads to their logical conclusions.

"I bet you're right. Laura told Helena about her own part in the affair but not her lover's name. She felt obliged to keep that a secret."

Evelyn nodded. "It might be someone with standing in the community. Like the mayor. Or president of the town council at the time."

"Do you remember who they were fifteen years ago?"

"No, but you can always look them up."

"I'll do that tonight." Another idea occurred to me. "If Laura was afraid to tell anyone the name of her lover, maybe she wrote about it."

"You mean like in a diary?" Evelyn laughed. "In my day, girls wrote in their diaries about the boys they had crushes on and wished would ask them out. I don't think grown women keep diaries these days."

"Nowadays, people of all ages keep journals where they write about their day's events, their feelings, their thoughts. Did you ever notice Laura writing while she was here in the library?"

Evelyn pursed her lips as she thought. "Funny you should ask. A few times, I noticed her writing at the reference desk when no patrons needed her assistance. Once I passed close by and was surprised to see her give a start and cover the page she was writing. I remembered thinking it odd, because I'd assumed whatever she was writing was related to work."

I tingled with excitement. "Laura could very well have been writing about her love affair. Why else would she care if you saw what she was doing?"

"Possibly," Evelyn said. "But even if you're right, we have no idea if she was writing on sheets of paper, in a notebook, or what-have-you."

"We know it wasn't an iPad. I don't think they were around then."

"Still, we're talking about fifteen years ago. If Laura was obsessed with keeping her affair a secret, she probably ripped up the pages as soon she wrote them. She probably wanted to vent her feelings and then destroy the evidence."

I sighed. "You're probably right. We'll never find out who this mystery man was."

"Or who killed Laura or Al Buckley." Evelyn shook her head. "Some mysteries remain unsolved, no matter how hard we try to solve them."

Chapter Twenty-Two

I left work a few minutes past five, eager to arrive home and start dinner. I'd marinated a chicken the night before and had plenty of veggies and salad in the fridge to choose from. I hadn't expected the heavy traffic en route to the cottage. Why was I surprised? It was rush hour all over the country. I'd been spoiled living with Aunt Harriet and Uncle Bosco, their house a short walk across the Green to the library.

Several people had texted me during the day to say they'd be coming to my birthday-housewarming party. Trish told me that Barbara would be in town that weekend, so I sent her an e-mail invitation too.

I thought about my conversation with Evelyn. We'd both agreed that Laura's secret lover might very well have killed her. Who could he be? Certainly not her next-door neighbor. As for the other men in her life—Jared, Ryan, their father, her brother, and Ken Talbot—my gut feeling was that none of them had killed Laura.

What had the police discovered at the crime scene? Had the murderer left any clues? His intention wasn't to kill Laura, or he would have brought a murder weapon. A gun or a knife.

Something that showed premeditation. Instead, he (or she) had picked up a vase and bashed Laura over the head.

Or had the killer been more calculating than I first thought? What if he or she knew exactly where the vase was and had planned to use it? The vase had been wiped of all fingerprints, which showed a sense of self-preservation. My mind raced with possibilities as I exited the road as soon as I could and drove back to the village. I wanted to talk to Lieutenant Mathers and get some background information on the case. Of course, he might not be in his office or willing to talk to me about Laura's murder, but it was worth a try.

A few minutes later, I parked in the lot behind the police station and entered the small brick building. I told the female officer at the front desk that I wanted to speak to Lieutenant Mathers.

"And you are?" she asked.

"Carrie Singleton." I decided to use my most potent influence. "Bosco Singleton's my uncle."

"That's nice." She stood, rising a head taller than me, and pursed her lips. "I'll see if the lieutenant's free to speak to you."

She returned a few minutes later. "He'll see you. Follow me."

"Thank you."

She flashed a smile, which changed her face completely. "You're the new head of programs at the library."

"I am."

"Your Halloween party was awesome. Can't remember the last time my hubby and I had so much fun. I'm Gracie, by the way."

We shook hands. "Hi, Gracie. Nice to meet you." So much for using Uncle Bosco to wield some clout.

Lieutenant Mathers was working at his computer when Gracie showed me in.

"Have a seat. Be finished with this in two minutes," he said.

I sat in one of the two metal chairs facing his desk. Was coming here a good idea? The police didn't like having civilians question them about ongoing cases, which was why I'd asked Uncle Bosco to find out what he could. I needed to learn everything that had been discovered about Laura's murderer.

"Hello, Miss Singleton. What can I do for you?"

"Please, call me Carrie."

He nodded but didn't ask me to call him John. Not that I expected him to. I cleared my throat, wishing I'd planned my opening. To my surprise, the words spilled out, sounding natural and logical.

"Lieutenant Mathers, I was in charge of the library event where Al Buckley was poisoned. The next day, you interviewed me at my uncle's home."

His blue eyes bore into mine. "I remember."

"It was the first time I'd met Detective Buckley, but I liked him immediately. I felt terrible that someone poisoned him." Tears sprang to my eyes. I blinked them back furiously. "I was wondering if you—the police—have made any progress in the case."

Lieutenant Mathers leaned back and steepled his fingers. "It's an ongoing investigation, Miss Singleton. Which means there's nothing I can share with you at this point."

I'd expected that. Still . . . "What about Laura Foster's murder? I know it was never solved. Are the records of that case available to the public?"

The lieutenant studied me for a minute and then let out a deep belly laugh. "Don't tell me you're trying to solve two homicides on your own, Miss Singleton."

"Of course not! I've gotten to know Jared Foster and can't help wondering who would want to kill his mother."

"She was a lovely lady."

"Have you any idea why the killer would take her gold bracelet and antique pin and nothing else?"

"Haven't a clue."

I let out a huff of frustration. "Can you at least tell me if the two murders are connected?"

He stood. "I'm afraid I can't tell you that either. However, there are plenty of newspaper articles about Laura Foster's murder online. You can read them in the library."

"I know." I got to my feet. "Thanks for your time."

Lieutenant Mathers tapped my shoulder. "I sincerely hope you're not out to solve these murders. There's a real killer in our midst. If he thinks you're snooping around, he might go after you. Take my advice and leave the investigating to the police."

"Of course." *Because you're doing such a great job.*

I headed for my car. *What did I expect?* I started out for the cottage once again. Not only had the lieutenant been less than helpful; he'd warned me not to do any investigating. Well, he couldn't stop me from talking to Jared and his family. I grinned as an idea occurred to me. Trish's dad, Roy, had been Al Brinkley's good friend. He'd been eager to talk to me about Al. It was possible that Al had spoken to Roy about Laura's case and named the person he believed had murdered her.

For some inexplicable reason, the traffic was lighter now. Eight minutes later, I turned onto the Avery property. I stopped at Dylan's house to collect his mail. I unlocked the front door, noting the small pile of business-sized envelopes and advertisements the mail carrier had slid through the mail slot. The house felt chilly; Dylan must have turned the heat way down in his absence.

I gathered up the mail, intending to read off the return addresses to Dylan when I called him later that night. The phone rang as I was leaving. *What to do?* I started for the kitchen and then stopped in my tracks. Dylan hadn't asked me to answer his phone. But then, he probably never expected it to ring during the few minutes I was at his house collecting his mail. What could be the harm?

"Avery residence."

"Where's Dylan?" a gruff male voice asked.

"Not here."

"Tell him he'd better . . . Forget it." He disconnected.

Shaken by the caller's manner, I hurried through the hall and locked the door behind me on my way out.

I stepped inside the cottage, glad to be home. I switched on the hall and living room lights and started dinner. The aroma of roasting chicken filled the kitchen. I sipped Chardonnay as I cut up lettuce, tomatoes, and a cucumber for a salad and then sautéed mushrooms and zucchini, which I topped with grated parmesan.

My first dinner prepared in my cottage was surprisingly delicious. Things were going well. I loved my new home and my job. I was making friends in Clover Ridge, and I had family. Oddly enough, moving had brought me closer to Uncle Bosco and Aunt Harriet. I even looked forward to seeing my cousin Randy at my party. Julia had e-mailed to say they'd be happy to come. For the first time, I felt grounded and like I was where I belonged.

Of course, I wasn't getting anywhere regarding the murders. Lieutenant Mathers was right. It was police business to investigate and track down the murderers. They had the know-how, the work force, the technical wizardry. Only, they hadn't managed to find out who killed Laura Foster fifteen years ago. I sensed they weren't making headway finding Al's killer either.

It had to be the same person. Which meant the killer had come to the meeting intending to kill Al. How he or she had managed to put the poisoned cookie on Al's plate without being seen was beyond me.

I enjoyed my dinner and then cleared the table and loaded the dishwasher. I made a cup of coffee using the Keurig machine Dylan had thoughtfully provided. Dylan. I marveled at the way things had turned out. Not at all as I'd expected when the curt male voice had answered my call.

I went into the small bedroom I was using as my office and called Roy Peters. He sounded happy to hear from me.

"Roy, I was wondering if you'd still like to get together so you can tell me more about Al Buckley."

"It would be my pleasure. When were you thinking?"

"I start work late tomorrow. We could meet for breakfast or an early lunch at the Cozy Corner Café."

"Much as I'd love to, I have two doctors' appointments tomorrow. Wednesday I bowl. How's Thursday?"

"Thursday I don't have to be at work until ten thirty. I could meet you for breakfast."

"Is eight too early for you?"

"A bit," I admitted. "How's eight thirty?"

We agreed to meet at the café Thursday morning. Next, I called Dylan's cell phone. It rang a few times. I was about to disconnect when he answered.

"Hi, Carrie. How are things going?"

"Fine. I picked up your mail. I'll send it to you tomorrow morning. Shall I toss the junk?"

"Yes, please. Here's the address." He rattled off a street in Baltimore and then asked me to read it back to him. After I did, he said, "Just a second." He muffled the phone, spoke to someone, and returned a minute later. "Sorry about that. Anything exciting happening in Clover Ridge?"

For some reason I didn't understand, I found myself telling him about my visit to the police station. I ended by saying that I didn't think the police were getting anywhere regarding the two homicides.

He laughed sarcastically. "Why am I not surprised? I hope you're not playing detective and trying to solve both cases."

"Jared and I have spoken to a few people, but no one seems to know anything. His mother's friend Helena said Laura was having an affair, but Helena didn't know who the man was."

"Some cases don't get solved."

"But it looks like Al's murder is linked to hers."

"Very possibly, though we can't be certain. What else is new?"

"My aunt and uncle are throwing me a party here at the cottage for my birthday. I decided to also make it a housewarming party." My heart hammered. "It's the second Saturday night in December. I'd love it if you could come."

"Thanks for the invite, but I can't say if I'll be home then. Hold on—"

I heard voices again and Dylan saying he'd be right there.

"Have to go. Talk to you soon."

"Someone called while I was at your house collecting your mail," I added quickly.

"Who?"

"It was a man. He didn't tell me his name, but he was abrupt. Sounded a bit ominous, actually. He hung up when I said you weren't there."

"I forgot to tell you, never answer the phone, okay? I can retrieve my messages myself."

Stung, I said that I wouldn't do it again.

"Good-bye, Carrie."

I disconnected, annoyed with myself. Now Dylan was mad at me, which bothered me more than I cared to admit.

Chapter Twenty-Three

The housephone rang loudly. Insistently. My eyes remained shut as I fumbled for it on the nightstand. "Hello."

"Sooo sorry," said a female voice in a deep Scottish brogue. "I thought, being a librarian, you'd be up at the crack of dawn."

"Is it dawn?"

"It's gone on eight o'clock. This is Mrs. Corcoran. Or Mrs. C, if you like. I'll be coming to clean the cottage today."

"It's pretty clean. I only moved in Saturday."

"Yes, I know, but Tuesday's cleaning day. Have you stowed your suitcases?"

I glanced across the room. "Not yet."

"I'll put them in storage for you. Any clothes need washing?"

"Well, I have a few things I was going to put in the washing machine."

"I'll see to it. Just leave them in a pile on the bedroom floor."

"Thank you, Mrs. C."

"Mind you, I can only care for your clothes when Dylan's away and the house requires no more than a general going-over. When he's home, it's another story."

"I understand."

"Good, because I don't want to mislead you. Of course, I'll be changing the linens and towels and running them through the washer and dryer. I'll stop back later to fold them and put them away."

"If that's what you do on Tuesdays."

"That's some of what I do, missy. I'll be by soon as I finish here in the house."

"Oh, you're there already?"

"For the past hour. I didn't call earlier because I wanted you to get your beauty sleep."

"Thank you, Mrs. C. I start work at one today, but I'm running errands this morning, so I probably won't be meeting you today."

"Don't you worry your pretty little head. Have a good day."

Suddenly energized, I showered and dressed quickly and then made myself coffee and toast for breakfast. I'd fallen into a mind-blowing situation. Not only was I paying an amazingly low rent, but the cottage came with all sorts of perks. It was like living in a luxurious vacation resort.

I stuffed Dylan's mail into one of the large envelopes he'd left me and drove to the Clover Ridge post office a few blocks from the library to drop it in the mail. That taken care of, I had three hours to myself. I decided to visit Aunt Harriet.

She was happy to see me and greeted me with a hug. "I'm meeting Betty Stiles for lunch at noon, but we have plenty of time for a visit."

"I thought we'd go over the party plans. I know it's a month away, but—"

"The sooner we get organized, the better. I've collected three catering menus. Choose the one you like. I'd like numbers as soon as you have them."

I pulled out my cell phone. "Twenty yes's so far, six no's, and fifteen I haven't heard from."

"I think you should contact the fifteen the beginning of next week."

I studied the menus she handed me. One was Italian food, one was Chinese, and the third was eclectic food with interesting appetizers and finger foods from various international cuisines.

"I like this one," I said.

Aunt Harriet laughed. "I told your uncle Bosco that would be the one you'd choose. They're all finger foods, which is perfect for a party."

We talked about drinks. Aunt Harriet said that she also planned to make cookies and mini cream puffs for the occasion. The cake would be a surprise.

"I'll buy the paper goods. Jared offered to take care of the decorations."

"That was kind of him."

"He's nice. We've become good friends."

Her eyebrows shot up. "Just friends?"

I nodded. "I think that's all we'll ever be. We're the same age, but at times, Jared seems so much younger."

"Poor boy. His mother's tragic death must have left terrible scars."

We chatted a few more minutes, and then Aunt Harriet glanced at the clock. "I'm sorry to have to chase you out, but

I must shower and dress. I offered to drive today, and Betty hates to be kept waiting."

I hugged her good-bye and drove to the nearby mall to browse and eat a light lunch before starting work at one. All that talk about food drew me to the gourmet food store. I studied the goodies on both sides of the aisles, wishing I could afford to treat myself to a jar of caviar and some of the expensive cheese I loved. Instead, I bought a box of imported crackers and a can of oysters for Thursday night's dinner with Angela. A sales clerk offered me a sample of dark chocolate filled with pistachios. Yummy! Though it was outrageously expensive, I bought a pound of it for the party.

I window-shopped my way to the health-food bar at the far end of the mall. As I stood in line to order my salad, I scanned the seating area in search of an empty table. I gasped with surprise to see Bryce Foster sitting at a table against the wall. He was speaking animatedly to the woman facing him. I moved a few feet to get a better view of her. The woman was Helena Koppel!

"Miss? What are you having?"

"Sorry. A chickpea salad with chicken and a cup of coffee."

"Your bread? Roll? Rye? Whole wheat?"

"Roll." I paid and went to stand in the waiting area.

From my new vantage point, I was close enough to catch snatches of Bryce and Helena's conversation. They were too wrapped up in each other to notice me.

"I think I'll take those bedroom lamps after all," Helena was saying.

"Good choice," Bryce answered. "They go well with the new bedroom set."

Helena sighed. “I appreciate your help. I didn’t realize what an undertaking choosing all new furniture was going to be. That and the move are sapping my strength.”

“No need to feel stressed. I’m here to help.”

Helena actually fluttered her eyes. “I appreciate it, though I feel bad, taking you away from the store.”

Bryce reached across the table to pat her hand. “I have to eat, don’t I? And so do you.”

“I suppose so. But you’ve been so kind.” She took his hand in hers.

I nearly gagged as they gazed into each other’s eyes.

“Number twenty-seven.”

Startled, I grabbed my tray and carried it to an empty table on the other side of the room and called Jared.

“Hi. I’m at Healthy Foods in the mall, and guess what! Your father and Helena are here having lunch.”

“Dad mentioned she was coming to the store to pick out furniture for her condo. The sale’s moving along quickly. Helena plans to move in right after Thanksgiving.”

I hesitated. Clearly Jared had no idea that his father and Helena were starting up a romantic relationship. “I thought they looked kind of friendly.”

Jared laughed. “I doubt it. Dad’s just being kind to an old friend. He hasn’t dated anyone in years.”

“If you say so. I was at Aunt Harriet’s this morning. We decided on the menu for my party. And I bought some goodies.”

“Very efficient of you. I’ll pick up the decorations in the next few weeks.”

“Thanks for taking care of that.” I paused. “I went to see Lieutenant Mathers yesterday, but he wouldn’t let me see anything in your mother’s file.”

"I'm not surprised. The case is linked to Al's."

"I'm talking to a friend of Al's on Thursday. Roy Peters is Trish Templeton's father. Trish is my assistant at the library."

"That's a stroke of luck. Maybe Al told him something about my mother's case."

"I hope so. We could use a good lead."

We said good-bye, and I concentrated on my salad. I almost missed seeing Bryce and Helena leave the restaurant, walking single file through the lunch crowd. Bryce had his hand on her shoulder.

As I drove to the library, I wondered why seeing Bryce and Helena together was so upsetting. They were both widowed and free to date whomever they liked. It wasn't uncommon for old friends to date and marry now that they were both single.

Was it because they were older? I shook my head vehemently. I enjoyed seeing older couples in love—probably because my own parents were always squabbling. I smiled as Uncle Bosco and Aunt Harriet came to mind. They were in their seventies and still adored one another. I could only hope to have a loving relationship like theirs when I reached their age.

Maybe Jared's dislike of Helena had rubbed off on me. He insisted that she wasn't to be trusted. That she exaggerated and distorted the reality of many situations. I remembered her standing up the night Al was murdered and saying that Laura had been unhappy in her marriage and had wanted a divorce. It had turned out to be true enough, but I thought it was cruel of her to announce it before Laura's family, friends, and neighbors. Still, it didn't seem to bother Bryce, so why should it bother me?

Trish was hard at work on our next newsletter when I entered my office. She gave me a rundown of the people who'd called, what they wanted, and who I needed to call back.

"I'll get to it as soon as I start the one thirty movie. And I want to look in on the first senior chair yoga class. Betsy's new to the library, but I hear from the grapevine she's an excellent instructor. I'm hoping she can continue to give us this time slot—at least through June."

Trish cocked her head. "Sally stopped by. She was wondering if you were busy this afternoon. I told her I thought you weren't too jammed up. She wants you to call her when you get in."

"Will do."

"And last but not least, my dad called to remind you of your breakfast date tomorrow morning."

I laughed. "I didn't forget."

"Why on earth are you two having breakfast together? He wouldn't say."

I was about to make a joke of it and pretend we were going on a date when I realized Trish was really concerned. "I want to learn more about Al Buckley. I feel terrible he was murdered on my watch."

"I don't think you should meet my dad to talk about Al."

"Why not?" I asked.

"Al claimed he knew who murdered Laura, and then he became the killer's next victim."

"We don't know that for sure," I said.

"My father likes being with people but doesn't get the chance to socialize much. When he's with people, sometimes he talks about things he shouldn't."

"You're afraid he'll tell me something Al told him about the case. And what if he does? Don't you want to see the murderer locked up?"

"I don't want anything to happen to my father."

I heard the desperation in her voice. "Nothing will, Trish. I think you're worrying about something that will never happen."

"Can't you tell him you can't meet him tomorrow?"

"I'm sorry, Trish. I can't."

"You mean you *won't*!" She turned back to her computer.

Not sure what else I could say, I called Sally's extension.

"Do you have time to run over to the restaurant supply store this afternoon?" she asked. "I'm free at three and thought we might drive over if it works for you."

"I have a few things to take care of, but three gives me plenty of time to work on my to-do list."

"Great. Meet me at the back entrance."

"I'll be there."

Thank goodness Sally's hostility toward me had worn off, but I felt awful that Trish, whom I liked so much, was mad at me. Was I being selfish, meeting her dad to pump him for information about Al? I didn't think so, especially since he was eager to talk about Al. I supposed it was his way of working out his grief. Besides, no one would dare harm Roy in the Cozy Corner Café, and he might prove to be the only lead in the case.

I started the afternoon movie—a foreign film I'd been meaning to see—and then stood in the doorway of the yoga class, observing the much-praised Betsy. In the dimly lit room, she was demonstrating the triangle pose as Indian music softly played. We waved to one another, and then I returned to my office to make some necessary phone calls. Trish nodded when I entered, but we didn't speak until I left an hour and a half later. I told myself I'd smooth things over tomorrow—after I met with her father.

Chapter Twenty-Four

Sally was in high spirits as we drove to the nearby town where the restaurant supply outlet was located. "I've never come home empty-handed. I've bought a wonderful set of kitchen knives for half what it would have cost me in a regular store."

"My aunt Harriet shops there regularly. Most of her baking pans and cooking utensils come from the outlet." I laughed.

"What's so funny?"

"I'll probably buy a few serving dishes for the party. The idea of my having a domestic side is hard to believe."

"Why? Most people have a domestic side. I got married when I was twenty-two. And soon I was working and preparing dinner every weeknight for the first time in my life. I learned how to cook real fast."

"Who taught you? Your mother?"

"No. Bob."

"Really?"

"He shared an apartment with friends in graduate school and proved to be the best cook of them all, so he ended up making most of the meals."

I pulled out my list of possible purchases and read the items aloud. "The chefs plan to bring their own sauté pans, utensils, and knives."

Sally smiled. "Still, we should have utensils and pots and pans on hand if we're going to make this a regular part of our curriculum."

"Great idea!" I appreciated her enthusiasm.

She finally turned off the road and into a parking spot at the side of a huge warehouse. "We've arrived."

I yanked open the gray metal door and gasped. Under fluorescent lights, the rows of kitchen supplies seemed to stretch on forever.

"Now, don't go crazy," Sally warned. "Even though you don't cook much, you're going to want every gadget you see."

We appropriated a shopping cart and moved slowly up and down the aisles, checking out items on both sides. What an array of appliances and utensils! We stopped at a display of two-burner electric hot plates and debated which of three possible units to buy. I knew nothing about hot plates, but I knew we needed one that was safe, sturdy, and capable of producing high temperatures.

A sales clerk approached to ask if we'd like some assistance. We explained why we needed a hot plate and asked which he recommended. While he was touting the virtues of each, a hot plate with four burners caught my attention.

"Excuse me," I interrupted his spiel. "Sally, don't you think this might be best? There might be an occasion when a chef needs a burner to keep something warm."

We debated the pros and cons of two versus four burners and then decided on the four-burner option. Jonas, our salesman, wrote up our purchase and then led us to the demo table section. I was shocked at how expensive they were. Jonas told us which he considered the best buy for our needs, and we followed his advice. He showed us where to go when we were ready to pay for our purchases.

"You can arrange for delivery there too."

"One of our custodians will pick them up tomorrow," Sally told him. "Right now, we want to wander around and select a few small utensils."

Jonas took the hint and left us. We chose a few frying pans and pots and a set of good knives. I bought plastic tumblers of various sizes and a set of stacking tables for the party. Sally bought a serving platter and two trays. It was six by the time we climbed back into her car.

"That was fun." I fastened my seat belt.

Sally turned on the motor. "Are you hungry?"

"I am, come to think of it."

"Let's stop for a quick dinner. I know just the place." She drove onto the road leading back to Clover Ridge.

"Shouldn't we be getting back to the library?"

"You were out on library business," Sally said firmly. "You're entitled to a dinner break."

"I'll call Susan. Let her know what needs attending."

When I finished my call, Sally said, "Susan's doing so much better lately."

I smiled. "She enjoyed working on the Halloween party. It made me realize she's creative, so I try to give her jobs that require decorating and artwork."

We stopped at a red light. Sally turned to me. "You're an even bigger surprise, Miss Singleton."

"I hope you mean that in a good way."

"I wasn't in favor of your taking P and E. You lacked experience. It irked me that your uncle, a library board member, was so insistent that I give you the position."

"Sorry about that. Uncle Bosco must have sensed I was about to leave Clover Ridge. The job was the only way to keep me here."

Sally patted my shoulder. "Well, it worked out in the end. You're a positive asset to the library. Patrons call me every day to say how much they like you."

"Really? I love my job. I love the library. Everyone's so nice and friendly." I paused. "Mostly everyone."

Sally frowned. "You're referring to Dorothy Hawkins."

"She's stopped her shenanigans."

"That's good, because I warned her I'd have to take action if she didn't stop her vendetta against you."

"She seemed to think the position should have been hers."

"It never would have. Dorothy doesn't have the necessary qualifications. Nor does she have the personality for the job. If you hadn't taken it, I would have had to undertake a nationwide search for applicants."

I knew that wasn't the entire story. "I got the impression she thought you'd give it to her because you're such good friends," I said.

Sally pursed her lips, and for a moment, I thought I'd gone too far. "I shouldn't have listened to her," Sally admitted, "but she led me to believe you weren't the right person for the job."

I laughed. "What did she say? I'm on drugs? A serious alcoholic? A kleptomaniac?"

I couldn't see Sally's expression in the dark, but I sensed she was embarrassed. "She said you were once arrested for theft. When I pressed her for the date and further information, she said the charges had been dropped."

"In college, six of us were brought to the local jail one night for being rowdy. We were never charged."

Sally went on as if she hadn't heard me. "After you started working, she claimed you were slacking off. Spending half your time on your cell phone."

"Is that why you gave me all those forms to fill out?"

"They do need to be filled out, but I'm afraid I was being difficult. How you managed to master them impressed me to no end."

"I had help," I admitted. "Why do people put up with her? Why do you?"

"She's not a person to cross. Besides . . ."

I waited, more curious than ever.

"Dorothy finds out things about people—private matters she holds over them," Sally said. "Only this time, she went too far."

What does she have over you?

I considered telling Sally about my experiences with Dorothy but decided there was no point. Dorothy was poison, and I was glad that I was no longer in her sights. She'd gone so far as to lie about me and, I suspected, threatened to expose a secret Sally didn't want known. Nice person she was!

Dorothy finds out things about people. Had she discovered Laura's secret?

After a quick bite to eat, we arrived back at the library at seven thirty.

"This was a fun day. It hardly felt like work," I told Sally while I gathered up my packages.

Sally laughed. "I enjoyed it too. I'm heading home now. See you in the morning."

I said good-bye and closed the car door. I'd stowed my purchases in the trunk of my car and was heading for the library entrance when Sally pulled alongside of me. "Let me know if Dorothy starts to bother you again."

"Will do. Good night, Sally."

In my office, I looked over the notes Trish and Susan had left me. Susan came in, and I told her what we'd bought at the warehouse.

"Now that we have four chefs scheduled for future programs, I was thinking we might put an article in the newsletter about our upcoming cooking demos," she said.

"Great idea. Want to write it?"

"Sure." She gave me a broad smile. "Like me to do anything before I take over at the hospitality desk?"

"I think I have everything under control."

I was reading my e-mails when I heard my cell phone jingle.

"Hi, Carrie. It's Gillian. Ryan's girlfriend."

"Hi, Gillian. Nice to hear from you, but I'm at work and really can't talk."

She laughed. "Sorry. I forget librarians often work evenings. I'll be quick. Ryan and I were wondering if you and Jared would like to have dinner with us Saturday night."

I'd meant it when I told Gillian I'd love to double date with her—if only Ryan weren't her boyfriend. He was an angry, obnoxious bully, and I doubted Jared would want to go out with them. I eased into the best way I knew to reject her invitation.

"I'd love to, Gillian, but Jared and I aren't a couple like you and Ryan. I don't feel it's my place to make social plans for us."

"Could you ask him? It would mean a lot to Ryan."

"Really? How can you say that when Ryan insults Jared every chance he gets?"

"Please, Carrie." Her voice quivered with anxiety. "Ryan wants the four of us to go out."

And he instructed you to do the arranging. "Why?"

"He doesn't mean to give Jared a hard time. He's so angry about their mother's murder, it spills out all over the place. He wants to talk to you both. To find out what you've learned."

"We haven't learned anything new since we last saw you. Thursday, though—" I stopped short, not wanting to bring Roy Peters's name into the mix.

"You're speaking to someone about the case?" Gillian sounded excited.

"It may prove to be nothing."

"Please ask Jared about Saturday night. It's time the two of them started to get along. Besides, I think you and I could be friends."

"I think so too, only—"

"Sorry, I have to go," Gillian said. "Call me after you talk to Jared."

I hung up, wondering what Ryan was really after. A chill shivered down my spine as I remembered his angry words to Al the night he died.

Had Ryan killed Al to stop him from presenting evidence that proved he had murdered his mother?

Did Ryan want to know if Jared and I had found something implicating him, and if we had, did he plan to do away with us too?

Chapter Twenty-Five

Wednesday was a quiet, peaceful day. Two more chefs called to say they were interested in doing demonstrations. And one had a friend who worked in another restaurant who was also interested in giving a presentation.

Max stopped by at noon to tell me he'd picked up the equipment Sally and I had bought on Tuesday. The only fly in my ointment was Trish, who remained cool toward me, speaking only about work. I was glad to attend the department heads' meeting Sally had called for because it took me out of my office. This couldn't continue. I'd talk to Trish after I had breakfast with her father.

I'd called Jared twice to tell him about Gillian's request to have dinner. Each time, his secretary told me that he was with a client. Finally he texted to say that he was flying to Rhode Island to see a client and staying overnight.

Thursday morning, I left the house a few minutes past eight to make sure I was on time for my meeting with Roy Peters. I was pumped with anticipation as I pulled into the library's parking lot. I hoped Al had talked to Roy about the new information he'd discovered regarding Laura Foster's murderer.

Roy waved to me from a table for two in the middle of the café. Every seat was occupied, and the place buzzed with conversation. Who would have guessed so many Clover Ridge residents ate breakfast out?

A middle-aged waitress came over with a pot of steaming coffee. She filled my cup and refilled Roy's. He recommended the Spanish omelet, which he ordered, but I opted for blueberry pancakes, my favorite breakfast on the rare times I found myself in a diner in the morning.

Our food arrived faster than I'd expected. As I poured syrup on my pancakes, I said, "Tell me about Al Buckley, Roy."

"With pleasure." He gulped down the last of his coffee and called over our waitress for a refill. "He was a good friend, and I miss him more each day."

"Did he tell you about the book he was writing?"

"A little." Roy chewed a mouthful of omelet. "I knew it was about the Laura Foster murder. He was furious with himself for not catching her killer back when he was on the force, but he was pretty sure he knew who had killed her."

My heart pounded. "Did he tell you?"

Roy chuckled. "Are you kidding? Al was a private SOB. Always played his cards close to his chest."

I swallowed my disappointment. Al hadn't told Roy what he'd discovered. Which meant he probably hadn't told anyone. But Roy was in a talkative mood, glad to have someone hear his stories. I forced myself to listen, though I was certain it would lead to another dead end.

"I remember the morning his phone call woke me when the sun was rising: 'Get up, Roy! I'm picking you up in half an hour and treating you to the best breakfast you've ever had,' he shouted into the phone.

"'What's this all about?' I asked.

"'I know who did it!'

"'Did what? I'm going back to sleep.'

"'Killed Laura Foster.' He said he'd been up all night reviewing the interviews again and again. He paid careful attention to everyone who'd had opportunity within the time frame of the murder. 'I've come up with the only logical person,' he'd said. 'Trouble is, there's no damn evidence to back me up. No prints on the vase. No witnesses. Nothing. The lucky SOB.'"

So for all his bluster the other day, Lieutenant John Mathers had nothing either. Had he found evidence pointing to Al's murderer? Either the killer was extraordinarily clever or just plain lucky.

"Is that why Al asked the audience all those questions about Laura?"

"I wasn't there," Roy said, "but Trish said people were offering up personal comments."

"They were. Helena Koppel said Laura told her she wanted a divorce."

"That was a lousy thing to announce in front of Laura's family and neighbors," Roy exclaimed. "Who cares about something like that after all these years?"

A few diners paused in their conversations to stare at us.

"Roy, keep your voice down. We don't want everyone to hear our business."

He lowered his voice to a soft rumble. "Right. Sorry. It's just that I get so riled up, thinking how mean people can be."

I couldn't resist sharing what I'd seen at the mall. "Would you believe I saw Helena and Bryce holding hands the other day?"

That brought a deep chuckle from him. "There's no accounting for taste."

"Laura's son Jared and I have been trying to learn who was behind his mother's murder, but her death is shrouded in secrets. Turns out, Laura was having an affair, but nobody knows who the man was."

"Goes to show nobody knows what happens behind closed doors. I'd always thought they were a happy family."

We returned our attention to our breakfasts. I could barely finish my pancakes but made myself eat every last crumb. They were too delicious to leave.

Our waitress cleared the table. Roy asked for more coffee and a piece of apple pie. He must have caught my expression of surprise.

"I know, I know," he apologized. "Trish's mother would be yelling at me if she saw how much I'm eating. But I rarely go off my usual breakfast of oatmeal."

"I can relate." I wished I didn't feel like a stuffed turkey. "Did Al say if the murderer was a man or a woman?"

He pursed his lips. "He wouldn't even say that much."

I stifled a sigh. Roy might have known Al well, but he wasn't privy to anything Al had discovered about Laura's killer. "What kind of proof did he hope to find?"

"Maybe someone who had slipped through the interviews had seen something suspicious that night. Better yet, maybe the murderer would show his hand. Kind of like revealing a tell when you're playing poker. He hoped that getting people to share their less-than-perfect memories of Laura might trigger some reaction in the person he suspected. Then he planned to talk to him or her. He was taping it all, you know."

I felt a sense of excitement. "How? With his iPad? That's missing." I thought a bit. "I wonder if the police know he was recording."

"I told John Mathers that Al was recording it all, but what good did it do, with his iPad gone?"

"Sally always films the major programs. I'll see if she saved it. See if I notice a pattern to Al's questions. To his responses to people's comments."

We chatted a bit longer, and I was left with the following: Al had figured out who'd killed Laura Foster. He had no proof but was hoping to get some through his Q and A with the audience. His questions had provoked the killer, and not in the way he'd planned.

Our waitress dropped the check on our table. "My treat," I said as Roy reached for his wallet. But when he insisted on paying, I realized it meant a lot to him and thanked him profusely for his information and the meal.

Walking to the library, I mulled over the various alibis at the time of Laura's murder. Ryan had been driving around, Bryce had been coming home from the city, Helena was—I couldn't remember where—and Jared was at basketball practice. I didn't remember where George was at the time, but checking would be easy enough. And who and where was this mystery lover we knew nothing about?

I ran into Trish in the room adjoining the ladies' room. She was making coffee for the current events group that met in our boardroom every Thursday from eleven to one. The room wasn't supposed to be used by patrons, but the man who'd been the library director thirty-four years ago had started the group, and it had continued ever since. The members brought their own lunch, and we served them coffee and cookies.

"Your dad and I had a lovely breakfast."

"That's nice. Did you get what you wanted?"

"I learned what Al Buckley was after the night he came to speak here."

"You had no business taking advantage of an old man! Knowing my father, half the room heard his story."

"I doubt it. Everyone else was busy talking as well." I touched her arm. "Please, Trish. Don't be mad. I only wanted to find out what Al might have told your father. It wasn't very much." I sighed. "I'm beginning to think the two murders never will be solved."

Trish shrugged, but she returned to the office with a plate of cookies for us to share. I went through my e-mails and called back three people who'd written to say that they had programs to offer. One wanted to give a talk on small-motored planes. A professor at a nearby college wanted to talk about drones. A third wanted to present a one-woman show about Hedy Lamarr.

The small plane expert didn't come across as a good speaker. I told him we were booked up for now and that I didn't think there would be enough interest in the subject. He started to object, but I interrupted and brought the conversation to a close. I found the other two charming—each in their own way. I told them how much we could afford to pay. They were agreeable, so I sent them each a form to fill out, asking them to choose one of the dates I had free in February or March. That taken care of, I went to see Sally.

She had someone in her office, so I mouthed that I'd be back and went to check on the various groups that were meeting. Everything seemed under control. The Civil War book club members were having an active conversation, as was the current events group. Downstairs, the afternoon movie was silent as a man crept through a house in search of the terrified girl hiding under the steps.

"How's your investigation going?"

Startled, I spun around. I heard a familiar giggle as Evelyn materialized.

"Did you enjoy your visit to the restaurant supply outlet?" she asked.

Interesting, since I'd never mentioned it to her.

"Loved it. I'm excited about the new cooking series. I think the patrons will really enjoy it. For the cost of five dollars, they'll watch the demonstration and sample the three or four dishes the chef has prepared."

"I wish someone had thought to do that when I was around," Evelyn said. "How was spending all that time with Sally?"

I grinned. "We're friends now. She thinks I'm doing a good job."

"You *are* doing a good job."

"How do you know?"

Evelyn gave me an impish wink. "I spend a good deal of time here at the library. More than you'll ever know."

"Have you found out where Laura might have hidden a journal?"

"Sorry, I haven't. I really think she destroyed any pages she might have written for fear someone would find them and read them."

"No one seems to know who the mystery man in her life might have been. In fact, nobody seems to know anything about the two murders at all."

Evelyn patted my arm, chilling me to the bone, which I knew wasn't her intention. "I'm sure something will turn up. As they say in the crime shows, everyone leaves a trace of himself wherever he goes."

"Very profound," I muttered.

We both laughed.

"Has Dorothy been behaving herself?" Evelyn asked.

"Since you're here so often, you must know."

"Just because I'm invisible doesn't mean I see everything."

I shrugged. "We keep out of each other's way."

"I'm glad to hear it." Evelyn sighed. "The poor girl is unhappy. I don't know what's bothering her, but I'm relieved she's no longer taking it out on you."

"I think she and Sally have had a falling out."

Evelyn tsk-tsked. "I was afraid of that. Dorothy never did learn how to keep a friend. She always had to have the upper hand, which isn't good for any relationship."

She faded away as I knocked on Sally's door. This time, she was free. I asked if she'd recorded Al's presentation. She had. The police had taken the recorder and would be returning it very soon. We talked about our purchases for the chefs' presentations, and then I told her about the programs I'd just acquired.

"They sound promising." She stretched her arms overhead. "Drones are a hot subject, and older patrons will love the Hedy Lamarr program. She was a fascinating woman."

I headed back to my office, pleased that everything was going so well. I opened the door and found Trish putting on her parka.

"Are you leaving? I thought your new hours are ten thirty to three thirty."

"I'm going to the hospital." She glared at me, her eyes glistening with tears. "Someone knocked my father down as he was unlocking the door to his apartment. He's concussed and his wrist is broken, and it's all your fault!"

Chapter Twenty-Six

I stumbled through the rest of the day as best I could. When Susan arrived at four, I offered to take her place at the hospitality desk, and she seemed happy enough not to ask why. At first, I told myself that there was no way my meeting with Roy that morning could have had anything to do with his being attacked. I even called the police to ask if he'd been robbed. An officer said robbery didn't appear to be the motive. There was no apparent reason someone would want to assault Mr. Peters.

Which meant I *was* responsible for the attack. A wave of guilt overcame me. Trish had begged me not to meet her dad to talk about Al. She hadn't wanted him involved. Did she know something that Roy hadn't told me?

I tried to remember who had been in the café at breakfast. The tables and booths, even the counter, had been jam-packed with diners. The only face I'd recognized was the police officer who had come to Uncle Bosco's house with Lieutenant Mathers after Al was killed.

I winced, remembering having to tell Roy to lower his voice as he spoke about Al. A few people had turned to stare at him, but I hadn't recognized any of them.

That was assuming I knew the murderer or the identity of Laura's secret lover. He might have overheard Roy talking to me about Al. I shivered. Would he come after me next?

"Hey, girl."

I looked up at Angela's smiling face.

"Are we still on for tonight?" she asked.

"Of course. Mac and cheese, like I promised."

"You sure?" She studied my expression. "If you'd rather postpone—"

"No!" It came out like a shout. "I'm upset because Trish's dad was knocked down outside his apartment. He's in the hospital." *And it's all my fault.*

"I heard. Poor Roy. Such a nice guy. But I'm glad we're still on for dinner."

"Me too. See you at six thirty."

As Angela headed back to the circulation desk, I wished I'd canceled our plans, but by the time I arrived home, I was glad I hadn't. It would be good to have company to take my mind off things. I called the hospital to find out how Roy was doing and was told that his condition was stable. They were keeping him overnight, and he was going home tomorrow.

Somewhat relieved, I opened a bottle of merlot and sipped a glass as I prepared dinner.

What can I do to atone for my foolishness?

I should have met Roy in a place where no one could hear us talk. I should have listened to Trish.

At six thirty-five, Angela greeted me with a hug and another bottle of merlot.

"Come, I'll show you around my new home." I put on a smile I didn't quite feel.

We'd gotten as far as the living room when I burst into tears. Angela sat me down on the sofa and pulled out a tissue from her pocketbook.

I blew my nose. "Roy's in the hospital because of me."

"What do you mean?"

"I met him at the Cozy Corner Café to find out what Al might have told him regarding Laura Foster's murder. They were good friends and poker buddies. Turns out, Roy doesn't know who Al suspected. Still, he tends to speak loudly when he gets excited, and he was excited talking about the two murders. The killer must have overheard us and followed Roy home to warn him not to talk about the case."

Angela handed me the glass of wine I'd left on the coffee table. "That's one hell of a conclusion to come to based on a conversation in a public place."

I gulped down the rest of my wine. "I'm not overreacting. The murderer probably lives in Clover Ridge. Trish told me not to talk to her father about the case, but I ignored her wishes."

"Why did you talk to Roy? Aren't the police investigating?"

I shrugged. "I suppose. And getting nowhere. Jared Foster and I decided to investigate on our own, but we're not doing much better. The only thing we found out is his mother was having an affair at the time she was murdered, but she didn't leave any clues about the man's identity."

"Maybe Laura's lover was a woman and that's why she kept it secret," Angela said. "Lesbian relationships were less acceptable fifteen years ago."

"I never thought of that."

"I admire you and Jared for trying to solve these cases. Roy talked to you because he wants the same thing."

I sniffed. "I guess."

Angela put her hand on my shoulder. "But after what happened today, maybe it's best to stop asking questions about the case—at least for a while."

"You're right. I still feel awful about Roy and Trish. I hope she'll forgive me."

"She will. I know how much she loves working with you. And Roy's a tough old dude. He'll be fine."

I wiped away my tears and felt considerably calmer after having shared my story with Angela. I poured her a glass of wine, and we talked and laughed through our salad, mac and cheese, coffee, and dessert. Later, as we sat in the living room gazing out at the river, she let out an enormous yawn.

"I'd better leave before I fall asleep on your sofa."

I walked her to the door, and we hugged good night.

"Thanks for dinner." Angela stifled another yawn.

"See you in the morning. Thanks for listening to me."

She waved her hand. "Don't be silly. That's what friends are for."

I hummed as I stacked the dirty dishes, glasses, and pots in the dishwasher and turned on my first wash. The machine—an expensive make—purred as it cleaned. I puffed up the living room sofa pillows and then got ready for bed.

Telling Angela that I felt responsible for Roy's attack had helped me move past the familiar black holes of guilt and self-pity. I should have arranged to meet him privately, but I wasn't an ogre with evil intentions. I was terribly sorry he'd been hurt and grateful he would heal.

Angela's my friend, and Sally's fast becoming one, I realized with some amazement. Drifting from one place to another, I'd never really bothered to make friends because I knew I'd be moving on. I was beginning to understand that friendships were an essential part of life. Friends supported you when you were upset. Friends shopped together, ate together, and shared good times and bad.

The phone rang, jarring me from my reverie.

"Hello." I wondered if it might be Aunt Harriet or Jared.

Silence.

"Who's there?" Perhaps it was one of those pesky callers trying to sell me something.

"Is this Carrie Singleton?" The voice was muffled. I couldn't tell if the speaker was a man or a woman.

"Who wants to know?"

"Someone who wants you to mind your own business, or you might end up in the hospital or worse."

"Who is—?"

The line went dead.

My heart thumped against my ribcage. Two people had been murdered. Roy had been assaulted. If the killer were to break into my cottage, no one would hear me scream. I wished I had a dog to warn me if someone was about to smash a window or break down the door.

I called Uncle Bosco. He sounded tired. "Hi, Carrie. Everything all right?"

I glanced at the clock. It was twenty to eleven. Past their bedtime. "Sorry. I didn't realize how late it was."

He chuckled. "Feeling a little nervous on your own? That's natural after staying with us so long. You'll be fine. The windows and doors have strong locks."

"Good night, Uncle Bosco. Talk to you soon."

"Night, honey."

I hung up, wondering if I should call the police. But somehow, I didn't think Lieutenant Mathers paid much attention to prank calls. Besides, the caller had threatened to hurt me if I continued to play detective, and I had no intention of doing that.

I jumped when the phone rang again.

"Yes?"

"Carrie, it's me, Jared. Sorry for getting back to you so late, but it's the first chance I've had all day."

"That's all right, but I can't talk long. I'm about ready to go to sleep."

"Then I won't keep you. I wanted to tell you that you were right."

"About what?"

"My dad and Helena. They've become friendly. Dad's kind of taken her under his wing. Not something he usually does."

"You mean they're dating?"

"Sort of, I guess."

"I'm sorry, Jared."

"Yeah, I know. My stupid brother thinks I'm making a big deal out of nothing. He says it's Dad's life and he should do what he likes."

"Maybe it's a passing phase," I said.

"Let's hope."

"That reminds me. Ryan's girlfriend called. She'd like us to go out with them Saturday night."

"That's why I'm calling. Dad wants all of us to go out for dinner Saturday night."

I paused to work out what he was saying. "All of us? You mean you and me, Gillian and Ryan, your dad and Helena?"

"That's the idea."

I didn't respond. I was being backed into a corner, and I didn't like it.

"Please say you'll go." He expelled a deep sigh. "It's my father's business if he wants to date Helena, but I don't like her. It would help if you were there."

"Jared, I don't feel comfortable having dinner with your family. I mean, we're not a couple like Gillian and Ryan."

"For God's sake, Carrie. It's only dinner!"

I was making a big deal out of it? But then again, it wasn't as if I had something important to do instead. "All right, Jared. I'll be your plus one on Saturday night."

"Thanks, Carrie. I don't want to force my family on you, but my dad rarely asks Ryan and me to get together socially. I'd hate to turn him down."

"Where are we eating?"

Jared laughed. "Due Amici. Dad likes the place too."

"I love their food, so I'm looking forward to that. And I like Gillian a lot."

"And me?"

I squirmed. "Of course you. That goes without saying."

"I wonder how she puts up with Ryan," he mused.

I'd wondered the same thing but thought it impolite to say so. "It should be an interesting evening."

We chatted a few more minutes and then said good night. As I brushed my teeth, I reviewed my relationship with Jared. As far as I was concerned, we were friends with a common goal. Lately, we'd been spending more time together socializing than sleuthing. I wasn't comfortable about it because now I knew for sure that I wasn't into him romantically. I had to let him know before I found myself attending more Foster family dinners.

I climbed into bed, glad that my conversation with Jared had helped me almost forget the distress caused by the anonymous call. I would stop questioning people about the murders—at least in the immediate future.

I drifted off to sleep wondering why I hadn't told Jared about the threatening phone call.

Chapter Twenty-Seven

I woke up Friday morning, struggling to recapture my dream, but all I could remember was a meowing cat. *Good thing it was only a dream*, I told myself as I hit the snooze button. My life was complicated enough.

I must not have heard the snooze alarm, because I'd overslept twenty minutes. Twenty minutes lost, when every second counted! I showered and dressed and then hurried into the kitchen for a quick breakfast. As I sipped the last of my coffee, I heard it again—the plaintive cry of a cat. Only this was no dream. I shrugged into my jacket, grabbed my pocketbook, and went outside to investigate.

I put my pocketbook on the passenger seat of my car, turned on the heater, and then slowly walked around the cottage, both curious and afraid of what I'd find. I loved cats and dogs but hadn't lived in one place long enough to consider keeping a pet. Once this cat caught sight of me, it would probably take off if it was feral. However, it was probably hungry and smart enough to have come to a house in search of food.

I'd come full circle when I saw it—a half-grown gray kitten with a bushy tail. It was sniffing the front tire on the driver's side of my car. I crouched down. "Here, kitty. Psst, psst."

The feline stared up at me with huge green eyes. He—I decided it was a male—was beautiful! "Where did you come from?" I crooned as I stepped closer.

He spun around and raced toward the cottage. I glanced at my watch. I had to leave now or I'd be late to work. A better idea would be to go inside and bring something out that the kitten could eat after I left. Frantically, I made a mental sweep of my supplies. I had some mac and cheese left over, but I didn't think he'd like that. I knew cats really didn't drink milk because it could give them diarrhea. My best bet was to buy some cat food on my way home tonight.

I opened the car door, welcoming the warmth emanating from the heater. A flash of gray flew over my feet and climbed onto the headrest of the passenger seat. I reached for him, but the little devil was too fast. He jumped onto the back seat.

I stepped out and pulled open the back door, hoping the kitten would get out of the car. Instead, he jumped back onto the headrest of the passenger seat.

"You're making me late!" I got behind the wheel and clicked my safety belt into place. I left the door open, hoping he'd take the hint and exit. Instead, he stared at me. "Meow," he complained.

I suddenly remembered the granola bar at the bottom of my pocketbook. I unwrapped it and broke off a tiny piece, which I placed in the palm of my hand. I smiled as the kitten climbed down the seat to sniff it and then take it in his mouth. I broke off another piece and let him eat that too. Then I put the car in gear and set off for work. When I stopped for a red light, I broke the rest of the bar into small pieces and watched him devour them.

"You were very hungry."

He stared at me and then curled up into a ball and went to sleep.

What am I to do with you? I hate to leave you in the car while I work, and I can't bring you into the library. Sally would have a fit.

By the time I pulled into the library parking lot, I'd decided to leave him in the car. I'd tell Sally I had to rush home because I'd left the oven on, drop the kitten off near the cottage, and buy cat supplies on my way home. He had a fur coat and was sure to survive until then.

But Smoky Joe, as I was beginning to think of him, had other plans. I'd no sooner opened my door when he scampered out. He scurried under an SUV parked in the next row. I followed after him when a car with two library aides pulled into the lot. Good thing they were engrossed in their conversation and weren't curious as to why I was peering under an SUV.

They finally saw me and waved. I waved back and watched them enter the library. I felt sick at the thought of leaving Smoky Joe here in the parking lot, where he might get hit by a car. I caught sight of him under the SUV. He saw me and ran under another car. I couldn't do this all day! But I could ask Max and Pete to try to catch him. Both custodians were kindhearted men.

With a heavy heart, I headed for the library door. As I was pulling it open, Smoky Joe made a dash across the lot. I reached down and scooped him into my arms. His body felt relaxed. "You silly boy," I crooned. I grinned when he began to purr.

Thank goodness I made it to my office without meeting anyone. I exhaled a deep sigh of relief as I closed the door behind us. At lunchtime, I'd buy some cat food in town, then drive Smoky Joe back to the cottage. And do my darnedest to see that he didn't escape in the next three hours.

While he climbed over my desk and Trish's, sniffing at everything, I ripped up an old newspaper and put the pieces in a shallow carton. I lifted Smoky Joe and set him down in the box. "That's where you go while you're here," I told him and laughed out loud as he started to pee.

"Such a good boy!"

Smoky Joe must have thought so too. After a bit more exploring, he settled down at my feet and went to sleep. All would have gone well if Angela hadn't stuck her head in to say hello.

"What was that?" she asked as Smoky Joe made a beeline out the door.

"A cat. And now he's loose in the library!"

"I know it's a cat. What's he doing here?"

"I'll explain later," I said over my shoulder as I ran out to see where Smoky Joe had gone.

A patron must have known what I was after because she was laughing. "He went thataway," she said, pointing to the children's room. I thanked her and hurried there, hoping Smoky Joe hadn't wreaked too much havoc. Not every child liked animals. Some were downright afraid of them.

I stopped short and took in the scene before me. Gayle was reading a story to a group of pre-K kids sitting cross-legged in a semicircle around her. At least, she *had* been reading, judging by the book resting on her lap. The half dozen children, including Tacey, were making a fuss over the gray kitten weaving his way among them.

Smoky Joe didn't protest as I lifted him into my arms, but the children complained loudly.

"Sorry to have disturbed you," I said.

Gayle waved a hand. "Cats are always welcome, especially sweet ones like him."

"His name is Smoky Joe." He started to purr as I raised him onto my shoulder.

"Please bring him back again, Cousin Carrie," Tacey said. Which gave me an idea. Smoky Joe wasn't afraid of the children or being in the library, for that matter.

"Maybe I will," I said.

Just then, Marion's office door opened. She and Sally came into the big room. Sally and I stared at one another.

"A cat in the library?" she said.

I took a deep breath. I felt a hand on my shoulder. I turned, glad to see Angela beside me. "Sorry. I should have discussed it with you first. This is Smoky Joe." I was relieved that my voice had remained steady.

"Why is he here?"

"Because Smoky Joe would make a wonderful library cat. He's friendly. Ask the children."

Sally opened her mouth, but I couldn't hear her over the cheering.

"Lots of libraries have cats," I said. "The patrons adore them. Many cats live in the library, but I'll bring Smoky Joe home with me at night."

"He does seem like a lovely creature," Marion said, petting him.

Smoky Joe purred louder.

"Well, we could give it a try," Sally said reluctantly. "You should have checked with me first, Carrie, before bringing him in."

"Sorry," I said.

"I suppose he'll need food and kitty litter. Call Max and tell him what you need. He's going out to buy supplies later this morning."

"Thanks, I will." I spun around, eager to be off.

Angela kept pace beside me as I headed for my office. "That was a stroke of genius! I thought she was going to hand you your head for bringing a cat into the library."

I laughed. "I saw how much the kids loved having Smoky Joe near them." I scratched his head. He looked up and yawned. "And I saw how much he enjoyed them. He's a stray that likes being with people. He'll be the best library cat around."

"He's the *only* library cat around," Angela said. "Are we still on for lunch?"

"I don't see why not. Max will be bringing him food, so he won't go hungry till I take him home tonight."

An hour later, Sally stopped by my office and handed me a camcorder. "A police officer just returned it. Now you can watch the video of Al's presentation—what I managed to get."

"Thanks so much, Sally." With all the excitement over Smoky Joe, I hadn't thought about the murders all morning.

She reached over to scratch Smoky Joe's head. "How is he adjusting?"

We both looked at him stretched out on Trish's desk. "Very well. He ate a small can of the food Max bought."

"Where did you get him?"

My pulse began to race. *Would she tell me not to bring him when I told her?* "He wandered over to the cottage, probably from one of the nearby farms. I'll make sure he gets his shots."

"Do that."

"Would you rather I not bring him in until then?"

Sally shook her head. "I know cats, and this one looks healthy. Just take him to a vet as soon as you can. The patrons are all asking about him." She grinned. "I think you can let him venture out among the stacks this afternoon for a short while."

She left, and I turned on the camcorder. My heart leaped with anticipation as the camera scanned the audience chatting and noshing on cookies and coffee. I looked carefully but didn't spot anyone placing the poisoned cookie on Al's plate. In fact, the table didn't appear until Al stood beside it, munching his snack.

I watched with an ache in my heart as he asked the audience for anecdotes about Laura. I listened to Ryan's outburst and Helena's unexpected disclosure. When Al fell ill, the video ended.

So much for that. I placed the camcorder on my desk to return to Sally.

Trish came in at eleven and made a big fuss over Smoky Joe. I asked how Roy was doing.

"He's fine. In fact, he was feeling pretty important when I drove him home this morning."

"Why?"

"When he told the nurses why he was attacked, they treated him like a hero."

"I'm glad to see you're not angry at me any longer."

Trish shot me a level look. "Dad said I wasn't to blame you for the attack. He's sorry he couldn't be of more help. He's glad you and Jared Foster are trying to find the killer, since he doesn't expect the police to catch him or her anytime soon."

"I'm afraid Jared and I have reached a dead end. We have no clues, no witnesses. Nothing."

Trish nibbled her lower lip. "It's hard to believe someone could kill two people and get away with it."

The rest of the morning, we worked in harmony on various projects. I was grateful that Trish was no longer mad at me, but it bothered me that Jared and I had gotten nowhere in our investigation.

At twelve thirty, after Trish reassured me repeatedly that she was capable of keeping an eye on Smoky Joe while I was gone, I returned the camcorder to Sally and then stopped by the ladies' room before meeting Angela at the back door. We were having lunch at a new Chinese restaurant a few miles south of town. As I drove, I told her about the previous night's anonymous phone call.

"How awful! You must have been terrified."

"I was, but the person won't harm me if I stop investigating. Which is exactly what I'm doing because we've hit a dead end."

The Chinese restaurant was in a strip mall. It was dimly lit, with booths along both long walls. A peaceful setting, especially as only four or five booths were occupied. I ordered chicken and broccoli. Angela ordered duck. As we ate our hot-and-sour soup, she told me a funny story about her boyfriend and his mother.

"You really like Steve's family," I noted.

"I do. I think they're nuts, but every family's nuts in its own way."

"I guess."

I must have sounded down because she asked, "Don't you like Jared's family?"

"I like his uncle George. I hardly know his father, and his brother's an angry cannon about to go off at any minute. I think Jared's a great guy, but I don't feel that special spark. Spending time with his family isn't my priority."

"Is there someone else you'd rather be dating?"

My ears grew warm. "Maybe. But he's not interested in me *that* way."

We stopped at the pet shop in town, where I stocked up on cat food, kitty litter, and a litter box. The sales clerk seemed very knowledgeable about cats, so I asked her to recommend a veterinarian.

Back at the library, I stopped in the ladies' room before returning to work. I was putting on lipstick when I heard the ping of a text message. I grinned as I read: "Mail has arrived. Sorry I snapped at you the other evening. Don't want you to answer my phone because I've a few tough characters working for me. I wouldn't want any of them to upset you. Talk to you later."

Later!

As I exited, I nearly collided with Dorothy. For a moment, we stared at one another.

"Sorry," we said at the same time.

She held a large book in her outstretched hands as if she didn't want it to dirty her blouse. I didn't blame her. The cover appeared old and dusty. *The History of Jewelry*, it read.

"Where did that come from?" I asked without thinking.

Dorothy pointed to the wall behind her. "From the attic. Now I'm all dirty, thanks to you."

I stared at the wall that I passed several times a day. "The attic? What attic?"

Dorothy laughed. "Didn't Sally give you a proper tour of our library? Behind the panel is a staircase to a small attic we use for storage. It used to be part of the underground railway for runaway slaves."

"I didn't realize the building was that old."

"There are lots of things you haven't realized." Dorothy took off at top speed.

Smoky Joe was asleep when I returned to the office. When he woke up, I fed him another small tin of cat food and some kibble. After he used his litter box, I carried him out to the main reading area, where a few patrons were reading magazines and newspapers.

I was afraid he'd disappear into the stacks, but I needn't have worried. He walked up to chair where an elderly man was reading a newspaper. When the man merely glanced at him and returned to the paper, Smoky Joe advanced to a woman reading a knitting magazine. She bent down to pet him.

"That's Smoky Joe, our new library cat."

"Hi, Smoky Joe. Welcome to the Clover Ridge Library."

And so it went. Half an hour later, I carried him back to my office, where he promptly fell asleep on Trish's desk.

Evelyn paid me a visit as I was getting ready to leave at five. Susan was on duty at the hospitality desk, so there was no chance she'd catch me talking to myself, as it would appear to anyone but my little cousin Tacey. But then, anyone else—including Sally—would knock first, and I could always claim I'd just put down the phone. She made a fuss over Smoky Joe, laughing delightedly when I told her how he'd come to be our library cat.

"That was quick thinking. Good thing you and Sally are friends now."

"Don't you look spiffy," I said.

She was wearing a gray silk blouse and a darker gray cardigan over black trousers, with a long string of pearls and matching pearl earrings.

"You like?" She grinned at me.

"I like." Someday I'd have to ask Evelyn where she kept her wardrobe of clothes and jewelry—along with hundreds of other questions—but there never seemed to be time.

"Are you looking forward to the weekend?"

I frowned. "I'm going out with Jared and his family tomorrow night."

"I thought you liked the boy."

"Of course I do. Jared's a good person. But he's a boy, while . . ."

"Someone else is a man," she finished for me.

To change the subject, I said, "I bumped into your niece this afternoon. Literally, I mean. She was bringing a book down from the attic—I imagine for a patron."

"Dorothy's very good at finding resources for our patrons. She's an excellent reference librarian. It's her people skills that need work."

"I never knew this building had an attic."

Evelyn laughed. "Our hidden room. The last several years, it's been used for storage. Sally mentioned wanting to assign some of us to clear it out but somehow never got around to it."

I felt a surge of excitement. "What was it used for before it became a storage place?"

"Nothing, really. There were some tables and chairs if a staff worker wanted a few minutes of privacy. Hardly anyone chose to go up there."

"What if someone wanted to write in private?"

"You mean, what if someone wrote in private and kept what she wrote up in the attic?"

* * *

I thought about my conversation with Evelyn as I drove home. The idea that Laura might have hidden her journal in the library's attic was a very distant possibility. For one thing, I had no idea if Laura ever went up to the attic. For another, this all happened fifteen years ago. Even if she'd hidden her journal, I had no idea where to look. Judging by the book Dorothy was holding, the place was dusty and jam-packed with old books and God knew what else.

It would take weeks for me to explore every nook and cranny of the attic. When, in my busy workday schedule, was I supposed to do this?

During lunch hours. And I'd come in early the days I worked evenings.

Aunt Harriet called on my cell phone. She laughed when I told her about Smoky Joe, who was purring away beside me. "I'm calling to remind you that Thanksgiving's less than two weeks away, and I expect you to come to dinner."

"Of course. Where else would I go?" I realized how tactless that sounded and began to apologize.

She let loose a rousing chuckle. "Don't be silly, Carrie. Of course I expect you to be here. I invited some of your cousins, but they're all going to their various in-laws for the holiday. Is there anyone you'd like to invite?"

"I can't think of anyone. Angela has a large, close-knit family, and I'm sure Jared will want to be with his father and brother." I wasn't at all sure about that, but inviting Jared to my aunt and uncle's would send him the wrong message.

"I've invited John and Sylvia Mathers, since their three children live out of state."

"*Lieutenant* Mathers?"

"Of course. The Mathers are good friends of ours."

"I had no idea."

Aunt Harriet sighed. "I should have extended my invitations earlier. Thanksgiving is my favorite holiday. I love preparing the turkey, sweet potato casserole, and cranberry sauce. And baking at least three desserts. It's the one time I enjoy being surrounded by people."

"I'll let you know if I think of anyone to invite."

"What about Dylan?"

"Dylan?" My heart began to thump. "I'll invite him, though he might not be home then."

"That would be nice, dear. He no longer has any family here in Clover Ridge."

"I thought you didn't like Dylan," I said.

"Bah, that was your uncle remembering the bad time when the farm was failing. Dylan's father took advantage of a good opportunity, as anyone would have. Besides, I always liked that boy."

"He was Jordan's friend."

"Exactly."

The house phone rang as I was unlocking the front door. "Hello."

"You sound out of breath," Dylan said.

"I just arrived home."

"I thought I'd catch you in after a busy day at work."

"It was busy enough. How was your day? Make any progress on your case?"

"Some. I'm hoping to tie things up soon."

"Well, that's an enigmatic response," I said, amazed that I was having a teasing conversation with Dylan.

"I work in an enigmatic profession."

We both laughed.

"Did you know the library has an attic?" I asked.

"I don't think so. Why, is that important?"

"I'm not sure, but I intend to find out." My heart started to race as I remembered Aunt Harriet's invitation. "Will you be home for Thanksgiving?"

"There's a good chance. Why? Need a break from sending me my mail?"

"Aunt Harriet asked me to invite you to dinner."

"Did she? I remember your aunt is one awesome cook."

"That would be great—if you can make it," I stumbled, suddenly tongue-tied. "She'll be glad." *And so will I.*

"I'll call to let you know my traveling plans soon as I find out. Tell Aunt Harriet thank you. Gotta go."

I set down the phone, feeling a grin spread across my face. Dylan had called as he'd said he would. Maybe he was interested in me after all.

Chapter Twenty-Eight

As I'd expected, the attic was dirty and crammed with boxes of books piled helter-skelter on the floor, on tables, and on top of one another. Tall bookcases lined the walls but were impossible to reach unless I started moving cartons. Where to put them? I barely had room to stand. I opened a box and sneezed from the debris flying into my nostrils. How Dorothy had found the book she'd been looking for was beyond me.

Minutes later, I climbed down the stairs, relieved to be breathing unpolluted air. I went about my usual day—introducing the Saturday afternoon movie, catching up on e-mails and phone calls until I left at five. I wasn't happy about my failed venture in the attic.

At home, I fed Smoky Joe and then turned the radio to a light rock station and poured myself a glass of Chardonnay. I wasn't looking forward to the evening. I was going to have to tell Jared we'd reached a dead end as far as finding clues or evidence was concerned. The killer was either very clever, very lucky, or both. As for us . . .

Jared was a caring person and good company, but there was no magical spark between us. I liked Dylan, but it was too soon to know how he felt about me. My pulse quickened. Maybe I'd find out Thanksgiving weekend.

I considered wearing one of my Goth outfits just to raise eyebrows but then decided to wear brown leggings, a beige blouse with a pattern of horses, a long beige cardigan and, of course, my new boots. I showered, dressed, and started on my makeup. I began to perk up as I lined my eyes with black eyeliner.

Jared came for me at a quarter to seven. As we drove to the restaurant, I told him of my unsuccessful venture into the attic in hopes that his mother might have left her journal there.

"It's not very likely, is it?" he said.

"I suppose it's wishful thinking, which is why nobody needs to know I'm going up there again. That way, no one will be disappointed."

"Unless you find it!"

As we approached the restaurant, I asked Jared if he was upset that his father was dating Helena.

"Not as much as I'd expected. Dad and I've spoken more in the past few days than in the previous six months. He sounds so happy. And Helena seems to like the idea of us all going out for dinner. Tonight was her idea."

"Does she have children of her own?"

"No. Either she or Lloyd couldn't have children."

"What happened to Lloyd?"

"He died a year or two after Mom. Heart attack, I believe."

The maître d' led us to Bryce and Helena's table.

Bryce surprised me by leaping to his feet and hugging first Jared and then me, a broad grin on his face. "It's so nice to see you, Carrie, under much more pleasant circumstances."

"Nice to see you too . . ."

"Call me Bryce."

I smiled. "Okay, I will."

"Jared, good to see you," Helena said when he kissed her cheek. "Carrie, I'm glad you're joining us tonight." She tucked away the brochures scattered about the table. "Bryce was helping me select new doors for my condo. There's so much more to do than I expected."

I sat next to Bryce, and Jared took the seat opposite me. Two uncorked bottles of wine and six glasses were already on the table.

"What's your pleasure, Carrie?" Bryce asked. "Merlot or pinot grigio?"

"Pinot grigio, please."

"Jared?" Bryce poured a generous amount into my glass.

"I'll have a Beck's dark."

"Of course. Of course. Whatever you want." Bryce looked around until he caught our waiter's attention.

Helena downed the last of her wine and reached for the bottle of white. "I sure love this pinot." She filled her glass.

Jared stared from Helena to his father. "How long have you two been chugging away?"

"Not long at all," Bryce said. "What would you say, Helena? Ten minutes?"

Helena laughed. "Certainly no more than twenty." She gulped down a mouthful of wine.

Oh, no. It's going to be one of those evenings.

The waiter arrived at the same time as Gillian and Ryan. He waited while they greeted everyone and took their seats next to Jared, across from Bryce and Helena.

Bryce pointed to Jared. "A Beck's dark for my son. Gillian, Ryan, would you like wine or something else to drink?"

Gillian chose the merlot, and Ryan ordered a double scotch straight up.

"Now that that's all settled," Bryce said, "we can relax and enjoy ourselves."

He finished his merlot and poured himself another glass. Jared and I exchanged glances. I felt as though we were the adults and Helena and Bryce were teenagers intent on getting drunk.

"Does he often get like this?" I murmured so only Jared could hear.

"Never." He pressed his lips together.

"So"—Ryan turned to each of us—"what has everyone been up to this past week?" He stared pointedly at me. "Carrie?"

I shrugged. "Working hard at the library."

"No more murders, I hope."

I didn't bother answering.

He turned to Jared. "Little brother, did you have a busy week too?"

"Yep. I flew to Providence to see a client."

"All on your lonesome, eh? Dad, what have you been up to?"

Bryce had a cat-that-ate-the-canary look. "I've been working hard at the store."

Ryan gave his father a devilish grin. "So I see. And Helena, what have you been up to lately?"

"I'm working feverishly on my new condo. Your father's been kind enough to help me pick out furniture."

"How nice for you."

"And you, Ryan, what have you been doing?" Jared asked.

Ryan shot him an amused look. "How kind of you to show interest. I've been busy lining up a new job."

"Really?" their father said. "That's good news. Want to tell us about it?"

"Not till it's all settled. I don't want to spook my chances. Right, babe?" He pulled Gillian close and kissed her cheek. "Gillian has her own good news. Tell them."

"I'm getting a promotion at the dealership where I work—to assistant manager."

"Bigger pay and perhaps a bigger apartment." Ryan winked.

Oh, oh. What are you thinking, Gillian?

Jared and I looked at one another. "She has no idea what she's in for," he mouthed as the waiter approached with six large menus.

I decided to order shrimp oreganata and put my menu aside when Helena said, "Why don't we order family style—a large antipasto for the table and four main courses with veggies and pasta?"

"Great idea, Helena," Ryan said. "I want a sausage dish. Gillian?"

"I'd love seafood marinara." She grinned.

"Seafood marinara it is! Dad, what would you like?"

"Meatballs in tomato sauce. Their meatballs are the best!"

"Chicken in white wine sauce would be lovely," Helena said.

"There are your four dishes," Ryan said. "A few sides and we're done."

"You didn't bother asking Carrie and me what we want to eat," Jared said stiffly.

"I could eat some seafood and chicken," I said.

"That's not the point! As usual, Ryan arrives late and takes over."

"Get over it, little brother. You can't have everything your way."

"I don't want everything—"

"Jared and Carrie, please order whatever you like," Bryce said. "Forget the meatballs."

"I didn't mean to start a family feud," Helena said. "I thought it would be easier and less waste if we ordered family style."

"Carrie, what would you like?" Jared asked.

"Shrimp oreganata."

"I'll have veal scaloppini," Jared said.

"We'll order all five," Bryce said. "No, six. I'll have the meatballs, after all."

Helena smiled. "It's all settled then. Ah, here comes our waiter."

Bryce ordered for us, and Helena asked for another bottle of pinot grigio.

"Are you sure?" Bryce whispered. "You've had a lot to drink tonight. You'll get a headache if you have any more."

"Are you kidding?" Helena said. "Believe me, I can drink a few glasses of wine without getting sick."

"Another bottle of pinot grigio." Bryce looked unhappy.

Gillian glanced my way, and I rolled my eyes. I should have trusted my instincts and avoided this dinner.

Our waiter brought us a plate of piping hot garlic twists and another with pieces of bruschetta piled high. He opened the new bottle of wine with a flourish. Ryan ordered another double scotch, and Jared ordered another beer. Bryce, Gillian, Helena, and I refilled our wineglasses and conversation resumed. Minutes later, our waiter placed a platter of antipasto and six salad plates on the table.

"I'll be mother and dole out the salad," Helena said.

We all stared at her, even Bryce.

"Sorry, that was tasteless of me."

We passed the dishes of salad around. When I handed Jared his, he whispered, "Sorry I asked you to come along."

"Dinner's almost over," I whispered back.

By the time our main courses arrived, I wasn't very hungry. I ate a small part of my shrimp dish and told the waiter I'd like to take the rest home.

"Would you like to taste the veal?" Jared asked.

"A small piece, please."

Jared cut it for me and held out his fork.

"Delicious and tender. I'll have to order it next time."

"You plan to come again soon?" Ryan asked.

I couldn't tell if he was teasing or jeering. He went back to giving his undivided attention to Gillian and gobbling down the large shrimp she'd offered.

Helena and Bryce fed each other forkfuls of their food. Eventually, everyone had eaten all they could.

A young man cleared the table and gathered up the leftovers to be boxed. *I can leave soon*, I thought hopefully. I was wrong. Bryce insisted that we order cappuccinos and three desserts for the table.

"Tell me, Jared, how's your little investigation going?" Ryan asked.

Bryce turned to Ryan. "What investigation are you talking about?"

"Don't you know? Jared and Carrie are conducting an investigation to find out who killed Mom and that detective who couldn't solve her murder."

"Is that true, Jared?"

Jared's face turned red, and my ears burned.

"We tried to find out what we could—"

"But had no success," I quickly added.

"Why, Jared, when I told you years ago not to get involved in your mother's case? The police—"

"That's the trouble," Jared said. "The police are hopeless. They have no idea who killed Mom or Al."

"You're forgetting the detective in charge of Mom's case was Al Buckley, the guy you thought so highly of," Ryan said.

"Yes, but Al finally figured out who the murderer was," Jared said.

Ryan snickered. "I don't believe that for one minute. If he knew so much, why all the questions that night? He was looking for information, not offering any."

"That's because he'd figured out who murdered Mom but had no evidence to back it up. He was hoping to get some that evening."

"What? Suddenly the killer was going to have an attack of guilt and stand up and shout, 'It was me! Call the police.'"

"Ryan, that's enough," Bryce said.

"Sorry, Dad."

Gillian stroked Ryan's arm. He took her hand and clasped it tight. Maybe he seriously had feelings for her. Not that it mattered. Ryan was full of anger and hostility. He lacked the loving traits I would want in a boyfriend.

"Do you think Detective Buckley confided his findings to anyone?" Helena asked.

"I doubt it. His closest friend had no idea whom Al suspected." I didn't feel like mentioning Roy had been assaulted and ended up in the hospital.

"He probably kept everything on his iPad," Jared said. "The killer took it the night Al was poisoned."

"Proof that the two murders are linked," Gillian said.

We all stared at her. It was her first contribution to the conversation.

Jared cleared his throat. "There's one possible lead, but it's only hypothetical."

I glared at him, but he seemed to be enjoying the spotlight too much to notice. "Carrie learned Mom was seen writing in the library the last weeks of her life. We're thinking she might have kept a journal. Carrie's investigating. There's a chance it's still there."

"A hidden journal!" Gillian said. "Awesome!"

I pressed my lips together, hating how this was playing out. So far, the existence of a journal was only guesswork and not something I wanted to discuss with Laura's family.

Ryan's eyes were scrutinizing me. "What aren't you telling us, Carrie?"

"Nothing! I only know your mom occasionally wrote during her free time at the library. No one said anything about a journal."

"If she kept a journal, it might have information about someone she was afraid of," Gillian said.

"Or the mysterious Mr. X." Ryan glanced at his father. "Sorry, Dad."

Bryce sighed. "I'll never stop wondering who killed your mother and why." He turned to me, his voice cracking with emotion. "Do you think Laura wrote down her thoughts and feelings and left the pages somewhere in the library?"

He sounded so sad, I had no choice but to answer him truthfully.

"It's possible she occasionally wrote in a room that's now used for storage. I checked it out. The place is a total mess. Full of cartons of books piled high. Finding some pages or a notebook would be an impossible task—that is, if she even left them there."

Helena put her hand on Bryce's arm. "Perhaps it's best to let sleeping dogs lie." She smiled as our waiter approached. "Ah, here come our cappuccinos and desserts."

Chapter Twenty-Nine

We finally left half an hour later. Gillian and I hugged Bryce good-bye, and we all thanked him for dinner. Bryce and Helena remained at the table, clearly in no rush to leave. She spread open one of the brochures she'd tucked away earlier and pointed to something. Bryce offered his opinion. Gillian and I walked to the exit together while Jared and Ryan followed behind, chatting amiably as if they had always been on good terms.

"Wow! That was one emotional psychodrama," Gillian whispered. "Are they always like this when they get together?"

"I hope not."

We both rolled our eyes and giggled.

"I could tell you didn't want to talk about the possibility that their mother had left a journal, but the idea that she might have is exciting."

"Yes, but there's no point in getting Bryce's hopes up if it doesn't pan out."

In the car, Jared said, "That didn't go too badly." He leaned over to kiss me, but I pulled away.

"What's wrong, Carrie?"

"Are you serious? It was awful! From the moment we arrived, I couldn't wait to leave."

"Really?" He sniffed as he backed out of the parking spot.

"For starters, your brother is obnoxious and mean-spirited and puts you down every chance he gets."

"That's Ryan," he muttered.

"For another, I asked you not to mention that your mother wrote during her free time in the library. It may have been a journal, or for all we know, she was composing a short story."

"What's wrong with their knowing? You can't think any of them murdered my mother."

I had my suspicions but thought it wise not to mention them. "Why get their hopes up when we have nothing real to go on? Your mom wrote in the library fifteen years ago. We have no reason to believe she hid whatever she wrote in some secret cranny. She might have brought the pages home with her. She might have ripped them up. That what she wrote still exists is pure speculation."

"Won't you reconsider going back up to the attic to search for her journal?"

I let out a snort of exasperation. "Sorry, Jared. It would be like looking for a needle in a haystack."

That said, we drove the rest of the way home in silence.

* * *

Though I was exhausted, I was unable to fall asleep that night. I kept rehashing the evening's conversations, trying to figure out exactly what was troubling me. So the Foster family wasn't the happy, close-knit unit they and their Clover Ridge neighbors would have had everyone believe. Bryce had been a workaholic. Laura had felt neglected and unhappy and had looked for love elsewhere. Ryan had serious anger management issues even before his parents' marriage began to fray.

And Jared? I believed he'd been a kindhearted boy who'd been buffeted about by his parents' and brother's dysfunctional behavior. Tonight I'd observed how desperate he was to win his father's and brother's goodwill and approval. Why else had he been so eager to tell them about the possible journal when we'd agreed not to share that with anyone? I'd made my feelings very clear on the subject, but he ignored both my feelings and me.

I finally drifted off and awoke at five thirty, unable to sleep any longer. A strange dream about digging in a cave was fading as I woke, and I knew I wanted to go back to the attic and try once again to find Laura's journal. Only this time, I wouldn't tell Jared.

* * *

Sunday at noon, I carried Smoky Joe into the library, which was suddenly bedecked with Thanksgiving decorations. As soon as I set him down, he sniffed at the pilgrims, turkeys, scarecrows, and dried bunches of colored corn arraying every nook and cranny. Many of our upcoming programs were in celebration of the holiday.

I was glad that neither Trish nor Susan was scheduled to come in that day. I needed to be alone to work out whatever was disturbing my peace of mind. I was disappointed in Jared. I had no idea if we'd be seeing each other again. What's more, I didn't know that I cared.

"You look down in the mouth for a sunny November afternoon."

I looked up from my computer into Evelyn's smiling face.

"What are you so happy about?"

"Nothing in particular. I sensed you weren't in the best of moods, and I've come to cheer you up."

"I could use cheering up," I admitted. "I was at the dinner from hell last night."

"Do tell."

When I finished my account, she tsk-tsked. "Not a fun evening for you. How did Jared and Ryan take to Helena dating their father?"

"Not as badly as I thought they would. When Jared first found out, he carried on about how she was the most awful person, but he didn't seem upset by her being with us last night."

Evelyn's eyebrows shot up. "And Ryan?"

"He was too busy being offensive and putting Jared down to go after Helena."

"He'll get to her yet," Evelyn murmured.

"Was he always so angry and scornful?"

"I'm afraid so. Even as a child, he gave his parents a difficult time. Poor Jared adored his older brother and tried to keep up with him."

"I was annoyed with Jared for telling them Laura might have kept a journal after I'd told him not to mention it. I explained that the storage place where she might have written was now full of cartons of books that no one could possibly go through."

"That attic is a mess."

"I was surprised to see Dorothy bringing a book down from there. That she managed to find anything amazes me."

Evelyn laughed. "Dorothy has many faults, but she's a fantastic organizer. I imagine she made sure that the old reference books were placed in cartons labeled 'Reference.'"

"But searching for Laura's pages is something else. I wouldn't know the first place to look."

Evelyn grinned. "As to that, I have a few ideas."

Having nothing pressing to do at the moment, I headed for the door that led to the attic. Evelyn kept pace beside me. A few patrons stopped me to ask questions about upcoming programs. I answered them as patiently as I could. I sensed Evelyn knew more than she was saying, and I was eager to find out what it could be.

Once upstairs, I turned on the light and closed the door, hoping no one would come up and ask what I was doing there. Not that anyone would. Sally wasn't working today either.

I looked around the room, glad for Evelyn's company. "Here we are. Where shall we start?"

Evelyn leaned against one of the three desks, their surfaces all laden with cartons of books. "I believe these desks were here before the attic became a catchall for discarded copies of books. And there are the chairs." She pointed to the far corner.

"Uh-huh." Where was this leading?

"The desks have drawers. I think you should go through them," Evelyn said.

"Well, okay. But I doubt Laura would put something personal in a desk drawer any member of the staff might open."

"True, but things have gotten shifted around here in the past fifteen years. It's worth a look."

I opened the narrow top drawer of the desk closest to me. It was filled with candy wrappers, paper clips, a few ballpoint pens, and rubber bands. There were two side drawers. The first held typing paper and forms that the library no longer used. A white cardigan was in the bottom drawer.

"No luck, I see," Evelyn said. "But there are two more desks."

They stood against the far wall, with dozens of piled-up cartons blocking immediate access.

Evelyn must have seen me hesitate, because she cast me a stern look. "They're worth investigating."

I moved the boxes impeding my path to the desks. After fifteen minutes of hard work—my hands filthy with dust—I reached the first desk.

"Nothing here." I opened the three drawers.

"One more to go," Evelyn said.

The drawers were empty, save for a pad of notepaper and a box of paper clips. Then I had an idea. "I'm going to look underneath and behind the desks, just in case Laura hid the papers there."

"That's the spirit!" Evelyn perched on top of a pile of cartons.

I examined the two desks carefully. I pulled out every drawer to see if there was anything glued to the desk's frame.

"Nothing," I reported.

"Don't forget the first desk," Evelyn advised.

"Of course not."

I moved the necessary boxes to retrace my steps and examined the first desk's underside. I pulled out the top drawer, found nothing. Same for the second drawer. But the third drawer that held the sweater seemed to be stuck. I yanked on the handle until the drawer came out. I saw nothing on the desk frame. I felt under the drawer and yelped as I detached a brown envelope taped to the bottom of the drawer.

"Evelyn, look!"

My fingers trembled as I unfastened the metal clasp. Inside were ten or twelve sheets of yellow legal-sized pages filled with a scrawling feminine hand.

Chapter Thirty

I hugged the envelope to my chest as I raced from the attic to my office. Once inside, I sat at my desk and pulled the sheaf of pages from the envelope. I scanned the first page.

". . . my mood swings from ecstasy when I think of what we share to absolute terror that someone will discover our secret. I wish I could shout it to the world. But I can't. He can't."

My heart thudded against my ribs. This was Laura's intimate chronicle of her adulterous affair.

As much as I longed to read every single word she'd written, I shoved the pages back inside the envelope. I'd read them at home, slowly and carefully. My exhilaration knew no bounds. Here was evidence neither Al Buckley nor Lieutenant Mathers knew existed. I'd found it! With Evelyn's help, of course.

"Evelyn?" I glanced around the office, but she was nowhere in sight. When had she left? I thought back and realized she hadn't accompanied me out of the attic. Had she begun to fade, or had she chosen to leave me to go wherever she went when she wasn't in the library?

Puzzled, I mused about Evelyn's sudden disappearance. Didn't she want to learn the identity of Laura's secret lover, the person who had probably killed her? Or had my sudden exit offended her?

Thank goodness there was a concert at two that required my presence from one forty-five until it ended at a quarter to four. That would keep my mind occupied. I was eager to get home and read what Laura had written. I left precisely at five and drove home at top speed. When I arrived at the cottage, I poured myself a large glass of Chardonnay and sat down in the living room with the stack of pages on my lap.

The first few pages, which began in early September, were mostly about Laura's feelings. She described the rush of happiness her new relationship brought her. The joy of being listened to, appreciated, and cared for. By mid-November, anxieties had begun to creep into her thoughts. Was she crazy to maintain an adulterous relationship? Though she and her love met in a motel two towns away, she worried that someone might have seen them together. She was terrified, imagining what Bryce would do if he found out.

She worried about her sons and how a divorce would impact their lives. They would hate her and blame her for ripping their family apart. As it was, she had no idea how to control Ryan's growing hostility. He was angry and out of control—getting into fights in school, arguing with his friends. She pleaded with Bryce to talk to him, but Bryce was ineffectual. She wondered if her affair was somehow responsible for Ryan's recent acts of vandalism.

As the new year approached, Laura's entries became filled with unhappy thoughts. She felt trapped in an intolerable situation. A divorce would solve her problems—but only if her lover was willing to break his marital ties and marry her. While they professed their love for one another, they never discussed a future together. He claimed to love and cherish her. He soothed her when she poured out her concerns about her family but never once suggested they leave their spouses and marry. And she was too afraid to bring it up.

How frustrating that Laura went on and on without mentioning her lover's name. I shuffled through the pages. On the next to last sheet, I came upon the letter *L*. Excited, I started reading.

"L insists we're best off staying the way we are. Keeping our relationship a secret will avoid the mundane, day-to-day patterns that drain the spontaneity from every love affair. I don't agree. I need to have him with me all through the night, day after day."

Who is L? Laura's neighbor, Lou Devon, visited her frequently to make small house repairs. Ryan thought he and his mother might have been involved, though Jared doubted there was anything between them. Lou Devon wasn't especially good looking, but he paid attention to Laura. That alone could be an aphrodisiac.

Helena's husband's name was Lloyd. But Lloyd was dead, so there was nothing to be learned there. Unless I questioned Helena. But I wasn't sure I wanted to do that. She'd told Jared she knew his mother had had a lover but that she didn't know who he was. Was that a lie?

I read on. The next-to-last entry was written in mid-January and described a terrible quarrel. Laura had asked L why they couldn't be together. L said he couldn't leave his wife. Each time Laura asked why not, he offered a different reason: "It's too complicated to explain." "It would devastate her." "We're partners for life." Laura left in tears. When L called a week later wanting to see her, her heart filled with happiness. Laura went to meet him, certain he'd changed his mind. Instead, he'd told her their relationship was over.

"L said our love has run its course, and we should be grateful for the joy we shared. I stormed out of the room, humiliated and wounded. How could I have been so stupid?"

I refilled my glass and returned to the first page to read all the entries in sequence. *Poor Laura*, I thought. Another woman led on by a devious male.

I ate my dinner—a roast beef sandwich on rye bread with spicy mustard—and contemplated what I'd learned. Laura had fallen badly for L and was devastated when he refused to take their love affair further. Had she become angry enough to tell L's wife that he'd betrayed her? Who was L? Lou or Lloyd?

I reached for my cell phone to call Jared when the jingle sounded.

"Hello, Carrie. Dylan here."

"Hi. Where are you?"

"Winding things up in Baltimore. I'm flying to Atlanta tomorrow morning, so please don't send any more mail to this address."

"Sure. Do you have your new address?"

"Not yet. When I do, I'll text it to you. On second thought, don't send anything. I'm flying home next Wednesday for Thanksgiving weekend."

Yay! "Does that mean you can come to my aunt and uncle's for Thanksgiving?"

"It sure does. Please let them know I look forward to seeing them both."

"I will."

"Have to go. Talk to you soon."

I put down the phone and twirled a pirouette. Dylan was coming to Thanksgiving dinner!

I closed my eyes and imagined us driving together to Aunt Harriet and Uncle Bosco's house. He'd probably bring a bottle of wine or flowers, and I'd bring . . . what could I bring that Aunt Harriet couldn't make better than me?

I was great at baking big, fluffy popovers—only they were best served the moment they came out of the oven. My double-chocolate brownies were always a big hit. Yes! I'd make a batch of them with walnuts or almonds.

I decided to wait awhile before telling Jared I'd found his mother's journal. I couldn't trust him not to tell Bryce and Ryan. I didn't think anyone in that family should have access to the pages Laura had written—at least not yet.

Was I obliged to hand over the pages to Lieutenant Mathers? I imagined Laura's case had been reopened, at least as far as it touched on the investigation into Al's murder. Not that the pages revealed anything beyond the fact that Laura's lover's name began with the letter *L*. I had no wish to go to the police station after the cool reception I'd received the last time. The police weren't willing to share what they knew with me, so why should I share my information with them?

Still, the pages were evidence of a kind. Perhaps one of their specialists could get more from reading them than I had. I stretched my arms overhead and let out a yawn. I would hold onto them for now. I could always hand them over to Lieutenant Mathers when I saw him Thanksgiving Day.

Chapter Thirty-One

Helena surprised me by calling Monday evening to ask if I'd mind going shopping with her for some accent pieces for her new home.

"I'm far from an expert when it comes to decorating." I hoped she'd take the hint and back off.

She laughed. "I can tell you have excellent taste by the way you dress. Besides, you don't have to feel responsible for any purchases I make. I've asked Gillian too. I figure, between the three of us, we'll make good choices."

"Sure." I was relieved to know Gillian was included in this outing.

"What evening this week is good for you?"

"I finish at five on Wednesday and Thursday."

"Gillian said Wednesday is good too. Do you like Greek food?"

"I sure do."

"Let's meet at the Hellenic Kitchen. My treat."

I wasn't about to argue, since Helena viewed our outing as a favor to her. What was she really up to? Did she have serious plans to snag Bryce as a husband and want to pump Gillian and me to find out what his sons thought of her? We arranged to meet at six at the Greek restaurant outside of town and shop in the decorating stores in the nearby strip mall.

I called Gillian. Like me, she couldn't figure out why she'd been invited to shop for decor items for Helena's new condo.

"Unless she's trying to get into Bryce's good graces through us somehow," Gillian said.

"My thoughts exactly."

We decided that we didn't care why she'd invited us out. We'd have a good time. I figured it might be a good opportunity to ask a few questions and find out what Helena knew. After all, she had been Laura's best friend.

That Wednesday, I arrived at the restaurant at exactly six. Helena was waiting in the tiny vestibule, as excited as a kid celebrating a snow day.

"I managed to have the closing changed to Friday! Now I can move in on Sunday. Bryce promised my new furniture will be delivered on Tuesday in time for Thanksgiving."

I looked at her in surprise. "Won't preparing a holiday dinner be too much work after moving in?"

Helena brushed away my concerns with a wave of her hand. "Bryce and I will have a quiet dinner ourselves on Thursday. I'm planning a small housewarming party on Saturday night. You and Jared will come, of course."

I opened my mouth to say I had other plans but found myself agreeing to be there.

"Delightful!" Helena showered me with one of her dazzling smiles. "It wouldn't be the same without the two of you."

Inwardly, I cringed. *Is my life to be forever linked with Jared and his family?*

The outer door opened and Gillian appeared. "Sorry I'm late. I got held up handling a last-minute sale."

I pushed open the door to the restaurant. As we waited to be seated, Helena repeated verbatim to Gillian what she'd said to me.

"Of course Ryan and I will come," Gillian said. "Who else are you inviting?"

"Ken and George and a few of my old neighbors."

"Sounds lovely," Gillian said. "I can't wait to see your new place."

A stocky, blonde, middle-aged woman led us to a booth. Helena sat opposite Gillian and me. The place was half filled with diners. On the walls were large posters with scenes of Greek islands: Santorini, Mykonos, Rhodes. Places I'd love to visit one day.

We studied our menus and ordered drinks. As we waited for our appetizers, Helena told us what she was looking for in the shops we were going to visit.

"I've discarded most of my knickknacks—I'm simply tired of them—and I want a few new items for my étagère and end tables as well as a centerpiece for my new dining room table."

She took out her iPhone to show us photos of the furniture, which I thought looked rather stuffy and formal. My soup and their salads arrived, and we settled down to eat. For a while we talked about decor, then Helena changed the subject to relationships—Gillian and Ryan's, Jared's and mine.

"Jared and I are just friends," I stated.

"That's too bad," Helena said. "I've watched Jared grow up, and I can honestly say he's one of the nicest young men you'll meet in Clover Ridge."

The world is larger than Clover Ridge. "He is very nice." I gave her my stare. I hadn't used it since Dorothy stopped harassing me and was glad to see it still worked.

Helena fluttered her fingers and gave a little laugh. "How could I have forgotten? You and Jared forged a partnership to find poor Laura's killer. Have you learned anything new in the past few days?"

"Nothing, really. One of the older librarians thought Laura was having an affair," I quickly made up.

"Did she see Laura with anyone?"

"Once or twice."

"Really? Who was the guy?" Gillian asked.

"I don't know." I turned to Helena. "Jared said you knew of the affair."

Helena nodded. "All Laura would tell me was that she was seeing someone."

"And you have no idea who it might have been?"

She threw open her arms melodramatically. "I've spent hours trying to figure it out but have no answer for you."

His name began with an L. It might have been your husband. In which case, the murderer might be dead. "And no one comes to mind?"

"Hmm." Helena put her finger to her chin. "I always thought Laura had a bit of a crush on one of our old friends. But that's all I thought it was—a crush."

My heart raced as I asked, "What was his name?"

"Harold Lonnigan. We called him Lonnie."

Our main course arrived, but I was too busy mulling over Helena's bombshell to bother with food. Who was Harold Lonnigan? Until now, I'd never heard him mentioned. Helena referred to him as "an old friend." Was he someone Laura,

Bryce, Helena, and Lloyd had socialized with? Was he married? He must have been, if he was the L in Laura's journal.

Or had Helena made up this entire story to turn attention away from her husband, Lloyd? But according to Helena, Laura had never told her the name of her lover. Helena would have had to have seen the pages Laura had written—the pages I'd found that were hidden in the back of my dresser's bottom drawer under my bulkiest, warmest sweaters—to know that Laura referred to her lover as L.

Unless Helena had found out that her best friend and husband were messing around. Wasn't that what usually happened, regardless of how cliché it sounded? A wife is charmed when her husband's best friend listens to her. A boss comes to rely on his secretary. Couples who spend time together—who know each other well enough to break down the usual social barriers.

"Carrie, is something wrong? You haven't touched your food," Helena said.

I gave a start. "Sorry." I cut off a piece of chicken kabob and started chewing.

"What's Harold Lonnigan like?" Gillian asked.

I could have kissed her for asking.

"Lonnie?" Helena shrugged. "I always thought he was good company. He works on Wall Street, like Bryce used to."

"Does he still live in Clover Ridge?" I asked.

"He moved to the city after he and Francine got divorced. The odd thing is, I saw him at Al Buckley's presentation." She lowered her voice. "The night he was poisoned."

"Really?" I said. "How did he know about it?"

"Francine must have told him, since they were sitting together. They remained on good terms for the sake of their kids. She sold the house a few years ago and moved into her condo in Devon Woods."

"Now you'll be neighbors," I said.

Helena laughed. "Francine can be irritating, but I'm glad I kept in touch with her and let her know I wanted to move back. She called me the moment the unit I bought went on the market."

I ate a forkful of grilled veggies and decided I'd asked enough questions about Lonnie and his wife. I'd call Jared later to find out what he knew about the man.

We finished our meals and decided to skip coffee and dessert so we could hit the stores. We climbed into Helena's car and drove the quarter mile to the first place on her list, Knickknacks and Things.

"Remember, I need something to put on my dining room table. Something classic, something dramatic. Something that will stand out."

"Uh-huh," Gillian said. "Got it."

"And I need a few accent pillows for the bedroom—burnt orange and moss green. When you see anything in those colors, give a shout."

She was also on the lookout for geese figurines and statuettes of young women less than a foot tall. And a three-foot-tall ceramic umbrella holder for the hallway.

The evening proved to be fun. We wandered about, looking for items Helena might like. By the time we'd combed the third store, Helena had bought four figurines and two possibilities for her dining room table and was considering an umbrella holder. She dropped off Gillian and me in the Greek restaurant's parking lot, where we'd left our cars.

"Thanks for helping me out, girls," she called to us. "See you a week from Saturday."

"Looking forward to it," Gillian and I called back.

When she was gone, we turned to each other.

Gillian wore a puzzled expression. "I wonder what she was really after, inviting us to shop with her."

Smart girl. "Maybe she wants to ingratiate herself with Bryce's son's friends."

"Or she's after information about Laura's secret lover," Gillian mused.

Very smart girl. I yawned. "Regardless, it was a fun night." I opened my car door.

"Do you think this Lonnie was Laura's lover?" Gillian asked.

I shrugged. "I have no idea. I'm afraid Laura Foster's murder is going to remain a cold case after all."

Chapter Thirty-Two

The week before Thanksgiving flew by. I no longer woke each morning with butterflies in my stomach and realized that I was settling into my position as head of P and E at the Clover Ridge Public Library. Smoky Joe was taking his role as library cat very seriously. Each day he wove through my legs as I put on my parka to remind me that he, too, was going to work. And no wonder! Library workers and patrons spoiled and petted him from the moment we entered the building. Trish was writing an article about him for our next newsletter.

At work, I saw to it that ongoing programs and events ran smoothly. I worked on the newsletter and returned e-mails and phone calls, always on the lookout for new and interesting presenters. Patrons stopped me to ask about a program or to share an anecdote. I attended a meeting with other P and E heads in the area and had lunch with Marion Marshall, the children's librarian.

The night before Thanksgiving, I met Angela at one of the local pubs known for its huge variety of beers. We found a small table in the corner and ordered tall glasses of their best brew on tap. They arrived chilled and foaming.

We clinked glasses and drank.

"Here's to Turkey Day, the holiday when we stuff ourselves and fight with relatives," Angela said.

I laughed. "I don't expect to fight with anyone—not even my cousin Randy. He used to torment me when we were young. I haven't seen him in years, though I met his wife and daughter at the library."

"My mom expects me at the house at nine thirty to set the table and make the sweet potato pies."

"You love every minute of it."

"Girlfriend, you caught me out." Angela raised her glass in salute and gulped down most of her beer. "I love seeing most of my cousins, aunts, and uncles. I think we're twenty-three at last count."

"Besides Randy, Julia, and their kids, my aunt and uncle's neighbors will be there, along with Lieutenant Mathers and his wife."

"Interesting group," Angela said. "Are you planning to hand over Laura Foster's pages to Lieutenant Mathers?"

"I think I will." I exhaled a mouthful of air I hadn't realized I'd been holding in. "Part of me wants to first show them to Jared, but I can't bring myself to do it. I haven't even told him I found them. I'm worried he'll blurt it out to his family the way he did at dinner last week, and . . ."

"And you think maybe one of them killed Laura and maybe even Al Buckley."

"Honestly, I don't know what to think. I know Laura's lover's name began with the letter *L*. I told Jared what Helena said about Harold Lonnigan. He remembered him but never saw him with his mother. He said Bryce speaks to him from time to time."

"That's not much help. Did Jared know why Lonnigan and his wife divorced?"

"He remembers Bryce once commenting that Lonnie couldn't take her exasperating ways any longer, and now he's happy living a free life in Manhattan."

"I don't suppose it makes much sense to go into Manhattan to question him," Angela said.

"Which is why I want to give Lieutenant Mathers Laura's pages. It might encourage the police to expend more resources to solve her murder. Maybe they can find out L's identity."

We drained our glasses and ordered another round, along with a quesadilla and a plate of zucchini sticks to share. Though we both had eaten dinner, we finished off the food in no time and ordered buffalo wings. Angela complained about her boyfriend and how he was going to his aunt's house instead of coming to her parents' the next day. I sympathized and then found myself the subject of our conversation.

"Carrie, you must be happy Jared's visiting a college friend over Thanksgiving."

"We're not a couple. I wasn't planning to invite him to my aunt and uncle's house."

Angela giggled. "That would have been awkward, don't you think, since you're going with Dylan Avery."

"In the same car. Not as a date."

"Call it what you like. Believe me, Dylan Avery wouldn't be going to your aunt and uncle's for Thanksgiving if he didn't like you."

"He's known them for ages." I spoke as calmly as I could, but inside I was lit up like a roman candle.

I'd been doing my best not to think about Dylan, telling myself not to weave fantasies that couldn't come true. Dylan was someone from my childhood. My brother's friend. My landlord. His job kept him out of town most of the time. But I'd been feeling euphoric since he'd called the night before to ask what time we were expected and to say he'd come for me at twenty to three.

Half an hour later, Angela and I asked for our check. Outside, we hugged in the chilly November air before getting into our cars.

"Remember, I want to hear all about tomorrow," Angela said.

I waved and set off for home.

* * *

Thursday morning dawned bright and sunny, with unusually warm temperatures. I ate breakfast and then placed all the ingredients I needed to make a batch of double-chocolate brownies on the counter. I hummed as I preheated the oven. Smoky Joe watched me from his perch on the windowsill.

I loved Thanksgiving. Even though my mother was never much of a homemaker, she'd made an effort to have a somewhat typical Thanksgiving dinner for Jordan and me. Since it was usually only the three of us, she roasted a chicken instead of a turkey. But I didn't care. She always made stuffing, sweet potato pie, green beans, cranberry sauce, and double-chocolate brownies—the only dessert she ever baked. The recipe I was following this morning was written out in her handwriting.

I decided to wear a pink sweater and a navy pencil skirt over navy tights. And, of course, my new boots. I took time with my hair and my makeup and redid my nails, painting them a screaming purple. I had the sudden urge to dye a streak of purple in my hair. Maybe I'd do it just before my birthday. I grinned. Even Sally couldn't object to a bit of color now that I'd turned respectable.

I expected to hear a car horn at twenty to three. Instead, the doorbell rang at two thirty. I opened it, and Dylan stepped inside.

For a moment, we stared at one another. He looked deliciously sexy in worn jeans, a light-blue denim shirt, and a brown suede jacket. He enveloped me in a hug.

"I thought I'd come in and see what you've done with the place." He followed me into the living room.

"Not much," I said when I'd caught my breath. "It was perfectly decorated."

Smoky Joe jumped down from the sofa. Dylan reached out, and the cat sniffed his hand. A minute later, Dylan was scratching him behind his ears, which started him purring.

"He looks like the feral cats that hang out near the Jenkins' farm. Glad this one got away."

I laughed. "He was hungry and came here looking for food. But I think he must have known he was a people cat and wanted our company."

I followed Dylan into my office.

"You've added your touches, as I knew you would." He peered at the two pictures I'd hung over my computer.

I went into the kitchen for the pan of brownies.

"Those look great," Dylan said. "Mind if I have one?"

"You mean . . . now?"

"Sure. I haven't eaten a thing since I worked out this morning."

I cut a brownie for him, and he demolished it in two bites.

"That was awesome. I'll have another at dessert time."

Dylan was helping me on with my jacket when I remembered Laura's journal. "Be right back." I dashed into my bedroom to retrieve the original pages from their hiding place and then went into my office for an envelope. The copy I'd made for myself was in a folder under a pile of towels in the linen closet. Dylan shot me a sidelong glance, but I wasn't about to explain what I was bringing with me or why.

We walked out to his car, a low-slung two-door BMW. I glanced in the back seat and saw a package with two bottles of wine. We fastened our seat belts and set out for my aunt and uncle's house.

"How long will you be home?" I asked.

"Through the weekend."

My heart thudded in my chest. "Will I see you before you leave?"

"That can be arranged."

What does he mean by that? Dylan didn't elaborate, and I didn't ask.

"Have you finished your latest case?" I asked instead.

"My part's done, at least for now. The gems have been recovered and the thieves arrested. I'll have to show up at their trials, but that'll be months from now."

"Will you start a new case immediately?"

"I don't know. I fly back to Atlanta Monday morning to report to my boss and take care of some paperwork. If they don't need me by the end of the week, I'm thinking of taking a short Caribbean vacation."

"Oh." I hoped I didn't sound as forsaken as I felt. Which was silly, given our nonrelationship.

* * *

Randy, Julia, and their children were already at the house when we arrived. My cousin was thirty-two and beginning to lose his hair. He was still rail-thin but had developed a bit of a paunch. Uncle Bosco started to introduce us when Randy reached out and pulled me into a bear hug. I found myself hugging him back.

"It's good to finally see you, cuz," he said.

"Same here."

"You made a big hit with Julia and our daughter."

"Hello, Cousin Carrie. How's Smoky Joe?" Tacey said.

"He's just fine."

Julie and I smiled at one another.

"And this is Mark." Randy rested his hand on his eight-year-old's shoulder.

Mark stuck out his right hand. "A pleasure to meet you, Cousin Carrie."

"Nice to meet you too."

We shook hands.

I went over to say hello to Aunt Harriet and Uncle Bosco's neighbors, Ruth and Chuck Claymont. They were in their mideighties and hard of hearing, so I had to repeat my greetings a few times. Dylan, I noticed, was in the kitchen with Aunt Harriet.

A few minutes later, Lieutenant Mathers and his wife, Sylvia, arrived. Sylvia was a warmhearted redhead in her midfifties.

They were introduced to everyone, and Uncle Bosco took orders for drinks. I asked for a glass of white wine and then went into the kitchen to see if Aunt Harriet could use a hand.

I found her chatting animatedly with Sylvia.

"Sylvia's bringing me up to date on her children," Aunt Harriet said.

I must have looked puzzled because they both burst out laughing.

"I've known your aunt Harriet since I was little," Sylvia explained. "She and my mom were close friends. Harriet and Bosco are my daughter Meg's godparents."

I made polite noises and left them to catch up in private. I looked about for Dylan and was surprised to see him conversing in the hallway with Lieutenant Mathers. Their expressions were serious, and I sensed that they, too, wanted their privacy.

But of course! They were both in law enforcement and had a good deal in common. Were they discussing their recent cases? I remembered the envelope I wanted to give Lieutenant Mathers when the opportunity arose.

Julie found me and told me how happy Randy was to reconnect with me.

"Really?" I asked. "When we were young, he teased me until I cried."

She grinned. "I think he wasn't used to spending time with little girls and didn't know how to act."

I laughed.

"Anyway, I won't let him tease you ever again," she said.

We bumped fists. "I think you and I are going to be great friends."

"I think so too."

I returned to the kitchen, where Aunt Harriet was removing a tray of stuffed mushrooms from the oven and Sylvia was stirring something on the stove.

"Can I help?" I asked.

"Would you please put these on that serving dish and pass them around?"

"Of course." I placed a toothpick in each mushroom, grabbed a handful of small plates and napkins, and went into the living room.

The Claymonts, sitting side by side on the sofa, each took a mushroom. My next stop was the den, where Uncle Bosco was chatting with Randy and his family. I placed the serving dish on the coffee table and helped the kids with their mushrooms. Julie said she was going to see if Aunt Harriet had another platter of hot hors d'oeuvres that needed serving. Tacey followed her mother and then made a beeline for me as I headed down the hall, where Dylan and Lieutenant Mathers were still talking.

"Carrie." Tacey tugged at my sweater, stopping me in my tracks. "How is Miss Evelyn?"

"She's fine, honey."

"I haven't seen her in a long time. Mommy's busy and can't take me to the library."

"Oh."

"Have you seen her?"

"I did about a week ago."

"Why can't she leave the library?"

"I don't know."

"Why doesn't she like my cookies?"

"Evelyn doesn't eat cookies, Tacey."

"She told me, but I think that's silly. Everyone likes cookies." She looked up at me. "You know Miss Evelyn's real, right?"

"She's real, but in a different way than us. And most people can't see her."

"But we can." Tacey gave me a broad smile and skipped back to her father and brother.

Chapter Thirty-Three

Uncle Bosco called us to the table, where our names were written on cards in lovely calligraphy. I silently cheered because my place was between Lieutenant Mathers and Dylan. Julia and I helped Aunt Harriet serve the butternut squash soup. When we were all seated, Uncle Bosco led us in a short prayer of thanksgiving. Then he asked us to say what we were thankful for. The kids giggled as they mentioned toys they'd received. The adults appreciated their good health, their families, or having the opportunity to share this Thanksgiving with dear friends.

"I'm thankful I had the good sense to come home to Clover Ridge," I said, suddenly all choked up.

"We're so glad you did." Aunt Harriet beamed at me across the table.

I finished my soup and looked at Dylan. He was trying his best to hold a conversation with Ruth Claymont, so I turned to Lieutenant Mathers. "Nice to see you here today, Lieutenant."

"Since today's a holiday, why don't you call me John?" His smile transformed his face. It struck me that he was a good-looking man.

"Certainly. If you'll call me Carrie."

"Will do." After a moment, he asked, "Are you enjoying your job at the library?"

"I love it."

"I hope you and Jared Foster have given up playing detective." A touch of his old seriousness returned.

"I think we've exhausted all our leads. Though I have something for you."

"Really? What is it?"

I retrieved the envelope with Laura's pages from the tote bag I'd brought and handed it to him. "It's kind of a journal Laura Foster wrote before she died. She hid it in the library attic."

I barely suppressed the giggles rising like bubbles when I caught his look of total amazement.

He held the envelope on his lap and glanced at the pages. "How the hell did you find this?"

I shrugged. "Just lucky, I guess."

John started to say something when Sylvia asked him a question.

Dylan was watching me, an amused expression on his face. "What have you been up to?"

"Later."

Aunt Harriet and Uncle Bosco left the table to bring in the rest of the meal. Julia and I collected the soup dishes and carried them into the kitchen. When I sat down again, John asked, "Do you have any idea who L is?"

My pleasure knew no bounds! Lieutenant Mathers of the Clover Ridge Police Department was asking my opinion about the murders.

"There are three possibilities," I said in a low voice. "Laura's neighbor Lou Devon; Helena's late husband, Lloyd Koppel; and Laura's old friend Harold Lonnigan."

John stroked his chin. "We'll talk later." He pushed the pages back into the envelope and placed it under his chair.

I put a little of everything on my plate—cranberry relish, turkey, green beans, stuffing, and sweet potato casserole. It all tasted heavenly. I'd hardly made a dent in my food when I realized I was full. Still, I kept on eating. When I'd finished all I could manage, I looked up and saw dazed expressions on the faces around me. Clearly, I wasn't the only one who had overeaten.

Julia, Sylvia, and I cleared the table. Aunt Harriet put away the leftovers while I loaded the dishwasher. We all agreed dessert would have to wait and returned to the dining room while the men wandered into the den to watch the football game.

Somehow we managed to consume a goodly amount of dessert as well. I ate a piece of the apple cake Julia had made, a nice-sized wedge of pecan pie, and a scoop of ice cream Sylvia and John had brought. I passed over my brownies, which I could always make. I was pleased to see Dylan take a brownie and hear Uncle Bosco praise them. After dessert, the men returned to the football game. Mark and Tacey ran around the living room until Julia told them to stop. Tacey began to cry and went to sit on her mother's lap. We cleared the dessert dishes, and Aunt Harriet insisted that everyone take home what was left of their desserts, or else she'd eat herself into a coma.

Too soon, it was over. The Claymonts said a general good-bye and took their leave. I hugged Randy, Julia, and Tacey good-bye. Mark shook my hand again. Sylvia and I went into the den, where the three remaining men were watching the game.

"Time to go, honey," she said to John.

He rose slowly from the sofa, his eyes still on the TV.

Dylan and I nodded to one another as though agreeing with Sylvia. We hadn't said much to one another all evening, but I was constantly aware of his presence.

"We'll be leaving too, Uncle Bosco." I leaned over to kiss his forehead. "Great dinner."

"Made especially wonderful because you were here."

Sylvia hugged me good-bye.

John gave me a solemn look. "We'll talk. Meanwhile, don't do anything foolish."

"Of course not."

I went into the kitchen to say good-bye to Aunt Harriet. She'd filled several containers of food for me to take home.

"This was the best Thanksgiving I've ever had." I grabbed her in a bear hug.

"Oh, honey, you've made it special for your uncle and me." Then she turned to Dylan, who'd been standing behind me. "I'm so glad you were able to come."

"Spending Thanksgiving with you meant more to me than you can imagine."

His words surprised me, but not as much as seeing him and Aunt Harriet embrace.

We carried the packages of food out to the car and started for home. Coming here, I'd felt both exhilarated and shy riding next to Dylan. Now I felt relaxed and comfortable in his presence.

"What were you and John Mathers talking about right after he and Sylvia arrived?" I asked.

"He asked about my latest case. And I wanted to know how the investigation into Al Buckley's homicide was progressing."

"Did you know Al?"

Dylan nodded. "Al's a major reason I became an investigator. We had a few good conversations after I graduated from college without the slightest idea what to do with my life. He was a great guy. Must have been a hell of a detective before he started drinking."

"I liked him too, though we'd only spoken briefly the night he died."

"Freakish, that—a retired detective poisoned in our local library."

"What did John have to say?"

"Not much. Seems they hadn't found anything conclusive pointing to any one person."

"I gave John a sort of journal Laura kept before she died. I found it in the library attic."

Dylan's body stiffened. "Carrie, I hope you haven't told anyone else what you've found."

"I was going to tell Jared, but—"

"Don't tell Jared or anyone else in that family!" Dylan swerved to the edge of the road and stopped the car. He grabbed me by both shoulders. "Promise me you won't."

"Okay, I won't. But why the alarm all of a sudden? I've met his family a number of times. I've never felt threatened by any of them."

Dylan leaned back and exhaled loudly. "This was told to me in the strictest of confidences, so keep it to yourself: John is convinced the killer is a member of the family. He can't move on it because he only has the testimony of one witness and no clear evidence."

I shook my head in disbelief. "Surely he doesn't think Jared murdered his mother. He's so intent on finding the person who killed her and Al. Now, his brother Ryan's a hothead, but even so, I can't see him as a killer."

"Did Jared tell you about the time he spent in a psychiatric hospital?"

"No. When was this?"

"A month or so after Laura's murder. He became violent, worse than his brother. Got into fights in school. Beat up a kid so badly, he almost lost an eye. Bryce couldn't control him and had him committed. He stayed in the hospital for a couple of months."

"It's hard to believe. Jared seems fine now. He has a job. I've never seen him angry, even when Ryan goads him."

"He's good as long as he takes his meds."

Dylan put the car in gear and edged back onto the road. As we headed for home, he said, "I know you guys are dating, and it's not my place to tell you not to see him, but steer clear of discussing the murders—with Jared and the rest of the Fosters."

"We're not dating."

Dylan had turned on the radio, and a blast of rock music drowned out my words.

When he pulled up in front of the cottage, I opened the bag that held the tin of brownies Aunt Harriet had returned to me.

"Why don't you take these, since you like them so much?"

Dylan grinned. "I won't say no."

"Thanks for driving me," I said.

"Thanks for inviting me."

He surprised me by kissing my cheek. "Be careful, Carrie. I don't want anything to happen to you."

Chapter Thirty-Four

I unlocked the front door and turned on the hall light. Something was different. *Felt* different. I walked slowly to the kitchen and studied the cabinets and the placement of the chairs. I was far from the neatest person, but I had this thing about making sure my kitchen chairs were pushed squarely under the table. The one I usually sat in stood slightly askew.

Despite my feeling of alarm, I moved slowly through the cottage. Nothing in the living room appeared to have been disturbed. Smoky Joe was asleep on the sofa. I turned on my computer. Judging by my browser's history, no one had touched it.

Someone had used the small towel in the guest bathroom and left it hanging with one end lower than the other. The toilet seat cover was down, and there were drops of water on the floor. My intruder had used the bathroom!

I was too frightened to check out my bedroom. What if the person was still in the cottage? I ran to the front door, ready to jump in my car and drive to safety when it dawned on me: Jack Norris had fixed the toilet in the guest bathroom.

I was still laughing when the phone rang.

It was Jared. "Hi. We just finished eating. How was Thanksgiving at your aunt and uncle's?"

"Great. I ate too much."

"I'm about to burst. I had to have two servings of Tommy's aunt's sweet potato pie. And the desserts were awesome."

We talked a bit more about our Thanksgiving dinners, and then Jared told me what he and Tommy planned to do tomorrow. As he spoke, I imagined him as a young teenager, hurt and angry at the world. He'd never mentioned his stay in a psych ward. It must have been hushed up, because my aunt and uncle hadn't known about it or they would have told me.

"I should arrive home around noon on Saturday," he said. "Helena expects us at seven thirty. I'll bring over a good bottle of champagne for the occasion."

"Good idea."

There was a long silence. "I guess that's it for now. See you in two days. I miss you."

"Enjoy the rest of your visit," was the best I could offer. I promised myself that after Saturday night, I'd tell Jared that since our investigation had reached an end, I wouldn't be able to spend as much time with him. No, I had to tell him I wouldn't be seeing him anymore. Jared thought we were dating. It was only fair to tell him how I felt.

I changed into my nightgown and flitted through channels on the TV. I was too restless to settle down and watch one program. My mind kept churning over what I'd learned in the last few days.

What had convinced John that Laura's killer was someone in her family? Did "family" include her brother, George? Close friends Ken and the Koppels? Was it because there had been no sign of a break-in that night? Because the only fingerprints found in the house belonged to family members?

Was Lloyd the L in Laura's life? Did he kill Laura because she threatened to tell Helena about their affair?

Or had Helena found out about Laura's relationship with Lloyd, killed her out of jealousy, and then murdered Lloyd a year later? I let out a humorless chuckle at the thought of adding another possible homicide to the mix. It was a preposterous idea! According to Jared, Lloyd had died of a heart attack. But there was no harm in finding out the circumstances of his death.

What about Harold Lonnigan? Had he been Laura's lover? Lonnie was a friend of the Fosters. His fingerprints might have been found in the living room where Laura was killed. And why had he come to hear Al talk about the old case? It could have been simple curiosity.

Or he might have been worried that Al had figured out he'd murdered Laura and wanted to shut Al up before he exposed him.

Or was his wife, Francine, the killer?

Was Jared dangerous?

I put my hands over my ears to silence the various homicidal possibilities clamoring inside my head. Dylan suddenly came to mind, blotting out all other thoughts. I smiled, remembering how much I'd enjoyed sitting beside him during dinner and driving to and from Aunt Harriet and Uncle Bosco's. Being in his presence, whether we were conversing with each other or speaking with other people, both soothed and excited me. I told myself not to get hung up on a guy who was hardly ever around. Who probably still considered me his friend's kid sister. Besides, if he was interested in dating me, he would have asked me out before he flew back to Atlanta.

I got ready for bed listening to Enya's soothing tones. I picked up my Kindle and started reading where I'd left off in the latest Jack Reacher thriller. Oddly enough, I found Jack's aggressive behavior comforting as he pummeled the bad guys for the sake of the good. By ten, I was fast asleep.

* * *

I woke up at six feeling energized and well rested. It was Black Friday, the biggest shopping day of the year, and I was glad to be working. There was nothing I was dying to buy, and besides, I hated crowds.

When I got to the library, I stopped by the circulation desk to chat with Angela. She gave Smoky Joe one of the cat treats she now kept on hand and told me she'd made up with Steve, who showed up at her mother's house after all. Then she asked for a Dylan Avery update.

"Nothing to report."

"That's a bummer."

I shrugged. "I told you nothing would come of it."

We made plans to have lunch together at the Cozy Corner Café. I ran into Sally, who was as ecstatic as I'd ever seen her. She and her husband had stood in line the night before until early that morning and managed to snag a huge 4K Ultra HD smart TV a local store was selling for less than a thousand dollars. I congratulated her and continued on my way.

I spent part of the morning responding to phone messages and e-mails. One of the chefs wanted to change his menu from a beef dish to a chicken dish. I'd written it up for the newsletter but still had time to make the change if I moved on it that day. I notified the printer and e-mailed the chef to say the change would be okay.

Trish called to say she'd be a little late because she was in a store with her children, and the lines were horrendous. I told her to take her time, as there wasn't much happening and I was going out for lunch with Angela at twelve thirty.

"Thanksgiving's the holiday I miss most of all."

I blinked as Evelyn materialized inches from my chair. She wore a gray dress with a full skirt, gray suede pumps with low heels, and a strand of pearls at least thirty inches long.

"Don't you look lovely."

"This is what I wore to my last Thanksgiving dinner."

I was about to ask Evelyn where she kept her wardrobe when she asked, "And what did your aunt Harriet serve yesterday?"

"The usual—turkey, sweet potato casserole—"

"With pineapple? Marshmallows?"

"There was pineapple in the casserole." I listed the other dishes we'd eaten. "I made brownies for the occasion. They went over big."

"Did you give Laura's pages to Lieutenant Mathers?"

"I did." I looked at her. "Don't you want to know what she wrote?"

Evelyn turned away.

"You know what she wrote because you read them!"

"I confess I read a few pages."

"Why didn't you tell me? Why did you have me waste time looking in the other desks when you knew exactly where Laura hid those pages?"

"I was too ashamed to tell you. One day, I found Laura scribbling away when I entered the attic. Years ago, it wasn't the holy mess it is now. A few of us liked to take our coffee breaks up there. The next time I was there alone, I found where she'd hidden the pages.

"At first, I thought Laura was writing a romance novel. Then I realized she was spilling out her passion for a man she didn't name. I was horrified and shoved the pages back in the envelope."

"Later on, she refers to her lover as L."

Evelyn's mouth fell open. "Don't tell me Lou Devon and Laura were having an affair."

"He's one possibility. Helena Koppel's late husband, Lloyd, is another."

"Lloyd Koppel," Evelyn said slowly. "The Koppels were good friends with Laura and Bryce."

"What was Lloyd like?"

"He was an architect. A nice-looking man who dressed well. He was reserved but had a charming smile."

"Helena said Laura seemed to have a crush on Harold Lonnigan."

Evelyn's face brightened. "Lonnie! Everyone doted on Lonnie."

"I told John Mathers about the three men. Dylan said John thinks a member of the family killed Laura. Who do you think it might be?"

"I couldn't begin to guess."

"Did you know Jared spent time in a psych hospital after his mother's murder?"

Evelyn shook her head. "No. How is he now?"

"All right, as far as I can tell. Tomorrow night, we're going to a party Helena's hosting at her new condo."

She reached out as if to grab my arm. I felt a chill as her hand nearly touched me. "Promise me you won't ask questions about Laura. If the killer hears you, he might think you know his identity and come after you."

"I'll be careful."

* * *

Angela's advice was the opposite of Evelyn's. I'd invited her over that night to help me finish off Aunt Harriet's leftovers. She brought along some of her mother's famous brussels sprouts casserole and half an apple cake. Angela thought the party presented the perfect opportunity to raise questions and look around.

"What am I looking for?" I cleared the table. "A hidden photo of Laura and Lloyd in an embrace?"

Angela downed the last of her diet soda. "You never can tell what you'll find. Or what someone will say. *In vino veritas.*"

I giggled. "Right. I'll make sure everyone drinks plenty of booze and then interrogate them."

"That's the spirit!"

I stacked our dishes in the dishwasher and then filled the Keurig with water for our coffee. "Tomorrow night's my last evening with the Foster family."

"You're dumping Jared?"

"I've decided not to see him anymore. Our investigation has come to a dead end. Unfortunately, we made little headway."

"Don't feel bad. Neither did the police."

After Angela left, I found myself too restless to settle down to read or watch TV. I wanted to solve the murders but hadn't the slightest idea how to move forward. Laura's pages reflected her state of mind but offered no clues. I decided to drive to the supermarket in town and do my grocery shopping.

I was halfway home when I realized a car had been following me. My pulse jumped when it continued onto the private Avery road. I grabbed my phone to call 9-1-1 when I heard two beeps. It was Dylan, who had stopped in front of his house. I waved, and he waved back. Smiling, I drove the remaining few hundred yards to the cottage.

Chapter Thirty-Five

Soft rock music and the aroma of warming canapés wafted toward us when Helena welcomed us into her condo. Tonight's getup was a purple harem outfit: a plunging, fitted bodice trimmed with gold-colored coins and gauzy harem pants gathered at the ankles. More gauzy fabric hung from the round, boxlike headpiece atop her blonde hair.

"Here you are at last!" She hugged and kissed us as if we were long-lost relatives. "Toss your coats on the sofa in the den and then come inside and join the party."

She thrust her hand, holding a wineglass, in the direction of the den and splashed wine on Jared's shirt. "Oh, sorry." She tried to wipe the damp spot with the fabric of her headpiece.

Jared pulled back. "It's okay, Helena. Really." He handed her the bottle of champagne. "For you. To celebrate your new home."

"Why, thank you. I'll put this in the fridge for later."

We added our coats to the pile on the den sofa, and Jared studied the wine spot in the mirror. "She's drunk already."

"At least it's white wine. It won't stain."

He grimaced. "Still, who wants to start off an evening with a wine-drenched shirt?"

We entered the living room.

"Jared! Carrie! Over here." Bryce, Ryan, and Gillian stood before the picture window at the far end of the room, drinks in hand.

We exchanged greetings, and Bryce gestured to the window. "Helena has a wonderful view of the lake from here and from her bedroom upstairs."

I nodded, though it was too dark to see anything outside.

"The condo's perfect for her," he enthused. "An updated kitchen, living room-dining room, den, and half-bath downstairs; two bedrooms and baths above."

"Don't forget to admire her new furniture." Ryan patted his father's shoulder.

"Very nice," I said, though the wood-framed, white-tufted sofa and matching chairs were not pieces I'd ever choose.

Gillian winked at me, and I knew she was thinking the same thing.

Jared went to the bar in the dining room to get a glass of wine for me and a beer for himself. Helena appeared with a tray of pigs in a blanket. She wobbled on her spiked heels, and I feared the canapés would end up on the Persian carpet. But she managed to offer them to her four seated guests and to us without incident.

I was about to follow Helena into the kitchen to ask if I could help when George and Ken Talbot left their seats to join us. I was delighted to see them and hugged them both. Besides Gillian, they were the only people I was going to miss when I stopped dating Jared. Two women stood hovering behind them.

George reached for the hand of the pretty brunette and drew her into our circle. "Carrie, meet Pam Hamilton, my significant other. Pam, you remember Jared."

"Hi, Pam."

We shook hands. "Nice to meet you," she said.

"My pleasure." She flashed me a friendly smile.

The overweight blonde in the tight red dress moved closer, forcing Pam and George to step back. "Hi, I'm Helena's friend, Francine Lonnigan."

"Oh!" I exclaimed louder than I'd meant to.

"Oh, what?" Francine asked belligerently.

"Nothing—that is, Helena mentioned you the other day."

"I told her you were the wonderful person responsible for my buying the condo of my dreams." Helena joined us.

I didn't dare ask Francine why her husband had come to hear Al Buckley's presentation. If he had, as Helena had told me.

"Our meal is about ready. Why don't we sit down at the dining room table?" Helena smiled. "I know you'll forgive me for catering instead of making it myself."

"Of course we do." Bryce slipped an arm around her waist. "You've been so busy these last few weeks; I don't know how you managed to pull this together."

"It was nothing." Helena stepped back from his embrace. She turned to Jared and me. "Would you like to see the rest of the place?"

"I'd love to," I said.

"Follow me for a fast tour." Helena led us past the dining room table set for ten and into the kitchen. "As you can see, the kitchen was remodeled only last year."

"Lovely." I took in the speckled granite counters and stainless-steel appliances as we walked through to the hall.

"You saw the den. I've ordered a large TV. It's being delivered next week."

The master bedroom was something to gush over. It was L-shaped, like the living room-dining room downstairs, with a sitting area and four windows that looked out on the artificial lake.

"You sure have plenty of closet space," I said as Helena opened two gigantic walk-in closets.

"Wait till you see my bathroom."

It was like a Roman bath, with four columns rising from the steps leading to a Jacuzzi. There were two sinks, a large shower, and the latest in commodes.

Jared and I oohed and ahhed, admiring the various shower nozzles that sprang from the wall.

"Of course, the guest bedroom and bath aren't as snazzy," Helena said as we walked back through her bedroom.

I scrutinized the room, on the lookout for places where objects might be hidden. I doubted the king-size bed and small nightstands—each with a narrow drawer—held any secrets, but the double dresser and closets were possibilities. The question was, how could I find out?

"The guest bathroom." Helena scowled as she pointed to the small, windowless room. "I can't imagine why they chose these awful bubblegum-pink tiles. And the wallpaper! Reminds me of a circus."

She's right. The striped pink, green, yellow, and white paper *was* garish.

I trailed Helena and Jared into the guest room. It held a bed, a lamp on a small nightstand, a desk in the corner on which stood a computer and printer, and a narrow chest of drawers I knew was a jewelry armoire. On it was a five-by-eight photograph of a man in a suit. He had nice, even features. From his smile, I got the impression he'd been warm and easygoing.

"Who is this?" I asked.

"My late husband, Lloyd. He died thirteen years ago. Lloyd's heart gave out while he was going over blueprints in a client's office."

"I'm sorry. He was very handsome."

"Wasn't he? Ready to go? I don't want our dinner to burn."

That was a weird response. No expression of love or caring. As Jared and I followed Helena downstairs, I frantically wondered what excuse I could use to return to snoop around the bedrooms. Surely if there was something to find, it would be in one of the drawers. But what was I after? What could I possibly uncover that might prove Lloyd or Helena had murdered Laura?

Jared tried to steer me into the dining room, where the others were seated, but I pulled away.

"Can I help you serve?" I asked Helena.

"I'd appreciate it." She smiled, once again the happy-go-lucky hostess.

She removed a large bowl filled with salad from the fridge and handed it to me. "Ask everyone to start serving themselves."

"Will do." I set the bowl on the dining room table.

Gillian followed me into the kitchen. "I've come to help."

I grinned, welcoming her company as Helena removed three foil-covered trays of food from the oven.

"The mitts are over there." Helena gestured with her chin. "Place the silver-colored hot-tray mats on the table and put a tray on each."

We followed her instructions.

"I'm amazed at how you were able to unpack everything in just a few days," Gillian said.

"I had a tag sale before I moved. Got rid of everything I didn't need."

But she kept the photo of her husband. What did she do with her wedding pictures? Photos of vacations?

"Carrie, there are two bottles of diet soda and seltzer and water in the fridge."

I carried in the bottles. Everything else was out on the table. Helena peeled back the trays' sheets of foil, revealing shrimp parmesan, chicken cacciatore, and baked ziti.

Bryce rubbed his hands together. "Everything looks delicious."

We all expressed our agreement.

Helena grinned. "Thank you all. I'm glad to see you brought the wine to the table. Eat, drink, and be merry."

Bryce stood. "A toast to Helena and her new home. We're glad to have her back in Clover Ridge."

I smiled at Jared, who had brought our glasses to the table, and sipped my wine in Helena's honor.

The food was delicious. Francine asked Helena where she'd gotten it, which led to a discussion of local Italian restaurants and then to restaurants in general. Jared commented on a few of the restaurants we'd been to. I remained silent, hoping someone would open up the discussion of the murders or mention Lloyd, but no one did.

We'd just about finished eating when Pam stood. She must have looked uncertain, because Helena said, "The bathroom's to the left of the den."

"Right."

I had my excuse! I waited a few minutes and then got up.

Helena noticed. "Why don't you use the guest bathroom upstairs?"

"Thanks," I murmured as Francine and Gillian helped her clear the table.

Where to first? I dashed into the master bedroom and pulled open the dresser drawers. I was careful not to mess the neatly folded bras and panties and the drawer full of nightgowns as I searched. I ran my hands over the sweaters crammed in the bottom drawer. Nothing.

Do I have time to check the closet? The nightstands? To cover my tracks, I flushed the toilet in the guest bathroom and turned on the faucet, aware of time rushing by. I had only a few minutes before my absence would be noted.

I crossed the hall to the guest bedroom. Lloyd Koppel smiled at me as I jerked open drawer after drawer of the jewelry armoire, exposing Helena's array of rings, necklaces, and dangling earrings. I let out a yelp of surprise when I saw them. Amid the gold chains strewn about the lowest drawer was a wide gold bracelet and a vintage peacock pin.

Chapter Thirty-Six

I heard footsteps on the stairs. I slammed the door shut and raced into the hall.

"Are you okay?" Helena asked. "We were beginning to wonder if you'd taken ill."

"I was feeling dizzy and thought I'd lie down for a few minutes."

Helena stared at me without speaking. *Does she know I just saw the two pieces of Laura's jewelry that were stolen the night she was murdered? Does she know I know they belonged to Laura?*

"I'm better now."

"Good. We're about to have dessert and coffee."

"Where have you been?" Jared asked when I sat down. "I was about to look for you, but Helena insisted on going."

"I'm sure she did." I folded my hands in my lap so no one would see they were trembling.

"What does that mean?"

I glanced around, glad the other guests were engaged in conversation. Francine had made herself the official cake cutter and was asking everyone which of the three cakes they wanted.

"Jared, we have to talk. But not here. Not now." I gave him a meaningful look.

His face took on a mulish expression. "I hope you'll explain everything on the way home."

"I will."

I did my best to be social the rest of the evening, but I had never been good at dissembling. I must have looked troubled, because Ken shot me a look of concern. I sipped my coffee and made mush out of the molten chocolate cake I normally would have devoured, but I was too upset to eat. I wanted to stand up and shout, "Everyone! Helena isn't the person you think she is! She killed Laura. The proof is upstairs in her jewelry armoire!"

What held me back? That I might be wrong? That Helena would claim Laura had given her those items and I'd look the fool? I needed to call John Mathers ASAP and tell him what I'd discovered. And pray that Helena didn't dispose of the items before the police came to search her condo.

Finally, Pam and George said they had to be going. I breathed a sigh of relief and helped Helena clear the table. Gillian got up to help too. When she returned from the kitchen, Ryan told her they were leaving and driving Bryce home. Bryce entered the kitchen to say good night to Helena. He tried to take her in his arms, but she brushed him aside, saying she was putting the kitchen in order and they'd talk in the morning.

Francine brought in the rest of the dessert plates and cups as I was pouring the pitcher of milk back into the carton. Then she, too, thanked Helena for a lovely evening and left. I wondered how Jared and I were the last to leave when I desperately wanted to tell him what I'd discovered.

At last we were out the door.

As we walked down the path to the street, Jared put his arm around my waist and drew me close. "Carrie, please tell me what you've discovered."

I looked around, afraid Helena might be following us, but the only person I saw was a man walking a fox terrier. "Wait until we're in the car."

Jared let out a grunt of annoyance, since we'd had to park two blocks from Helena's condo.

As soon as we climbed inside, I began. "First of all, I found the pages your mother wrote about her secret lover."

"You did?" Jared's eyes shone in the near darkness. "When? Where were they?"

"In the library attic." I paused. "I found them Sunday."

"*Last Sunday*?" He gripped my arm.

I pulled away, suddenly afraid. "You're hurting me."

"Sorry." He let go. "Why didn't you tell me?"

"I didn't want you telling anyone. Not your father or Ryan—or Helena."

"Like I did at dinner the other night." He started the motor. "I get it."

He sped down Devon Woods Drive and exited the development.

When we stopped at a red light half a mile down the road, he turned to me. "I'd love to read the journal, Carrie. After all, my mother wrote it."

"I know, Jared. I gave it to Lieutenant Mathers. I'm sure he'll let you have it when they're done with it."

"What does it say? Does she mention the man she was involved with?"

"She writes about him but doesn't say who he is. She refers to him as L."

Jared thought as he turned onto the main road leading to my cottage. "That's why you mentioned Francine's husband, Lonnie."

"Helena told me your mom kind of liked him."

Jared shrugged. "She spent more time talking to our neighbor Lou Devon and to Lloyd Koppel."

"She used to talk to Lloyd?" I was surprised.

"Sure. My parents were best friends with the Koppels. You knew that."

"But—" The headlights of a car behind us blazed in the side mirror. I turned. Though the lane beside us was empty, an SUV was tailgating us.

"Jared, there's an SUV on our tail."

"I know." Jared sped up.

The vehicle kept pace.

"What's wrong with him?" I asked.

"There are plenty of crazy drivers on the road."

The SUV moved to the lane to our left.

"Good," I said.

I'd spoken too soon. Now it was veering into our lane, trying to push us off the road and onto the shoulder. Only there wasn't a shoulder. Beyond the guardrail, the land ran downhill into a gully below.

Jared drove faster. The SUV did too and inched farther into our lane. Jared tried to drive straight ahead, but the SUV was bigger and heavier and kept edging us over. Another few inches, and we'd hit the guardrail.

I was terrified, but I bit back my scream. I didn't want to distract Jared, who was doing his best to stay on the road.

The SUV sideswiped us. Jared swerved and rammed into the guardrail. I looked back. The SUV had reversed several feet. Now it was heading straight at us to send us to the ravine below.

Suddenly a black car passed both our vehicles. It veered across the road not ten feet in front of us, blocking both lanes.

"Oh, my God! What's happening?" I screamed.

The SUV screeched to a stop. I stared at the driver and saw a tuft of blonde hair. "It's Helena. She was trying to kill us!"

Dylan Avery stepped out of the BMW, his gun aimed at Helena Koppel. "Out of the car, Helena. The police are on their way."

Helena didn't move. Sirens sounded in the distance. Dylan approached the SUV. Helena climbed out and raised her hands.

I stared at Dylan. *How did he know? How had he figured it all out?*

Three squad cars arrived. Lieutenant Mathers spoke to Dylan and then to Helena. I heard her say she was driving past us when she noticed we were in trouble. Thank God they didn't believe her! I was relieved when an officer handcuffed her and put her in the back of a squad car.

Jared backed up slowly and turned off the ignition.

Dylan walked over to the car and knocked on my window. In the police cars' flashing lights, his face looked ashen. "Are you all right, Carrie?"

"Yes."

He gestured to Jared. "What about you?"

"I'm okay, but my car's going to need a ton of work."

"That's the least of it. Are you well enough to come down to the police station?"

"Sure." Jared turned to me. "Are you, Carrie?"

"I think so." I opened the car door. "But if you don't mind, I'll ride with Dylan."

Jared looked at Dylan and then at me. "You two have a thing going. You should have told me, Carrie."

"I'm sorry. I never found the right time to say I want us to be friends, nothing more."

Jared revved the motor. I closed the car door and watched him drive away.

Hours later, after I'd given my statement, Dylan drove me home. I unlocked the door to the cottage and plopped down on my living room sofa, thoroughly exhausted. But I wasn't too tired to ask a few questions of my own. "How did you know I was in trouble?"

Dylan sat beside me.

"I only found Laura's jewelry this evening," I continued.

"Could be Helena sensed Laura's journal existed. When she knew you were looking for it, she grew suspicious of you."

"Why? She didn't know I'd found the pages Laura had written."

"You were curious about Laura's lover. Helena must have figured you knew it was Lloyd or that you'd find out very soon. I was worried about you. So was John Mathers."

I looked at him. "Were you following me last night when I left the supermarket?"

Dylan grinned, making my heartbeat quicken. "Maybe I followed you there too."

"Did John tell you to keep an eye on me?"

"We both agreed you needed looking after. I knew you wouldn't agree to skip Helena's party tonight. Since John didn't have the manpower to send someone from the force, I offered my services."

I smiled. "Poor Dylan. You had to hang around all evening, waiting for Jared and me to leave."

"At least I was saved from having to stand guard outside the cottage all night."

I turned to him. "You would have done that?"

He nodded. "I would have."

"That's very sweet."

"You're sweet."

I yawned as he moved to kiss me.

"I'm sorry." My ears grew warm with embarrassment.

"So am I." He gave me a quick hug. "You're exhausted. We'll talk tomorrow. Are you scheduled to work?"

"From noon till five."

"How about I pick you up at six for dinner?"

I smiled. "I'd like that."

As he got to his feet, I said, "I have one question. Did John really suspect the murderer was someone in the Foster family, or did he suspect Helena?"

"Helena, of course. She must have been furious when she found out her husband and best friend were having an affair. She went over to the Fosters' house to have it out with Laura. Judging by her choice of weapon, she hadn't intended to kill her. When Al announced he knew who the killer was, Helena had to get rid of him too. The police found his iPad in her bedroom closet. It had been wiped clean."

I missed the closet. "Poor Bryce. Falling for his wife's killer."

"Helena's an egotist," Dylan said. "The affair must have rankled her all these years. She made a play for him to get back at Laura."

"And to get her new furniture faster and cheaper, no doubt." I thought a moment. "Do you think she gave her husband something that caused him to have a heart attack?"

"I'll discuss it with John and leave it in his hands. Now that his wife has confessed to killing two people, they may think it wise to exhume Lloyd's body."

I stood, and Dylan walked me to my bedroom.

"I'll say good night." He took me in his arms and kissed me.

This time I didn't yawn.

Chapter Thirty-Seven

Word of Helena's arrest had spread throughout Clover Ridge by the time I arrived at work at noon. I'd just taken off my parka when Angela and Sally came dashing through my office door, eager to hear every detail of the previous night's events. I told them I'd gone snooping and discovered Laura's jewelry that had been taken the day she'd been killed.

"I told you you'd find something if you looked hard enough," Angela crowed.

"But was that good advice?" Sally asked. "Helena came after Carrie and almost succeeded in driving the car into the ravine. She and Jared would have been killed."

"That's when Superman came to the rescue," Angela teased.

My face heated. "I was lucky Dylan was watching out for me. He saved my life."

"Anything else you'd like to share?" Angela asked.

"Not at the moment." I kept the knowledge that I'd be seeing Dylan in six hours to myself.

"You're hiding something," Angela said.

Sally looked pointedly at the clock. "Angela, why don't we let Carrie get some work done." She winked at me. "I'm sure she'll share whatever else there is when she's ready."

I watched them leave before turning to my computer to check my schedule for the day. *My two friends.*

I did some necessary paperwork for an hour and a half and then headed down to the meeting room to introduce a folk-singing trio to the audience. It took me longer than usual to get there because several patrons stopped me, wanting to know if I was all right and if it was true that Helena Koppel had murdered Laura Foster and Al Buckley. I introduced the trio, stayed long enough to take a few photos, and then headed upstairs to return to my office.

"Carrie."

I turned to see who was calling me. My stomach lurched. Dorothy Hawkins was beckoning to me from the reference desk. We'd been on civil terms since she'd paid for the car window she'd smashed. Still, I approached warily.

"I heard Helena Koppel tried to run you and Jared Foster off the road."

"She's down at the station being questioned for murdering Laura Foster and Al Buckley."

Dorothy frowned. "I never did like that woman. Too bad Connecticut no longer has the death penalty for murderers. At least she'll spend the rest of her life in prison."

I turned, and then I remembered. "You're part of the reason Helena was caught."

"Really?"

"I saw you come down from the attic last week. I never knew the library had an attic. That's where I went looking for the journal Laura used to write when she worked here. Your aunt Evelyn helped me find it."

A look of longing and nostalgia crossed Dorothy's face. "Tell Aunt Ev I think about her every day."

"I will." I smiled as I headed for my office.

Evelyn paid me a visit minutes before I was about to drive home. Her eyes glittered with excitement.

"The patrons can't stop talking about how you proved Helena Koppel killed Laura and Al."

"It's getting to be a bit much. Two reporters want to interview me, and Uncle Bosco's called three times today to make sure I'm okay."

Evelyn's face took on a stern expression. "Still, I wish you hadn't put yourself in danger by nosing around her condo. If Dylan hadn't stopped Helena, you and Jared could have been killed!"

"I promise to be more careful next time," I teased.

"I hope you mean that."

"Why?"

"Because helping you find Laura and Al's killer turned out to be my mission. And since we did such a good job of it, I was told we'll be working together on future 'projects.'"

"What exactly does that mean?"

But Evelyn had gone, leaving me as suddenly as she'd arrived. I put on my parka and headed for the parking lot. I hummed as I started my car, wondering where Dylan and I would have dinner. My life at that moment was perfect. I had a good job, friends, loving relatives nearby, and the start of a romantic relationship. I knew it wouldn't stay perfect—nothing ever did—but for now, I was utterly happy.

Acknowledgments

A special thanks to my hardworking, wonderful agent, Dawn Dowdle; to my terrific editor, Faith Black Ross; and to Megan Grande for the great and thorough job she did copyediting *Death Overdue*.